IN YOUR WILDEST DREAMS

USA TODAY BESTSELLING AUTHOR

REBECCA JENSHAK

CHAPTER ONE

Ash

YOU WANT A PUCK?

My pulse races as we walk down the tunnel. With every step the noise of the crowd gets louder. I hold my stick horizontally across my body, twirling it to release some of my nerves.

I let out a breath, roll my shoulders, and force my mind to focus. My eyes are locked on my teammate Declan in front of me. His broad back covered with the green jersey we all wear blocks me from seeing anything else, but when the first guys' skates touch the ice, I know it. The roar inside the arena vibrates inside of me.

One by one, we take the ice for the first home game of the season. The buzz of excitement in the arena is electric. The night is ours and this moment is magic.

Fans have waited months for this. *We've* waited months for this. There is no better high than gliding around the rink while thousands of people jump to their feet and cheer. They need us to put on a show, but I don't think they realize how much we need them too. The music is loud, the announcer louder, and my heart thumps wildly in my chest, nearly drowning out everything else.

When it's finally my turn and my right skate touches the ice, I push out everything except the quiet sound of my skates gliding over the smooth surface of the ice. Fresh ice. There's nothing better. It has this smell that I've never been able to describe, but I breathe it in with a huge smile. It smells like home.

Muscle memory sends me through my usual routine, skating around half the arena, finding a puck, and then firing it at the net before I skate back to center ice.

Slowly, everything else comes back into focus. My buddy and teammate, Leo Lohan, waits for me to stop beside him. His eyes scan the arena like he's taking it all in for the first time. He's been like this a lot lately—more aware, more in tune with everything.

"Have you ever seen this place so packed?" he asks, finally tearing his gaze away and looking at me. His eyes are wide with a wonder that has me smiling at him.

"First home game of the season is always like this," I tell him. "But damn, it never gets old."

"It feels different this year."

"Would that have anything to do with the little guy sleeping in your wife's arms?" Lifting my stick slightly, I aim it at Scarlett making her way down the steps of the packed arena with baby Callum.

Leo's face lights up when he spots them, and he automatically starts moving toward them. I go with him. The little guy is cute as hell. Scarlett holds up Callum when we get close, showing off his Wildcat shirt, then turns him so we can see it has Lohan on the back. Baby's first jersey for his first NHL game.

I know everyone says babies are all screaming, crying, pooping life-ruiners, but Callum is chill. He sleeps about ninety-five percent of the time, at least when I've seen him.

"How's he doing with all the noise?" Leo asks even though the kid is wearing ear protection that looks like fuzzy, baby earmuffs.

She cradles him back in her arms. "Good. I'm going to take him up to the suite where it's quieter and he can play with the other babies, but we wanted to say hi first."

Leo places his gloved hand up to the plexiglass. I swear Callum tries to move his chubby little fist to meet it.

"Hey, Ash," Scarlett says to me as her husband coos at their baby.

I nod toward Callum. "The little guy just needs some pads and a stick. I bet Coach Miller would make a spot for him."

She smiles, expression soft even as she speaks with sass. "Don't give them any ideas. They're already talking about getting him in skates as soon as he can stand."

Chuckling, I tap the glass like I'm offering Callum a fist bump, then I skate off to give them some time together, just the three of them.

It's crazy watching Leo become a husband and father. It suits him though. Never seen him happier.

Stopping at the blue line, I drop to my knees and stretch. Just like every other part of the warmup, I have a routine here. I go through a series of stretches to loosen up, singing along with the music pumping through the arena. I have the best job ever in the best city ever. I don't take even a single second for granted.

My teammates are all going through their own routines. Some of the guys like to focus only on warming up, others like to interact with the fans. More than a couple of guys are over by the glass to talk to their girls or families. The last two years, I've seen a lot of my teammates settle down. Married, kids, the whole shebang.

I scan the crowd. It really doesn't get old no matter how many games I play in this arena. It's still a trip every time I see someone wearing a jersey with KELLY across the back. A couple of girls holding a big glittery sign are waving at me. When I give them my attention, they hold the sign higher. *Hey, #53. Put it in my five-hole!*

Damn. I chuckle and wave at them, then keep scanning. A couple of kids have much tamer signs asking for pucks or sticks.

When I'm finished stretching, I skate over to the bench to get a marker, sign my stick, and then head over to one of the kids. A little girl with big brown eyes stands next to the glass with two other people who I assume are her dad and brother. She's wearing a Wildcat jersey and her hair is in braids. She bounces in place as I stop directly in front of her.

"I like your jersey," I tell her, then nod at her dad and smile at her brother. He looks to be about fourteen or so. He gives me a chin tip.

"They didn't have any of yours, so I had to get this one." She turns to show me our captain Jack's last name and number. He's easily the most popular guy on the team, but her lip curls like she's really put out having to wear his jersey instead of mine.

"Jack's a great hockey player and captain. Hel—" I catch myself before I swear in front of her. "Heck of a guy too."

I hand my stick over the top of the glass. Her dad takes it and presents it to her. Her face lights up when her small hands wrap around the carbon fiber shaft. She gives her dad something and then he motions with his hand to indicate he's going to throw it over. It takes two tries, but when I catch the item, a big smile stretches over my face. The little girl made me a friendship bracelet. Green and white beads surround my name and number. It's small, obviously made for her tiny wrist.

I close my fingers around the adorable gift. "Thank you. I love it."

Her smile grows a little shy. With one last wave, I head back to the bench to drop off my bracelet and the sharpie.

Lewis, one of our equipment managers, hands me a new stick.

"Thanks," I say. "Can you hold on to this for me?"

I drop the bracelet in his hand. With a grin, he nods. "Sure thing."

I start to skate off, then pause. "Can you get me an extra jersey?"

"Of course, no problem." His eyes drop to take in the one I'm wearing. "Something wrong?"

"Nah. Just want to give it to a kid that couldn't get one of mine from the gift shop."

He nods in understanding. "Stop being so popular, Kelly."

"Yeah, right. That store is basically a shrine to Jack."

Lewis laughs it off, but he knows I'm not wrong.

I pull off my jersey, then run a hand through my hair to get it out of my face. Feminine squeals catch me off guard. Mr. Popular himself comes to a stop next to me.

"Seriously, Kelly?" Jack shakes his head. His slicked black hair doesn't budge. "Ten minutes into the season and you're already taking your shirt off for the ladies?"

"Shut the fuck up." I set my jersey on the top of the half-wall in front of the bench and scribble my name. "It's for a little girl. She gave me a friendship bracelet."

He quirks a brow. "A friendship bracelet?"

"Yep. I'm her favorite."

"One out of twenty thousand isn't so bad, Kelly."

Fucker. I leave him to skate back over to the girl. She's surprised to see me, but as soon as she realizes I'm giving her my jersey, she starts bouncing in place again.

Her dad thanks me about a dozen times, but her excitement is all I need. I'd play hockey for free with no one watching, but damn if this isn't so much better.

"Enjoy the game," I tell them.

More women are squealing and calling out for me. I have on pads, but without my jersey, my abs are on display. I wink at a brunette screaming so loud that I worry for the eardrums of the people around her.

Jack is still stretching near the bench and he gives me that same disapproving headshake as I approach. "Show off."

Lewis tosses me a jersey and I pull it on to a chorus of disappointed boos. Time is ticking down for warmup, so I head back out to hit a few more pucks and get ready for the game. It's then that a blonde on the other side of the arena catches my eye. Possibly it's because she's one of the few women not looking my way.

Her long hair is curly and falls over her shoulders. She stares ahead with a blank expression, watching the ice but not really seeing it. The guy next to her has his nose buried in his phone. Lots of couples come to games together, but if a guy is ignoring his date at a hockey game, it's usually because he's enthralled with the action on the ice, not his phone. Especially a girl that looks like her.

I glide around our half of the ice with a puck, but my gaze keeps going back to the blonde. She and her date sit at center ice a few rows up. For reasons I can't imagine, he's not at all interested in talking to the woman next to him. He gets up and walks up the stairs, stopping a few rows higher to talk to someone.

My skates take me to her before I've even decided to approach. I stop hard in front of her, spraying ice. She finally looks at me. My pulse goes into overdrive as our eyes lock. I can't tell what color her eyes are from here, but I'm struck with this overwhelming desire that I want to find out. I want to move closer and memorize every inch of her face.

A small smile curves her lips and her left brow quirks up in an expression I can only describe as tempting. I stand dumbstruck eight feet away. It's when she glances over her shoulder and checks to see if her date is paying attention that I finally snap out of it. (He isn't, for the record. Idiot.)

I flip the puck up with my stick and catch it.

"You want a puck?" I ask, knowing full well it might look or sound like I asked her something else. I'd also be down for that. This girl is even more gorgeous the longer I look at her. She's dressed casually in jeans and a black sweater. Casual but still striking. All that blonde hair. I want to wrap it around my fingers and tug.

She barely moves her head, but the no is clear from the tiny shake. Her rejection shouldn't sting; it's a stupid puck for fuck's sake, but I want her to have it. People around her are starting to notice I'm giving away a puck and start clamoring for it. I point to her, making my intentions clear, and then toss it over. A guy in the front catches it and (reluctantly) passes it to her.

"If you don't want to keep it, you could write your number on it and throw it back," I suggest, raising my voice to be heard over the noise.

A faint blush paints her cheeks, and her lips pull higher. She has a great smile. Perfect full lips and dimples.

"I'll give you my number," some guy yells at me and the people around him laugh.

"Thanks for the offer," I say, not taking my eyes off her. "She's prettier though."

She sits a little straighter, cradling the puck in both hands.

"What do you say?"

Still silent, she runs her fingers over the black disc in her hands. Her fingers are adorned in gold rings, but the important finger is empty. "I don't think so."

"Is that your boyfriend?" I ask and tip my head toward the guy that was sitting next to her. He's still chatting away with someone a few rows up like the hottest girl I've ever seen isn't waiting for him.

"Shouldn't you be, I don't know, skating around?" Her stare lifts over my head to my teammates warming up behind me.

"Can't. I just met my future wife and I need to know if she's single."

I can't hear it, but her body language tells me she laughs quietly. "Yes."

"Yes, you're single?"

"No. I meant, yes, that's my boyfriend."

Damn. But not a total bust. People break up all the time. And he's clearly not the guy for her. If she were mine, I'd never take my eyes off her.

Her date finally looks back down at her, notices her attention has been captured and then scowls toward the ice. When he finds me standing in front of his girl, he takes a step toward her possessively. I can hardly blame him. I'd fight me for her too.

Maybe I crossed a line hitting on his girl, but I regret nothing. Skating away is physically painful, but I don't want to cause a scene and the game is about to start. I chance one more look at her. A rush of pleasure jolts up my spine when I find her eyes on me. With one last smile, I head to the bench. Time to go to work.

"To the start of a great season!" Declan raises his glass.

"This is the year," Leo adds as he does the same.

"To shutouts." Tyler grins smugly.

Each one of us says something along the same lines, flying high after winning our first game, and then we slam back our drinks. The first of many to come, judging by the atmosphere tonight.

Wild's, the closest bar to the arena and unofficial team hangout after games, is packed, and it's still early. I had to push my way through. Luckily, they always hold a couple of tables for us on home game nights in case we stop by.

My empty glass is quickly replaced with a full one. The guys scatter off to their girlfriends and wives, a few move toward the pool tables and dartboards. I linger at the bar and glance around to see who all came out to help us celebrate.

I smile when I find a familiar face. She moves through the crowd to get to me, hand raised over her head to get my attention. Everly, my teammate Tyler Sharp's younger sister, comes in for a hug when she finally reaches me. I get a mouthful of her blonde hair as she lunges with enthusiasm.

"Congratulations. You were on fire today." She squeezes me hard and then pulls back, smiling proudly.

"Thanks, Little Sharpie." I lean back against the bar. "Are you here alone?"

I look past her and search for her best friend and constant sidekick.

"No." Her smile is apologetic as she glances over her shoulder and stands on her toes. I follow her line of sight. "Grace and her boyfriend Lane snagged us a table. You want to come say hi?"

"Nah, probably shouldn't."

"Lane's cool. He won't mind."

It's not Lane I'm worried about. For a short time, I considered making a move on Everly's best friend. She's beautiful and smart, but since she's only twenty and still in college, I decided we were at two different places in our lives. I told her as much when she tried to kiss me at a pool party over the summer. She was embarrassed and I felt like an ass, but it was for the best. At least I hope so. The thought of going home alone tonight has me seriously questioning my choices.

"Give her my best."

Ev nods. "I will."

"You want something to drink? Soda? Water?"

"I'd love a glass of champagne."

"Your brother would kick my ass."

Her quiet laughter is barely audible over the noise. "We're heading out soon anyway, but I wanted to say hi first."

"I'm glad you did. How's school?"

While she fills me in on all the classes she's taking this semester, my attention wanes a little. I love chatting with Everly, but I'm still so wired from the game and it's hard to focus. Out of the corner of my eye, a mane of curly blonde hair snags my attention.

I stand taller to get a better look as the crowd of people between us parts, giving me a clear shot. My pulse quickens as I confirm it's the woman from the game. She's near the door, arms crossed at her waist as her date towers over her, glowering as he speaks. I don't need to hear what he's saying to know he's being a dick. Looks like a breakup is on the horizon even sooner than expected.

"Earth to Ash Kelly." Everly waves a hand in front of my face.

"Fuck. I'm sorry. I just saw someone I know."

"A girl someone?"

"Maybe." I grin. "But I'll find her later."

"Go." She chuckles. "I'll see you soon."

"Thanks, Little Sharpie. Good to see you." I squeeze her shoulder as I pass her to head for the couple at the door.

But by the time I get there, they've moved. I turn in a circle, looking for them. His angry voice is what finally leads me in the right direction. Standing outside of the bar a few feet from the entrance, he backs her up against the building as he speaks. "Are you cheating on me?"

"What?" Her voice is stronger and more assertive than I imagined for her small frame. Her boyfriend is tall and broad. It'd be totally reasonable if she was intimidated, but she speaks loud and clear. "Of course not. I told you, I have to go to work."

"Can't you just call in? I've barely seen you this week. It's not like you're performing surgery or something. How much help can you really be?"

Her gorgeous features twist in annoyance. "Screw you."

"I'm sorry. Fuck, it's just that I want to hang with you and you're blowing me off."

"No. I'm not. I told you that I'd have to leave right after the game."

I have an overwhelming desire to high-five her for sticking up for herself while this prick talks down to her and then switches to victim-mode.

"Hang out a little longer. I'll drive you there when it's time." His tone is pleading and pathetic.

"I need my car. Otherwise, you'll have to pick me up in the morning and take me home. Last time you forgot."

"It was one time," he says sharply. He wraps his fingers around her bicep. "Come on. Please?"

"I can't. I really need to go."

"One drink. You can stay for one drink." He pulls her along by the arm.

She winces but doesn't protest again as she stumbles after him.

I step in front of them. "Let her go."

Her sharp inhale precedes him shooting daggers at me. "Fuck off, man. This doesn't concern you."

His hold on her must tighten because her face contorts with pain.

"The fuck it doesn't." My jaw tightens as I watch her face pale. "You're hurting her."

He looks down to where he's gripping her and lets go. "Sorry. I didn't hurt you, did I?"

Her lips part and form an O, but it takes her a second to speak. "No," she says finally. "I'm fine."

"See?" He flashes a cocky smile at me. "She's fine."

"She doesn't seem fine. I think you should take a walk and cool down." I take another step toward him. He's taller than me, but softer. He looks like he works out just enough to have the appearance of a fit guy, while I've trained nearly every day since I was fifteen. My muscles aren't for show. Although, that is a nice bonus.

He huffs a laugh and sticks out his chest as he comes toward me. Too dumb to know he can't possibly win this fight. "Run along before I kick your ass. She doesn't want anything to do with you, Ash Kelly. You're a has-been they should have traded years ago."

Now I'm pissed. A rush of heat spreads through my body. I assumed he didn't recognize me, but calling me a has-been? Fuck that. I take a step and curl my hand into a fist.

"W-wait." The girl grabs on to his arm. Some of her long, blonde curls fall over her shoulder. I couldn't make out her eye color earlier, but they're a greenish-blue, almost turquoise. "This is stupid. Let's grab a drink at that place we went last week and then you can drive me to work."

It doesn't take a lot of effort on her part to stop him. She shoots me a look that tells me to get lost. I don't want to leave her alone with this guy though.

"Go," she mouths. I hold my ground until she adds, "I'm fine. I don't need your help."

Her boyfriend sneers when I eventually step back. "Yeah, that's what I thought."

With a huff, he shrugs out of her hold and heads down the sidewalk in the opposite direction with her walking quickly to keep up. I stand there and watch, feeling all sorts of conflicted about letting her leave with him.

My body tingles as my temper cools. What a fucking asshole. Who manhandles a chick like that?

As they turn the corner, she looks back and smiles, but it's fake as hell. Her dimples don't even pop. Then they disappear out of sight.

CHAPTER TWO

Ash

DID IT COUNT?

ONE MONTH LATER

Coach enters the locker room thirty minutes before we go out for warmups. His suit is unbuttoned, and his face is downcast as he paces in front of us. Even without looking up, I can still make out the deep lines burrowed in between his eyes from scowling for the better part of a month.

A quick look around at my teammates and their expressions are just as grim. We're frustrated, tired, and playing like shit. Everyone stops dressing and gives him our attention.

"I don't have to tell you that Vegas is going to be tough. They're going to push the tempo, try to rush us, and force mistakes. We can't let them. We need to go out there and play our game. Take your time, move the puck around, and fight like hell in front of the net. It doesn't have to be pretty. A goal is a goal." He stops pacing and places his hands on his hips. Briefly, his gaze lifts to the doorway. Standing just past our equipment managers is the GM of the Wildcats, Jim Smith. Next to him is a younger guy, early to mid-twenties, wearing a suit almost identical to Jim's. I can't place him, but something about the kid is familiar.

"Who's the guy with Jim?" I whisper to Declan, who sits on my right in his stall.

He looks over to where they're standing. "I'm not sure."

I stare harder, still unable to figure out who he is. There's something about him that makes unease crawl up my spine. Maybe Jim got a new assistant. Though this guy is dressed way nicer than any assistant I've seen following him or the other executives around.

I refocus on Coach, who has started pacing again. We haven't won a game in two and a half weeks. The home opener was a fluke. I don't know what happened since then, but things just aren't meshing out there. Passes are long, shots on net are wide, and we're not giving our goalie any help at all. It's like we're a bunch of rookies playing together for the first time. We desperately need a win to turn things around.

"Let's go out there and take care of business. Remind everyone what a great team we are because *we are*. But even great teams need to show up ready to go. Every guy counts, every shift counts." He claps his hands together. "Let's get the energy levels up. Captain, give us the starting lineup."

After Jack calls each name, we all cheer, and by the time Coach leaves, the energy has shifted. Frustration has leached into anticipation.

When it's time, we march down to take the ice with determination radiating from our bodies. I go through my usual warmup, only allowing myself to look for the mystery blonde for a moment. She hasn't come to another game, at least not where I could spot her. It's weird to be disappointed about a chick I barely spoke to, but sometimes you just get a feeling with people. I got that with her.

My thoughts drift to her turquoise eyes and the way she stood her ground against that jerk she was with.

"Is she here?" Jack asks as he drops beside me to stretch.

My hair falls into my face, blocking me from seeing the smug expression I'd bet he's wearing. If it were anyone else, I could play dumb, but I confided in Jack last weekend after I turned down three different girls' offers to take my mind off hockey. He was concerned I was having a quarter-life crisis.

I'm not, I just…can't stop thinking about her. She had a grit and a backbone that I admire. It was sexy as hell.

Hooking up with someone else while I'm thinking about another girl is not my style. I'm all in when I'm hooking up, totally and completely in the moment. Sure, sometimes that moment lasts only for a night, but I'm never banging one person and wishing I was somewhere else.

"No. I don't think so."

"Too bad."

I flip my hair back. "It's whatever. Let's go out tonight. Somewhere other than Wild's. I need a change of scenery."

"Yeah?" he asks, one side of his mouth pulling into a pleased smile. "Finally tired of holding out for your soulmate?"

"Shut the fuck up, I never called her that."

His upper body shakes with quiet laughter. "I know just the place. And just the girls to call."

Of course, he does.

"Ash is gonna get laaaaaaid tonight," he says on beat with the music.

"You're a little too enthusiastic about my sex life."

"As your captain, I take all your needs very seriously. Your goals are my goals."

"Well, in that case I only have one goal tonight."

"Win," we say in unison.

He flashes a smile, extending his hand. We bump fists and then return to stretching silently.

By the time they play the anthem, announce the teams, and do all the other pre-game bullshit, I'm vibrating with adrenaline. Some games I just have this unshakeable confidence—a perfect combination of resolve, preparation, and grit. I'm ready to make a difference out there.

And I do. My first shift out, I get an assist for a slick pass to Jack between defenders. That lifts the entire team's spirits, and we score twice more before the end of the first.

I take the ice for the start of the second period, almost feral in my need to keep pushing us. Vegas has come back from the first intermission with a renewed determination though. Their hits are harder and they're checking tighter.

After an icing penalty, Jack wins the face-off. He tips it to me, and I pass it off to Leo. I cut through the defense, moving away from the puck, opening up the ice to give us room to work. Only two of their guys get tangled up, leaving me alone with no one between me and the goalie.

"Yep, yep!" I call to let them know I'm open. Jack passes the puck to me and I move toward the net. There's a defender on my right, and another not far behind him coming to help. I'm too fast, easily pushing past them. I fire it into the net and over the right shoulder of the goalie. Before I can raise my hands in celebration, I'm hit hard.

I wasn't bracing, so my body careens fast toward the ice and I don't have time to stop the fall. My feet come out from under me and my head slams against the ice.

Stars dance in my field of vision before blackness creeps in. The noise in the arena quiets to a dull roar. My right shoulder kills, but it's the least of my worries. I try to get to my feet, but my head spins and I can't quite tell which way is up. I think I see Jack taking a swing at the guy who hit me, but they're blurry shapes.

Giving up on standing, I rest my forehead against the ice. I don't know where my helmet is, but I'm glad it isn't keeping me from letting the cold numb the ringing in my head.

I take a couple deep breaths and blink. My stomach lurches and I fight back the need to get sick. Eventually the medical staff comes out to check on me. They ask me questions that I struggle to answer.

"Get me off the ice," I mutter incoherently.

Someone mentions a backboard and I sit up as best as I can. "No. I can skate. Help me."

They hesitate, but Jack and Leo flank me on either side and lift me up. They all but carry me off, but at least I'm upright. The crowd is on their feet, clapping and cheering as I go.

I don't remember much of the walk back to the locker rooms, but after the team doctors check me out, I'm told I likely have a concussion and a separated shoulder. I'm still struggling to focus, probably because of that concussion thing, but I hear enough to know they're sending me to the hospital to fix my shoulder and check out my head. I feel like I'm outside of my body, watching myself in slow motion.

"Did it count?" I ask Hunter, the young trainer tasked with helping me out of my skates and uniform.

His brows pull together in confusion as he unlaces my right skate and yanks it off.

"The goal. Did it count?"

A slow smile spreads across his face. "Yeah, man, it counted."

The pain dulls. At least we got a goal.

CHAPTER THREE

Bridget

YOU WOUND ME

I hurry out of the break room, pulling my hair back and securing it with a clip.

My coworker Hannah falls into step beside me. Her brows lift and a playful smile tugs at her lips when she scans my face. "You look tired. Did you get any sleep today?"

If it were anyone else commenting on my appearance, I'd be offended, but Hannah's words and scrutinizing gaze isn't her being mean, she's just one of those people who tells it like it is. And sadly, she's right. I do look tired, but I guess there's no hiding the fact I only got three hours of sleep.

"I slept," I say with a hint of defensiveness in my tone.

"Oh yeah? How many hours?"

A small laugh escapes. "Hopefully enough to make it through another night."

We slow our pace as we approach the nurses' station to begin our shift.

I work nights as a registered nurse on the orthopedic floor of the hospital. I got placed here a month ago after six months working on the cardiac floor and a short stint on the psychiatric wing. I'm going to school to get my bachelor's degree in nursing. Once I have my BSN, I want to be a pediatric nurse. I fell in love with peds during my RN clinicals, but so far, a spot hasn't opened up.

For now, I'm bouncing around different areas of the hospital, getting experience and filling in wherever I'm needed. Moving around in the hospital means I haven't stayed in one spot long enough to form many friendships with my coworkers, but Hannah is one of my favorites.

She offers a sympathetic smile. "I don't know how you manage it all. Working all night and then going to school all day. You need more rest."

"I got a nap in at lunch, and I slept a couple more hours this evening."

Her mouth falls in a straight line, silently communicating her disapproving thoughts on my schedule.

Back-to-back night shifts during the week are the worst. I get off work at seven in the morning, head to my place for a quick shower, then go to a full day of classes. When I'm done, it's basically time to be back at work. Despite the lack of sleep, I love my job. Totally worth the bags under my eyes.

"I'm fine. Let's just hope it's busy tonight or I might fall asleep on my feet."

"You haven't heard?" she asks as we stop to look at the board.

"Heard what?"

"We've got a VIP." Her lips curve into a smile.

My brows lift at her excited expression. "That's good news?"

"Ask me who it is." She nudges me with an elbow, and her smile widens.

"I don't care who it is."

"Just ask me," she insists, practically vibrating next to me.

"Okay, fine. Who is it?"

Before she can answer, the charge nurse on the day shift shouts my name. Sandy is a frightening woman who has worked at the hospital longer than I've been alive. Her patients love her, but everyone that works with her gives her a wide berth. One of her jobs is to create the schedule for the nightshift. We had a new hire last month that talked back to her and barely lived to regret it. She quit on day two.

I happen to like Sandy's no-nonsense, slightly prickly personality. She still scares me, but I like her.

After startling, I aim a wobbly smile at her. "Yes?"

"I'm assigning you the VIP in 601 tonight."

"Lucky," Hannah hisses and then leaves me to start her shift.

Lucky? Is she joking? I once overheard a nurse trade two vacation days to avoid taking a VIP patient. No one wants to get stuck with a VIP.

All I've heard since I started working here is how management hovers nearby VIP rooms, popping in and out unexpectedly and scrutinizing care decisions, and that the patients are often more demanding. Sometimes it's a doctor's family member or a loved one of someone in administration, or it could be a donor who gives large sums of money to the hospital each year. The criteria for who makes a VIP is broad and not clearly defined.

But as I look around, I notice a few more jealous gazes turned in my direction, which makes no sense to me.

Sandy brings both hands up to rest on either end of the stethoscope around her neck. "Let's do the bedside report for 601 first."

Nodding my agreement, I follow her toward the room of who I'm sure is going to be the most stressful patient of the night. On the plus side, I probably won't be bored enough to realize how tired I am.

The hospital is laid out in an L-shape. One long hallway with patient rooms extends out from the nurses' station, and on the other side are four more patient rooms—though these are bigger, nicer, and often reserved for cases the hospital deems a higher priority. Room 601 is one of the nicer rooms. Maybe the nicest since it sits at the end of the hallway. Every floor has one room at the very end of the short hallway with windows that look out onto the city. The executive offices are on the top floor on this side of the building for that very reason.

"So, who is the patient?" I ask her as we pass by empty rooms, trying to shake any negative thoughts. Whoever it is, they're just another person that needs the same empathy and care.

She stops in front of the supply closet and hands me two extra pillows and a blanket. "Are you a hockey fan?"

"Hockey?"

She nods.

"No. Not really. Why?" As I ask the question, my throat goes dry.

"I never really cared for it either, but my husband is a diehard. We always go to a couple of Wildcat games each season. He'll be so jealous when I tell him I got to meet one of his favorite players."

The implication of her words hits me with force. A Wildcat hockey player is *here*?

I can't seem to find my voice to ask her which player. Besides, there are a dozen other guys it could be. There's no way it's him. It can't be.

Without another word, she shuts the closet door and continues down the hallway toward the last room. I follow behind her, heart racing even as I repeatedly tell myself I'm overreacting for no reason.

The door for Room 601 is open a crack. Light seeps out along with muted voices. Memories of the last time I was face to face with a Wildcat player swirl through my mind and my fingers tremble.

"Sandy! Wait up."

We both turn to find Hannah jogging toward us. She stops in front of Sandy. "Someone from administration needs to see you."

"Tell them I'll be there as soon as we do the handoff on 601."

"She said it can't wait. They have a question on some paperwork for him." She tips her head in the direction of our VIP.

"Maybe I should go," I offer.

"No. You go ahead and check on your patient," Sandy says with a sigh. "I'll deal with administration and then hopefully they'll leave you to do your job the rest of the night. I'll be back as soon as I can."

As soon as Sandy is gone, Hannah latches on to my forearm with a firm grip and pulls me over to the wall where we're partially hidden behind a crash cart. "Did you see him yet?"

"No, not yet. Who is it?"

Please don't be him. Please don't be him.

"Ash Kelly!"

My heart drops and a high pitch ring drowns out the background noise the hospital. It's been a month since Ash Kelly hit on me in front of an entire arena and then almost got into a fight with Gabe outside of Wild's bar. A whole month and that night still haunts me.

"Can you believe it?" Hannah asks.

I can't, but I can't seem to form words to reply either.

When I still don't respond, she adds, "Ash Kelly? The hockey player. He plays for the Wildcats."

"Right." My voice comes out tight, but I do my best to force my body to appear calm and relaxed. "I've heard of him. Why's he here?"

He's hurt obviously, but just…*How?* How can this be happening? And how do I avoid going in there and facing him?

"He got injured in the game tonight. Concussion and shoulder separation. Dr. Weston was on her way to the hospital for an emergency ankle repair, so they sent him here."

Despite my shock at finding out who our VIP patient is, the nurse in me wants more details. "AC joint? Does he need surgery?"

"Yes, and I don't know. They just brought him up a few minutes ago." Her smile gets impossibly bigger. "God, you're so lucky."

"We could switch." I try to hand her the pillows and blanket. I cannot walk in there and be Ash Kelly's nurse. My face flames hotter at just the thought. I have no desire to relive any part of that night.

"And face the wrath of Sandy? No way. Besides, Weston's letting me help on the ankle repair."

"And you think I'm the lucky one?" Though to be fair, there are few things that sound less humiliating than walking in Room 601 and facing Ash again. I can still see his expression as he watched me walk off with an angry Gabe. He seemed so confused and a little concerned. It's the concern that surprised me the most. It was genuine.

"Ash Kelly or a surgery with the best doctor in this hospital?" She moves her hands in front of her like she's weighing the options, then drops them with a laugh. "I'll tell you about the surgery if you promise you'll tell me what he's like?"

I manage a small nod.

"Have fun," she chirps before taking off in the other direction.

"You too," I mutter back, too quiet and too late for her to hear.

I pace in front of the door, hugging the bedding to my chest. Flashes from that night play in a loop. Ash skating around the ice with women screaming his name. His cocky smile as he tossed me the puck. And that puzzled expression as I left him on the sidewalk.

Part of me wonders if I'm being silly. There's no way Ash Kelly remembers me. I'm certain that I am one of many, *many* women he's charmed with his little pre-game warmup. But on the off chance he does recognize me, I'd prefer not to have a conversation about what happened outside of Wild's that night. Especially here in my place of employment.

I've just about talked myself into going into the room, keeping my head down, and faking an accent, when the door opens. A guy with gray hair wearing a white polo shirt with the Wildcat hockey logo embroidered over his chest steps out, then pauses when he sees me loitering in the hallway.

A practiced, closed mouth smile falls into place. "Hello."

"Hey." The man steps to the side to allow me to enter. "Can we get some more water?"

"Absolutely." I nod with more confidence than I feel. I really wish I could shove the pillows and blanket at him and run off, but I am a professional, dammit. Holding my head high, I walk over to deposit the extra bedding on the far chair. Normally the first thing I'd do is make eye contact with the patient, but I avoid staring at Ash until it's nearly uncomfortable.

Looking up and directly into his blue eyes, I hold my breath as I wait for his reaction. Immediately, I know he recognizes me. I can't even begin to think about how that's possible, but I know it's true. The corners of his lips pull up on either side and he opens his mouth to say something, but I'm saved by Dr. Weston as she enters the room. She's a badass orthopedic surgeon that just transferred here from Virginia. She's one of the best in the country. The Wildcats scooped her up this season as a team doctor, so it's not all that surprising that a Wildcat player would be here, I guess, but it's the first time I know of that it's happened.

She stops at the side of his bed. "How's your pain? Better or worse since they checked you at the arena?"

"Fine. Same." His gaze flicks back to me for a second, then returns to the doctor.

While they go over his pain and the tests that have already been run, I take the opportunity to get more water and then see what else the room needs. I check all the closets for supplies and even make sure that he has fresh batteries in the TV remote. Busy tasks so I don't have to look at him.

"But I won't need surgery, right?" A hint of fear in his voice beckons me to finally redirect my attention his way.

He's wearing only black athletic pants with his jersey number stitched in green on the left hip. I've successfully managed not to gawk at his bare chest since I walked in, but all that restraint goes up in a plume of smoke now. And dammit, his body is just as spectacular as I remember from the stunt he pulled at the game, whipping off his jersey to give to a little girl in the crowd. He's quite the charmer, I'll give him that. The fans love him.

Light hair along his chest is trimmed short and trails down his washboard abs before disappearing into the band of his pants. He's lean and cut and his muscles are defined even in the awful fluorescent lighting overhead. His left arm is covered with a sling, keeping it close to his body and elevated.

I spot two tattoos—a butterfly on his left bicep, and script on the right side of his chest that I can't quite read without giving away that I'm checking him out.

"I don't think so, but we can go over all of that tomorrow when you're feeling better. For tonight, I think you should stay here where we can keep an eye on you. It'll be easier for everyone, considering your limited mobility with your shoulder and the concussion. Any more nausea or vomiting?"

"No," he answers quickly.

Doctor Weston pauses, giving him a chance to change his answer.

"A little nausea, but it's better. No vomiting."

"Good," she says. "Blurry vision? Problems walking or talking?"

"No." His voice is more assured this time.

She nods, but still pulls out her penlight and checks his eyes. When she's satisfied, she turns it off and stands tall. "All right. I'll check back in a couple of hours, but for now, the best thing you can do is rest and let your body start to recover. Your pain level will likely increase as the adrenaline from the night starts to wear off." For the first time, she looks at the other gentleman in the room. "Any questions?"

They're both quiet, and with another nod, she takes a step toward the door.

"Thanks," he calls after her.

I feel Ash's gaze immediately switch to me, but the man in the polo shirt speaks first. "I should get home to the wife and let you rest up. If you need anything, give me a call. I'll be back first thing in the morning."

While Ash says goodbye to him, I finish reading his chart. Ash Kelly, twenty-nine years old, no allergies, shoulder separation and concussion, just as Hannah said. They didn't list his six pack or panty-melting smile. An obvious oversight.

"I can't believe it's you," Ash says when we're alone.

My heart skips and I shuffle awkwardly, having no idea how to respond.

"It is you, right? I'm not hallucinating, am I? You're the girl from the game last month?"

"Bridget," I say, not directly answering his question.

"Bridget." The way he says my name sends a shot of unprofessional heat climbing up my neck.

I should tell him I'm his nurse for tonight, but maybe I can still get someone to switch with me. I settle for smiling and asking, "Can I get you anything, Mr. Kelly?"

"Mr. Kelly?" He quirks a brow, then lets out a soft laugh. "Nah. Only thing I need right now is a shower."

Now that he's mentioned it, I can tell he came straight from the game. His hair is a little messy, though still somehow sexy. The dusty brown locks fall just below his chin, and he has it tucked behind his ears to keep it out of his face and covered with a backward hat.

His wrists are still taped, something I noticed at the game that a lot of the guys do. It's a wonder he isn't still in pads and skates.

"Sure." I walk over to the bathroom and open the door wide. "Everything you need should be in there."

His stunning blue eyes sparkle with excitement and disbelief. "I can't get over it. You're really here."

I can't get over it either. My stomach is doing a series of somersaults that make it hard to catch my breath.

"I've looked for you at every home game."

Thrown off guard by that comment, but eager to guide us back to a more professional topic, I decide to take this moment to go through my usual spiel when entering a patient's room. As much as my coworkers would love to trade me places, no one would dare go above Sandy's head.

"I'm taking over as your nurse tonight. The room is all stocked, and I'll put in a request for a late dinner tray. Any food preferences or dietary restrictions not noted on your chart?"

"I'm not hungry," he says.

"Okay. Well, if there's anything else you need, press the red call button on the side of your bed."

I'd usually go show him, but stepping any closer feels like a terrible idea. Even six feet apart he can probably see the impact he's having on me. "I'll bring in a dinner tray anyway in case you're hungry later. Do you need any help with the shower?" My face heats. "I mean getting out of the sling or getting undressed? I can ask a male nurse to assist."

Do not think of him naked. Do not think of him naked.

His lips twitch at the corners like he knows exactly what I'm trying not to think about. "I can manage."

"Good."

He doesn't move and his gaze stays locked on me. "This is such a trip! Wow. I think I'm in shock. A nurse, huh?"

"Yep." I smile at him. It's a little forced, but hopefully convincing and doesn't show how much I'm inwardly freaking out.

"Nurse Bridget." His smile widens. "How long have you worked here?"

"Not that long, but I promise you're in good hands." God, why does everything I say suddenly sound so dirty? I back up toward the door. I need to get out of here and regroup. "I'll be back in a little while to check on you."

"I look forward to it, Bridget." Ash swings his legs to the side of the bed and stands. He winces a little as the movement pulls at his shoulder. He takes a step, then sways and wobbles as he takes another. My instincts kick in and I'm at his side quickly, aiding him like I would any other patient. His skin is warm and my fingers tingle as I steady him on the right side. I glance up to meet his gaze. He's taller than I realized. I'm five foot five, but my chin barely reaches his shoulder and I have to tip my head back to look at him.

"Are you okay?"

He looks first at where my fingers wrap around his bicep before answering. His voice is gruff. "Yeah. Shit. Guess I'm still a little unsteady on my feet. I got it now."

Stepping away from him, I wait while he crosses the room. He's almost to the bathroom when he stops and asks, "Do you still have the puck I gave you? Maybe sleep with it under your pillow at night?"

I resist rolling my eyes. I'd say he's going to be just fine if he's feeling good enough to hit on me. "Sorry to disappoint, but I gave it away."

"You wound me, Bridget."

I swallow hard. His teasing and flirty demeanor is disarming, even if I think he's full of crap. "No, I think you did that all on your own."

"Me and the guy that rammed into me," he mutters, all traces of that playfulness gone.

I wince. *Crap.* The guy might be a total flirt and egomaniac, but he's hurt and under my care. "I'm sorry. I don't know why I said that."

My reaction to him has my guard flying up in defense. I will not fall for another guy who uses charm like a weapon.

His lips pull into a half-smile that's cocky and endearing. "It's okay, Nurse Bridget. You have all night to make it up to me."

CHAPTER FOUR

Ash

NURSE BRIDGET

Jack, Leo, Tyler, and Declan stop by after the game. The guys are crowded around the far side of the room, leaning against the wall. All except Jack, who's sitting in the chair next to me.

I'm showered and sitting up in bed while they fill me in on the game. They won. Our first W in weeks. I freaking *hate* that I wasn't there.

My head and shoulder hurt, but the painkillers keep it to a dull ache. More than anything I'm worried about how long I'll be sidelined. A couple of weeks if I'm lucky, if I'm not, maybe a month or more. It's a huge blow to me and to the team. This is supposed to be our fucking year.

"Wait, your nurse is the girl from the game?" Leo asks, brows lifted. "The one you've been searching for at every home game? The one who has you turning down girls left and right?"

I chuckle at his assessment, and playfully glower at Jack. The only way Leo would know that is from our dear captain because Leo hasn't been out much since Callum was born.

"With good reason. I met a ten. You don't shake off a ten that easily."

A knock sounds at the door and I perk up, excited for the guys to meet Bridget. She's cute as hell in her scrubs.

Her eyes widen as big as a hockey puck as she notes the four guys in the room with me. She's carrying a cafeteria tray in front of her. That long, curly hair is pulled back in a clip, and falls over one shoulder. My memory of her didn't do her justice. If she's a ten, then every other girl I've ever called a ten was really a six. I'm going to have to redo my entire scale. Zero to Bridget.

She covers her surprise quickly, smoothing out her expression and smiling stiffly. "I'm sorry. I didn't realize you had visitors. I can come back."

"No, come in. I was just telling them about you." I wave her over.

Her brows lift and she hesitates before she steps farther into the room.

She sets the tray on the table next to my bed, then eyes the bags of takeout my teammates brought.

Leo takes a step forward and offers his hand to her. "You must be Bridget. I'm Leo."

"Hi, Leo." After a short hesitation, she takes his hand, then nods to the other guys. They're all giving her these big, cheesy smiles, which is hella awkward. She doesn't seem to notice. Or if she does, she's hiding it well.

"I was just dropping off your dinner and checking to see if there was anything else you need before I take my first break, but it looks like your friends are taking good care of you."

"Anything for Ash. He's a great guy." Declan gives her an approving nod.

"The best!" Tyler adds enthusiastically. "Everybody loves him. Most genuine guy you'll meet."

Jack chuckles and then covers it with a cough.

Dear god. How am I the single one when these guys are this bad at talking to girls? Do they really think they're helping me out?

Bridget hesitates like she isn't sure how to respond before she says, "Visiting hours end in twenty minutes. I can ask for special permission if you'd like someone to stay with you overnight, but you need to rest."

And have them continue to talk me up to her like I'm their kid brother that can't get a date? No way. "I'm good. They were just heading out anyway. Right guys?"

"Yep," they all say at once and start shuffling around to leave.

"I am sorry to kick you guys out," Bridget says, genuine sympathy in her voice. I like that she's not afraid to tell my buddies to take a hike, but yet she still seems apologetic about it.

"We understand." Jack places a reassuring hand on my good shoulder. "Text if you need anything. I'll stop by in the morning."

Each of the guys says their goodbyes and thanks Bridget on their way out. Leo gives me a thumbs-up as he disappears out the door.

When we're finally alone, she motions for me to lie back. "How's your pain?"

"With them around? Excruciating."

She laughs lightly. "And now?"

"Same as before. Not too bad."

"You can have more meds in thirty minutes."

I melt back into the pillow, relaxing for the first time since I got here. "Does that mean you'll be back in half an hour?"

"Yes, if someone else doesn't beat me to it."

I tilt my head to the side in question, and Bridget laughs quietly. "I'll be shocked if the other nurses don't fight over who gets to cover my break. Your presence has everyone losing their minds."

"Everyone but you."

Her stare holds mine as she adjusts the bed's incline to relieve more pressure from my shoulder. "I was surprised to see you."

"Excited?"

"Surprised."

"I guess I'll take it. Surprised is better than horrified."

Our gazes lock and several beats pass while we silently smile at each other. Her turquoise eyes hold me hostage.

Bridget looks away first, checking the watch on her left wrist. "Do you need anything else?"

"No, I guess not." I don't want her to go. The thought of lying here all night with nothing but my own thoughts sounds downright awful. But I also don't want her to miss her break.

"I'll be back at the top of the hour. Buzz if you need anything."

The minutes tick by so slowly. My head hurts too much to focus on TV or scrolling on my phone, which means I'm basically staring at the wall waiting for Bridget to come back. I have so many things I want to ask her. I don't know her at all, really, but I feel this connection to her somehow.

When she finally returns, she's joined by Dr. Weston, so I don't get a chance to talk to her alone. Bridget hits the lights as they leave, orders me to get some sleep with a sexy glare, and tells me she'll be back in a couple of hours.

Sleep? Unlikely.

I replay tonight's game from the beginning to the hit that took me out. The Vegas player who delivered the late hit received a game misconduct penalty and was ejected, but it hardly makes up for the fact I'm lying here in this hospital bed. Damn. I cannot believe one month into the season and I'm injured. The thought of sitting around for weeks, or longer, has me getting to my feet. I head out into the hallway, not sure where I'm going but needing to move around.

The hospital is quiet. All the lights are dimmed, and the only noises are the air conditioning vents humming as they pound out cool air (it's freaking freezing in here) and the distant chime of an elevator. I pass by several empty rooms on my way down the hall. I don't particularly like hospitals—then again, who does? But I'm pretty stoked that it's given me a chance to see Bridget again.

Which is why it shouldn't really surprise me when my steps lead me to the nurses' station. Bridget sits behind the desk with another woman. A few other nurses work behind them. Each of them are quiet, busy doing their own thing. My girl has her head bowed over a book, wearing a pair of cute glasses. Sexy nurse meets sexy librarian. That's a fantasy mash-up I never saw coming.

"Ash Kelly. Holy crap, you're tall." The woman I haven't met notices me first and elbows Bridget.

She rubs her arm and glances up at me. "Mr. Kelly. What are you doing up? Did you need something?"

"You can just call me Ash."

"Ash." She pauses after saying my name like she isn't sure how she feels about using it. "Is everything okay?"

"Fine. Just bored."

A small smile lifts the corners of her pouty mouth. "You're supposed to be sleeping."

"Impossible."

"Is your pain increasing?" She gets a cute little furrow between her brows.

"No. I meant sleep is impossible because I know you're down here."

The girl next to her giggles, but Bridget cocks her head to the side and gets this sexy annoyed look in her eyes. "Mr. Kelly."

"Ash," I remind her.

"Ash. You really need to try to rest. Your body has been through a lot tonight."

Don't I know it, but it's just another reason that I don't want to sit and stare at the walls.

"What are you reading?" I ask her, then finally give the other nurses enough attention to realize their gazes volley between me and Bridget.

"She's studying," the girl next to her says. She smiles at me. "I'm Hannah. Huge fan. Go Wildcats!"

Ah, an ally.

"Nice to meet you, Hannah." Smiling, I rest my good arm on the desk and lean forward. "Busy night?"

"Yes," Bridget says, returning her gaze to her textbook at the same time Hannah says, "No."

I look at Hannah. "Did Bridget tell you we're old friends?"

"We are not friends," Bridget interjects quickly.

Ignoring her, I keep my attention on Hannah. "We met at a game. I gave her a puck during warmups and tried to get her number. I've been looking for her at every game since. Imagine my surprise when I end up here and she's my nurse."

The accusatory glare Hannah sends Bridget makes me chuckle. "You went to a Wildcat game? And met Ash Kelly?" Her voice climbs higher. "When?! And how could you not tell me something like that?"

"It was forever ago and it wasn't a big deal."

"Last month," I clarify. "The home opener."

Hannah tips her head to the side. "With Gabe?"

Bridget says nothing but gives her coworker the tiniest of nods.

"Is that the boyfriend?" My jaw clenches remembering the way that asshole talked to her. I'd forgotten about him in my excitement at seeing Bridget again.

"*Ex*-boyfriend." Hannah's big grin matches mine.

Giddiness I haven't felt since I was a kid spreads through me. *They broke up.* Hell yeah. Best news I've had all day.

CHAPTER FIVE

Bridget

BEEN CALLED WORSE

t's been a weird shift. Everyone's lost their mind over Ash being here. All night I've fielded questions about him. What's he like? Is he nice? Is he just as hot as he looks on TV? And on and on. The guy is obscenely good-looking from every angle, and it just gets worse the closer you get to him. It's like a contact high. But there's no way I'm admitting that to anyone.

He's signing scrubs and scraps of paper for all my coworkers while I try to drown it out and study. School is kicking my butt this semester and I need every minute of study time I can get. But Ash's presence has thrown me off completely. Before he walked up, I'd reread the same section of my homework notes five times and I still don't remember a word of it.

I'm not usually so easily shook, but today has been one too many things piling up on my plate. First, I found out my landlord isn't extending my lease. I live in this cute one-bedroom guesthouse. It's tiny, barely more than a bed, bathroom, and a counter with a hot plate and sink, but it's within walking distance to the Whittaker campus and the rent is cheap.

Crisis number two: I went to get my morning coffee and saw my ex-boyfriend. Gabe didn't see me (thank goodness), but just seeing him added to the already crappy start of the day. A sighting of my dick ex would be enough to put me in a bad mood, but at my coffee spot? Surely I should get custody of the Starbucks near my house and school? He doesn't live or work nearby, so I'm pretty sure he was there just hoping to run into me. We broke up a month ago and he still thinks there's a chance we'll get back together (never going to happen).

And finally, after a day of stewing over points one and two, I forgot to put my favorite scrubs in the dryer and had to wear my backup pair that are too tight on my butt.

I thought coming to work tonight I could unwind, forget about everything and just get lost in work and studying.

Then Ash Kelly happened.

I've spent all night ignoring the butterflies in my stomach when I'm near him while trying to remain an objective and considerate caretaker.

I adjust my glasses and then turn the page of my book at the same time the group of nurses surrounding Ash break out in boisterous laughter. Instead of the words on the page, all I can concentrate on is the hot patient charming my coworkers. I look up and inadvertently meet Ash's gaze. He's smiling, but it looks strained. I wonder if his shoulder is hurting him. He put on a shirt before he left his room earlier—small mercies, but he looks too good to be true in a basic gray T-shirt and his athletic pants.

I'm not too proud to admit that I looked him up after he tried to get my number at the game. I knew, or I sort of assumed, that Ash was as big a player as he seemed. I was one hundred percent correct. His hockey stats are impressive, but so are the girls he's dated.

All the women he's been pictured with are stunning. His last girlfriend was an actual model. He doesn't post on his social media accounts that often, but there were still several images of the two of them on beautiful vacations and attending fun, local parties.

The phone on the desk in front of me rings and I jump like a girl in a horror film.

While I answer, Ash and Hannah slowly make their way to me. Hannah takes the seat next to me again. Ash stands in front of me on the other side of the nurses' station.

He watches me as I chat back and forth with the guy in the emergency room department downstairs. My face warms under his gaze. He has this way of watching me that's unnerving. Like he's checking me out but noticing more than my physical appearance.

Ignoring him the best I can, I hang up the phone and direct my attention to Hannah. "That was the ER. They're sending up a broken pelvis."

She nods and glances back at the board with our room assignments.

"Do you want me to take them?" I ask. Since I have a VIP patient, Sandy gave me fewer rooms than everyone else.

"No. I've got it. Why don't you go ahead and go to lunch?"

"Sure. I'm just going to check on my patients first." I glance at Ash. "You should try to get some sleep. Lying down will help your shoulder."

"I can't sleep in this place." The flash of vulnerability in his eyes is there one second and gone in the next. A flirty smile kicks up one side of his mouth. "Maybe you want to come keep me company while you're on your lunch? I have lots of food."

"What you're proposing sounds like the opposite of rest."

"Did you think keeping me company was code for getting naked or something? I'm shocked, Bridget." The way he says my name sends goosebumps racing up my arms. "I was only suggesting we sit and hang out. I want to hear what you've been up to since the last time I saw you." His smile couldn't be any smugger if he tried.

"I'm not allowed to *hang out* while I'm on the clock. I have other patients."

"Professionalism, I dig it. So, check on them first, then come hang out." He glances around the empty halls. "Looks like everyone is sleeping, anyway."

"Everyone but you," I correct him. "I'm sorry. I can't hang out with you."

"Unless I need something…" He shifts his attention. "Tell me, Hannah, if I were to go to my room right now and buzz my nurse, would Bridget be the one to come check on me?"

"Yes, she would." She stands and stretches.

The traitor.

He's charmed all my coworkers to taking his side.

"And she'd tell you—" I start, but he cuts in.

"That I need rest. I know, I know. I got it." He blows out a breath and runs a hand through his messy light-brown hair as he moves away from the desk.

"I'll be by in a few hours, but if you need anything—really need anything—just buzz."

"All right. Three hours. I'm gonna hold you to that. Later, Nurse Bridget."

The man is infuriating, but somehow so likeable that it's hard to be annoyed with him. As he strolls away, I stand to work off some of the anxiousness in my body.

"That is one good-looking guy." Hannah moves a step closer to me when he's gone.

"And he knows it," I mumble.

She turns and leans against the desk. "I don't know. A flirt? Yes, but he seems to have a good head on his shoulders. I know for a fact he does a lot of charity work for the Wildcat Foundation and he just spent the past thirty minutes signing everything we pushed at him."

"Fine. He's a decent human, but he's still arrogant."

"Sweet, good-looking, and a world-class athlete. I think he's allowed to be a little cocky. He's quite the triple threat in my book," she says. "Single too, but not for long if I have anything to say about it."

"What is John going to say about that?" I quirk a brow. Her husband is fiercely protective and adoring. He picks her up every morning after her shift. Gets out, kisses her, and opens the door. It's heartwarming. And I can't imagine him sharing, even if they're both Wildcat fans.

She throws her head back and laughs loudly. "Not me. I am very happily taken. My cousin just graduated college and moved back home."

"Oh." A pang of jealousy hits me unexpectedly.

"Unless *you're* going to cut the guy a break and stop ignoring his blatant attempt to get your attention."

Heat climbs up my neck. "I'm not interested in dating right now."

She's quiet for a moment, considering me with a pensive gaze. "I didn't meet Gabe, so I know I don't know the situation, but I know what it's like to be fresh off a breakup and feel like you'll never find a decent guy. You will. I promise. I felt the same way so many times. I would swear off dating because of shitty dates or asshole boyfriends. It was exhausting. I couldn't fathom going through it all over again. But you know what?"

"What?" My lips quirk up at the corners just listening to Hannah talk. She never ceases to put me in a good mood. If we weren't at such different stages of our lives, I think we could be good friends.

"All I really wanted was someone who would work harder to tear down the walls I built. I wanted to feel like I was worth the trouble." She pushes off the desk when the elevator dings and a nurse from the ER pushes our new patient out onto the floor. "Then again, that was just me. I was hard to love when I was your age."

"I find that very hard to believe."

"It's true. I wouldn't let anyone close enough to get to know me, so the only men that bothered asking me out were the ones that didn't care about knowing me more than one night. Until John."

"What made him different?"

"Everything."

My chest tightens. My situation is different, but there's probably more to her words than I want to analyze right now.

Room 612's call button flashes on the desk. I'm happy for the distraction.

"I got it," Hannah says. "Go take your lunch."

"It's fine. I should probably go check on Ash anyway and make sure he went back to his room. If Sandy hears that he was walking the halls and flirting with nurses, she'll lose her shit." I chew on the inside of my cheek. A terrible habit I've had since I was a kid whenever I'm nervous or agitated, or sometimes just bored.

"Okay, fine. You handle Ash, but then go eat. You look tired. You need food and caffeine. Are you going to see Liza?"

"Oh, shoot." I check the time. "I forgot."

"Go now. I've got you covered." She shoos me with a wave of her hand as she heads down the hall toward Room 612.

I give myself a pep talk on the way to check on Ash before I leave the floor. I can do this. I love my job. I've wanted to be a nurse for as long as I can remember. How I make people feel while they're here matters. Even when I leave here exhausted, there's a sense of accomplishment that no other job has given me.

Ash is charming and he's a flirt, but he isn't the first patient to hit on me. I can handle him for a few more hours.

When I walk into his room, Ash is in bed. Leaning back, one ankle crossed over the other, he stares up at the ceiling.

"I thought for sure I was going to find you in here bouncing off the walls."

He lets his head fall to the side. "That was either the fastest three hours ever or I blacked out."

"It hasn't been that long."

"That must mean you missed me then." One side of his mouth quirks up.

"You're incorrigible."

"Been called worse." He sits up. "Been called better too."

I stop by the side of his bed, hands in my pockets. "Are you going to be able to sleep at all?"

"Doubtful."

"I'm sorry."

"Eh, it's fine. It seems like I'm gonna have plenty of time to rest over the next few weeks." His lips pull into a straight line and a muscle in his cheek flexes.

"I meant I'm sorry about the injury."

He nods slowly. "Thanks."

I walk around the bed and pull the curtains.

"It's such a trip that I'm here and you're here. Fate."

"Getting a concussion is fate, huh?"

He chuckles softly. "It brought us together and now I can ask you out, so yeah."

I'm almost relieved he finally put it out there because I can tell him no and we can move on.

"I'm not dating right now."

"Because of the jerk ex-boyfriend? I've never wanted to hit someone so much in my entire life. I was worried about letting you leave with him, but I didn't know what else to do."

I break his stare and swallow down the emotions rising to the surface when I think about that night. He couldn't have done anything. I know that, but the what-if scenarios still taunt me. "No, not because of him. I can take care of myself."

"I have no doubt," he says in a playful voice that causes me to look back at him. He really is too handsome for his own good. Some of that playfulness takes on a serious edge when he adds, "I really did look for you. Every game I kept hoping you'd show up again."

I have no idea how to respond to that. Do I even believe him? I finally settle on, "I don't really like hockey."

"How come?"

"I don't understand it, and everything moves so fast."

"No, not that. How come you aren't dating right now?"

"Oh. I'm too busy."

"With?"

"School and work." I wave a hand around the room. "The stress of dealing with patients who won't sleep at night."

That pulls a smile out of him. "That's it? I'll be on my best behavior. Promise."

"You? Doubtful."

"I'll have you know I'm a gentleman."

"Sorry."

"Too busy," he says quietly. "That's an excuse I haven't heard in a while."

We both know I could make time for dating if that was the real issue. He manages, and I know his schedule must be insane. Then again, everyone Ash dates probably lets him dictate everything from when and where they go out to how often they have sex. Which I bet is a lot, as cocky as this man is. And now I'm thinking about having sex with him. Dammit. Why can't I keep my thoughts out of the gutter?

Frustrated, I shake my head. "I'm going to lunch. I'll check in again when I get back."

"Okay," he says, voice despondent.

I get all the way to the door before I pause and reconsider, but I force myself to go. He needs rest and I need to catch my breath. This day, this month, has been a lot.

On my way downstairs, I eat a protein bar. The elevator doors open on the pediatric unit. Mindy, the charge nurse on the floor, looks up and smiles when she sees me.

"Is she up?" I ask her, tipping my head toward the direction of the patient rooms.

Mindy nods. "Yeah. I think she was hoping you'd stop by."

"Thanks." I smile and head down the hall. Everything on the pediatric floor feels warmer, happier. It's decorated basically identical to every other unit, but the air is different I swear.

Kids have this amazing ability to find joy in every situation. It's one of the big reasons I want to work here eventually. I don't ever want to stop finding the joy. No matter how bad things seem.

At Liza's room, I knock quietly and peek in.

"Come in," she calls over the TV. She sits at the end of her bed watching the screen on the wall in front of her. She turns quickly to see who it is, then does a double take and a big smile spreads across her face. She tries to hide it quickly, but her smile won't cooperate. "Hey."

"Hi." I walk all the way into the room and toss a new book of Sudoku puzzles on the bed next to her. "Can't sleep?"

"It's barely midnight." She snorts and tosses her red hair over one shoulder. "Besides, I have three episodes left in this series."

I glance at the screen. "What is it about?"

"It's too hard to explain, but that girl in the hospital bed fell off a cliff as she was about to get with the guy she likes. He confessed that he'd been in love with her for years, but now she has amnesia and doesn't remember any of it."

"She was going to get with that guy?" I ask as on the TV a dark-headed, broody-looking guy appears next to the hospital bed with tears in his eyes.

"No. That's a different guy. She was dating him, but secretly had feelings for the other guy. This dude is all wrong for her."

I laugh and take a seat on the bed next to her. "Sounds complicated."

She shrugs one shoulder and takes a drink of juice.

"How's your blood sugar?"

"Shit, obviously. I'm here."

I laugh softly and she gives me a rueful smile. "I'm dehydrated and my sugars are a mess."

I check her chart while she keeps watching the TV. She's improved since they admitted her this morning, so that's good.

Liza was my very first patient. I was doing clinicals when she was admitted to the hospital and diagnosed with Type 1 diabetes. For the past nine months, she's been in and out as they struggle to get her levels steady. Her parents both have big corporate jobs and most of the time she's here by herself. They visit, but it's not like the other kids who have parents hovering over them for their entire visit. Even when she was here the first time, her mom only stayed the first night and the rest of the time she visited for an hour or two once a day.

Liza's sixteen, plenty old enough to be left alone, I guess, but it frustrates me that they leave her alone so much while she's sick. That's probably why I bonded with her so deeply. I felt this huge responsibility to make sure she had someone looking out for her.

Mindy lets me know any time Liza is admitted and I try to come down during my lunch break. The sassy teenager is a total night owl, which works out nice for me since I don't take my long break until around midnight.

"I heard you had some famous hockey player on your floor. Is it true?" She takes her attention off the screen long enough to look at me as she asks the question.

"How'd you hear that?"

"Please. That's all anyone has been talking about. Have you met him?"

"Yep. I sure did."

"Really?" Liza pauses the TV and turns on the bed to face me. Her eyes light up. "You met Ash Kelly?!"

"A second ago he was 'some famous hockey player.'"

She rolls her eyes dramatically. "My dad watches hockey and sometimes I sit with him so we can spend time together."

My chest squeezes at her admission and I like her dad even less than before. I wonder if he has any idea his daughter is trying so hard to get his attention.

"So, tell me, what's he like?"

"He's...fine."

"Fine?" She studies me closely, then stiffens. "Is he an asshole? Was he mean to you?"

The fire in her eyes at the thought of someone treating me badly is heartwarming.

"No," I say quickly. I don't want her to get the wrong idea. Ash might be frustrating, but I'm pretty certain that he's not a jerk. "He's fine. Normal."

"I'm not buying it. You're not telling me something."

Now I'm rolling my eyes. "There's nothing to tell. He just won't sleep."

"O-kay," she says the word slowly like she's trying to decide why that's a problem.

"He needs rest to heal and instead of doing that like I keep suggesting, he's wandering the halls and signing autographs for every person on the floor."

Liza nods slowly. "He's probably just bored or lonely."

"It's only been a few hours."

"Yeah, but hospital time isn't like normal time. I swear the minutes go by twice as slow here. There's nothing to do and nowhere to go.

Everyone inside either feels crummy or is preoccupied taking care of the people that feel crummy and at this time of night everyone outside of here is sleeping or busy."

I try to hide the pity in my expression at her admission, but she must see it because she's quick to smile and add, "I'm used to it by now. That's why I always make sure to bring my own entertainment."

Liza presses play on her show and turns back to watch it. Guilt settles in as I think over everything she said. Maybe I was too quick to dismiss Ash's need for socializing. He's a professional athlete who is going to be sidelined for weeks. Who wouldn't want to take their mind off that?

Dammit. I think I screwed up. Standing, I head for the door.

"Are you leaving?" she asks, a hint of disappointment in her voice.

"I am, but I'll be back. I forgot something."

CHAPTER SIX

Bridget

WILDLY TALENTED

After getting the okay from Mindy, I call up and ask Hannah to bring Ash down to the pediatric floor. I'm standing in front of the elevators waiting for him when it dings and the doors slowly open.

He wears a skeptical but humored expression as he steps out. "Are you exiling me?"

"Where's Hannah?"

"She got a call as we were about to leave. I told her I could find it on my own." He looks up and around. "Where am I?"

"Welcome to the pediatric floor."

I'm not sure what I expected his reaction to be, but when he smiles, my stomach does a flip. "We're going to hang with kids?"

"Just one. The others are sleeping."

"Right." He nods and falls into step beside me as I lead him back down the hall toward Liza's room. "I don't have any merch or anything with me, but if I make a couple calls—"

I stop abruptly in the middle of the hall and look him square in the face. "This isn't about what you can do for her, it's about what she can do for you."

"I'm intrigued," he says, aiming that arrogant and flirty grin at me as I walk backward a few steps. I can feel my smile widen in response to his. I'm glad he's on board. I think this will be good for Ash and Liza.

As I always do, I knock on Liza's door as I enter.

"What'd you forget?" she asks, staring ahead at her TV show. She's still sitting on the bed, legs crossed. The book of Sudoku rests in her lap.

When I don't immediately answer, she glances over and goes very still.

I take another step and look back at Ash hovering in the doorway. "Liza, this is Ash. Is it okay if he hangs out in here with me for a few minutes?"

She still doesn't speak. I'm worried I might have broken her brain.

Ash walks farther into the room. His good looks mixed with his friendly and flirty demeanor make my good sense want to take a permanent vacation. At the game last month, I thought it was all for show, but now I'm starting to think it's just him.

"Hey," he says. "What are you watching?"

Snapping out of it, Liza rushes to pause the show. "It's this anime series a friend recommended. Wow. It's really you."

The way she looks at him, equal parts awe and shock, has me covering my mouth to hide a smile.

"Nice to meet you, Liza." He nods toward her Sudoku. "I love those. I play a lot on road trips. That and Royal Match."

"Bridget brought it for me because she knows how bored I get in this place."

He looks over his shoulder at me with an expression I can't quite decipher.

Bringing him here was my idea, but now that we're all crammed into this room together, I feel even more aware of him. His VIP room is twice as big, and at least upstairs, I had a getaway.

"That's cool. How do you two know each other?" he asks her.

"She was my nurse the first time I was here. Diabetic," Liza says. "Bridget's the best. Bummer that she's on another floor now. But good for you, I guess."

I was anything but the best on my first day. I was scared and unsure, but I tried not to let Liza see any of that.

"Yes, great news for me." Ash smirks at me and I'm certain my face is turning red.

I clear my throat. "Ash was bored with us upstairs, and you're the most entertaining patient in the hospital so I thought you should meet."

"What she means is I'm a giant pain in the ass and making her life difficult. She's pawning me off on you," Ash says.

"Do you want to do one?" Liza offers him her book.

He takes it with a grateful smile.

"Sit," I command, pointing toward the chair in the room.

He does and I grab an extra pillow to put behind his shoulder. Liza has fully come out of her earlier shock. For the next five minutes, we all watch the end of the current episode and Ash works on a Sudoku puzzle. I have no idea what is happening, partly because I find myself continually watching Ash instead of the screen. Best-case scenario I thought Liza would chat his ear off long enough for him to get his mind off everything, but he looks like he's enjoying being here.

When it's over, Liza fills him in on the earlier plot points of the show and then starts peppering him with questions about his injury.

"That sucks," she says when he's told her about the hit during the game and that he'll likely be out for a few weeks. "I broke my arm in seventh grade and missed twelve weeks of tennis."

"Tennis, huh?"

"Yep, just like Bridget."

Ash's gaze lifts. "You play tennis?"

"I did. Not anymore."

"She was, like, really, really good," Liza says.

"How would you know?" I ask her. We talked about it a couple of times, but I know I never claimed to be good. I was decent as a kid, but I didn't put as much effort into it as I got older and hit a plateau.

"I saw some old videos on YouTube. She won a couple of local tournaments."

"Is that right?" Ash asks her, but his eyes are locked on me. "How did I not know this?"

"Maybe because we met four hours ago."

"That's not entirely accurate."

I glare at him. If he tells Liza the whole story like he did the nurses upstairs, I'll duct tape his mouth closed. As if he can see my thoughts, Ash's upper body shakes with quiet laughter. He turns his attention back to Liza. "I might need to see some of these videos."

"I'm out of screen time until tomorrow," she says with a frown.

Thank goodness.

"Good thing I have mine." Ash's voice is saccharin sweet as he reaches into his pocket and pulls out his phone.

"Knock, knock," Mindy says as she stands in the doorway of Liza's room. "Sorry to interrupt, but I need to check your blood sugar."

"Now?" Liza asks with a whine.

"We should get back anyway," I tell her. "Ash needs to sleep, and my lunch break is almost over."

"All right." The disappointment in her voice always tugs at my heart.

"I'll stop by tomorrow," I promise.

"Nice to meet you," Ash says to her. "Thanks for keeping me company."

When he tries to hand her back the book of Sudoku puzzles, she shakes her head. "Keep it. I have a stack of them."

We say our goodbyes and Ash and I head out.

He doesn't say anything until we get on the elevator.

"Is she going to be okay?" he asks.

"Yeah." I nod. "She's a brittle diabetic, which means her blood glucose is harder to control. She's had to stay in the hospital quite a bit since her diagnosis."

He nods thoughtfully as he leans back against the elevator wall.

"How are you feeling?"

"I'm all right."

"Liar. Your head hurts, doesn't it? You keep clenching your jaw."

A small smile tugs up one side of his mouth. "It kills."

"I'm sorry. I shouldn't have dragged you down here."

"No," he says quickly. "I'm glad you did. Liza was cool and I got to learn more about you. A tennis player, huh?"

"I was, yeah. I quit the team last year."

"I'd love to watch you play sometime."

"*You* want to watch a college tennis match?"

"I want to watch *you* play."

I don't even try to resist rolling my eyes at him.

"I play a little. My uncle owns a country club. I spent every summer working there until I graduated college. I could take you to dinner and then we could hit the ball back and forth a bit."

The doors open on the orthopedic floor and we step out and slowly walk back toward his room.

"With one arm?" I ask.

He flashes a cocky smile. "I'm wildly talented with the right incentive."

Yeah, I'll bet he is.

"And my nurse will be there in case I need anything."

I can't help but laugh. "I'm not dating right now."

"Right. Because you're *busy*."

"I am," I insist, voice on the verge of a screech. "I have a lot going on."

When we get to his room, he walks right in and climbs into bed. He rests his head back on the pillow and waits for me to continue.

"I work all night, go to school all day. Any spare minutes I find, I'm usually studying or figuring out what I'm going to feed myself. Seriously, who knew the worst part of being an adult would be deciding on and cooking dinner? I haven't read a book for fun or watched TV or gone to the tennis court in so long, I basically have no hobbies."

Something in the way he looks at me, half-amused and wholly focused, pushes me to keep going. "And today I found out that I'm going to have to move from my rental, so that'll take days or weeks of searching for something close to campus that I can afford. See? I definitely don't have time to date."

"I happen to be great at deciding what to eat for dinner. I'd be happy to help. Two birds, one stone." He looks so proud of himself.

"How's tomorrow?"

I imagine that for a moment, what it would be like to go to dinner with Ash. He'd be charming and attentive, and I'd have fun for a few hours. But I'm not ready to get involved with anyone right now. Definitely not a hot hockey player who is a notorious serial dater. "I don't think so."

"Why not?" His voice climbs with lighthearted outrage and his eyes twinkle. "You can't be too busy to eat."

"Maybe I just don't want to go out with you."

"I did consider that, but then I remembered you checking me out earlier when I had my shirt off."

"I was doing my job."

"Ogling my body is the job, huh?"

My face heats with the accusation. He isn't wrong, I was checking him out, but some of it *was* for professional reasons.

"I'm not going out with you."

"Is it because of the jerk ex-boyfriend? Are you still in love with him?"

"No," I say too quickly. The only emotions I feel when I think of Gabe are anger and shame. Anger that he turned out to be such an asshole and shame for not realizing it sooner.

"Good. He didn't deserve you. I'm glad you broke up with him. You should date someone that treats you a hell of a lot better than he did that night. Even if it's not me, though I think it should be me."

I wish he'd forgotten about that night outside the bar. "How do you know he didn't break up with me?"

He scoffs. "Nobody is that stupid."

I'm at a loss for words again and distract myself by checking the time. I need to get back to the desk and relieve Hannah.

"I should go check on my other patients, and you need sleep."

He nods. "I am starting to get a little tired. Don't know how much sleep my shoulder is going to let me get though."

"Is the pain okay?"

"It's better now that I'm lying down. What time do you get off?" he asks.

"Seven."

"Will you come see me again before you leave?"

"Only if you promise to stay in bed and rest until then."

He laughs. "If I do, will you have breakfast with me?"

"You just don't give up."

"Never."

Against my better judgment, I find myself nodding. "Fine, but just coffee."

"Really?" His obvious glee makes my stomach flip.

"I'll stop by once I clock out, but I only have thirty minutes before I have to leave for classes."

"I'll be ready. Not how I pictured our first date, but I can work with cafeteria food."

Even with excitement bubbling under my skin, I feel an instant twinge of regret. What the hell am I doing?

"It's not a date. I'm just letting you buy me coffee to make up for being the worst patient ever."

He laughs that deep, throaty chuckle again. "Fair enough."

"Get some sleep."

"Goodnight, Nurse Bridget."

CHAPTER SEVEN

Ash

LET'S NOT GET CARRIED AWAY

"**Y**ou didn't even get her number?" Jack pulls into my driveway and kills the engine.

"I was working on it. We were gonna get coffee, where I'd convince her she should go out with me. But then the doctors sent me for a second X-ray this morning to double-check my shoulder and that took forever. When I got back, she'd already left."

"Damn. That sucks."

I nod in agreement. "But at least I know her name now and where to find her."

My body aches as I climb out of his car. As the pain in my shoulder and head has lessened, the rest of the bumps and bruises from the game are starting to hurt. I can't wait to get to the rink and have the trainers work their magic before we leave for Nashville.

No sooner than I've thought it, I realize that's not going to happen. I'm not going to Nashville or any of the other upcoming road games.

Jack follows me into the house. It's been less than twenty-four hours since I left to go to the rink before the game, but damn, it's good to be home. I'm a homebody. Don't get me wrong, I love to hang with friends and throw parties, but I prefer doing those things here.

Since my teammate Tyler and his wife Piper moved out, it's been too quiet around here. It might be time to throw a party. Just as soon as I get out of this sling.

In the kitchen, I toss my stuff on the counter, then notice the takeout bag from my favorite breakfast spot.

My stomach grumbles. "You know the way to my heart, man. I won't even question why you were already in my house this morning."

"I just made sure you had a few things on hand."

At his words, I walk over and open the fridge. I scan the many containers of food stacked up on the shelves and look back at him. "A few things? This looks like meals for a month. You didn't need to do all this."

"It's nothing."

It's not nothing. The fridge is packed with pre-cooked meals that I'd bet his chef cooked last night or this morning. That guy needs a raise for putting up with Jack.

I shut the fridge and lean a hip against the counter. "I'm not helpless, you know. I've still got one good arm."

"I know. Just trying to help how I can. The team leaves this afternoon and we'll be gone until Friday. I'll feel better knowing you aren't sitting around eating Ramen and DoorDashing burgers."

A burger sounds fucking fantastic right now.

"Well, thanks." The reality of my situation is starting to really settle in, and it sucks.

Not long after, Declan stops by and then Leo. The four of us all live in the same neighborhood. Leo is across the street, Declan just next to him, and Jack is at the end of the cul-de-sac. One big, slightly dysfunctional, but hella fun family.

We settle in the living room. Leo is telling us about how Callum projectile vomited on Scarlett's dad (also our coach) last night after the game and Coach had to go into the media room smelling like baby puke.

Sitting around, shooting the shit does wonders to help me forget about my injury, but when they all start checking the time and making excuses, I realize they need to head to the team jet.

"Scarlett wanted me to invite you over for dinner tonight," Leo says.

"Sounds good."

Declan tips his head. "Take it easy. I'm counting down the minutes until you're back."

"Me and you both." I walk them to the door.

Jack hangs back. He pulls his sunglasses down over his eyes. "I'm having a party next Saturday after the long road trip."

"What's the occasion?"

Jack throws a lot of parties, but there's always a reason. If this is on my behalf, some pity party to make me feel better about sitting out for four weeks, I want to know beforehand.

"I met someone last night and her birthday is coming up."

Well, that's unexpected. My brows rise. "You met someone last night and you're throwing her a birthday party?"

"That's what I said."

Jack does not bend over backward for chicks. Certainly not one he just met. "Who is she?"

"Meredith." He hesitates, working his jaw back and forth. "She's a sports reporter."

I bark a laugh. "A reporter?!"

"For the Twins. She doesn't cover hockey," he quickly adds.

I fight another laugh. "I have so many things I want to say right now, but I don't want you to take back all the food you brought over. You hate reporters."

"She's cool."

"And super hot?"

His lips curl into a smile. "Yeah, that too."

"Wow. You don't mess around. You left the hospital late, somehow met a chick and got to know her well enough to throw her a party?"

"Ha ha. It's not a big deal. I asked her to go out next weekend and then when she said it was her birthday, I asked what she wanted to do. She said to keep it simple."

"And you thought throwing a party with all your teammates was keeping it simple?"

"She's new to town and doesn't know that many people. I repeat, not a big deal."

"I can't wait to meet her. The great Jack Wyld may have finally met his match."

"Let's not get carried away. Saturday night, eight o'clock, bring a date if you can find one."

"Maybe I'll ask Bridget."

"Yeah, text her…oh, wait. You can't because you somehow didn't get her number."

I give the finger to his back as he jogs toward his car.

"Thanks for everything, asshole," I call out.

He opens the car door with a smirk on his face. "See you in a week. Try to shower before then, my car stinks like sweat and hospital food."

I shake my head as I go back inside. God, he's a pain in the ass.

The days go by in a crawl while the team is on the road. They played in Nashville, then New York, and tonight they're in Toronto.

I'm just sitting down in front of the TV for the opening face-off when there's a knock at the door, followed by Everly's voice. "Ash? Are you home?"

"In the living room," I call.

A few second later, three women walk in and give me the same pitying, hopeful look.

"We brought snacks," Scarlett says. She's holding a platter of cookies in one hand and Callum in the other.

"And wine." Jade, Declan's wife, holds up two bottles—a red and a white.

Ev plops down beside me. "We're here to make sure you aren't moping around."

"There's food in the kitchen," I say and motion with one hand for Scarlett to give me Callum. "I ordered those little pretzel bite things you like, Jade."

"With cheese?" Her eyes light up and she hugs the wine bottles to her chest.

"Of course."

She takes off to the kitchen.

"Did Leo tell you we were coming?" Scarlett carefully places her sleeping baby on my right side. He squirms a bit, but then goes limp against my chest.

"Nah, but it's been almost twenty-four hours since any of you stopped by, so I figured there was a good chance you were going to do a group attack to watch the game."

"You do have the best TV." Scarlett takes a seat in a chair next to the couch and gives the giant screen her attention. "They have to win tonight."

"They will." Jade returns with three glasses of wine. She gives one to Scarlett, puts mine on the coffee table in front of me, and takes a seat with hers.

"Where's mine?" Ev asks.

I make a sound like a buzzer. "I'm gonna need to see some identification first, young lady. You don't look twenty-one."

"I'll be twenty in a month."

"Then in thirteen more months, you can drink my booze," Jade says with a playful wink.

The game starts and the four of us watch, screaming when the other team gets a power play goal and cheering when Leo scores. At the first intermission, Jade and Scarlett disappear into the kitchen.

"You look pretty good with a baby," Ev says, leaning forward and taking a sip of my wine before I can stop her. "Eww. That's gross."

I swipe the glass and drain the rest of it. Wine isn't really my go-to, but it's not bad.

"It's a little sweet," I admit, slowly leaning forward to set it back on the coffee table without waking Callum. "How've you been?"

"Okay. School is harder this year. I need a tutor in just about every subject."

"It's that bad?"

"Nearly. I had to stop going out on weekdays to stay home and study. Bleh."

I chuckle softly. "You poor thing."

She sticks her tongue out at me. "But Grace and I are loving the new place. You need to come by and see it. It's so cute. I'm pretty sure Ty is renting it to us at a steal, but I love it too much to protest too loudly. When he and Piper have kids, I'm gonna owe them so much free babysitting."

Her brother bought a house near campus for Everly to live in while she's going to college.

"He's happy to do it, and real estate near Whittaker is smart."

"I guess so. It's a three-bedroom, so Grace is going to ask her cousin if she wants to move in. Or we're going to turn it into one giant closet."

My phone buzzes in my pocket. Little Callum, who's slept through everything else, protests swiftly and loudly.

"Uh-oh." Everly reaches over and takes him from me. She holds him away from her body like she's scared of him while I dig my phone out. I scowl at the message.

"I'm guessing by your expression that it isn't from the nurse."

"How do you know about Bridget?"

"Oh, please. You're the hottest gossip around right now. Now that you and Jack are the only ones still single, Ty and the others just sit around talking about their women and any fresh gossip about your dating life."

Yeah, that sounds about right.

"I heard she turned you down. Several times." She's still holding Callum all awkward, so I slide my phone back into my pocket and motion for her to hand him back.

"She only turned me down once. We were going to have coffee but then it didn't work out."

"Okay. So text her and ask her to go out tonight. What else are you doing?"

"Thanks for the reminder I'm out of commission," I grumble. "I didn't get her number."

Everly's eyes widen. "Oh, crap. So she really is playing hard to get. I like her already."

"There was something there. Her ex was a dick, so she's hesitant, but I'm patient."

"Of course, you are. You have random girls texting you to fill the void." She pointedly glares at my pocket where I slid my phone.

"It was just Talia and I'm not interested in seeing her again."

"Good. She was kind of a bitch when you weren't around."

Which is exactly why I ended things. My team is family. I could never be with someone that didn't get along with them.

"Are you going to Jack's party for Meredith?"

"Yeah," I say. "I was hoping to bring Bridget, but that's not looking like it's going to happen."

"I was summoned to stop by but not touch the alcohol." She gives another eye roll.

"Jack invited you?" Those two are at each other's throats more often than not. Mostly because Jack is an asshole. He's a great captain and friend, the best actually. But when Everly came to live with Tyler, we all took on some of the responsibility of looking out for her. Jack's way of doing that was just a little more abrasive than the rest of us.

"Yeah, but probably just because he wants Grace to come and talk baseball or whatever."

"Ah." I nod. Grace's dad was a pitcher for the Twins before he retired.

"I'm thinking of filling an empty bottle of vodka with water and bringing it with me just to watch his head explode."

Knowing Jack, that's probably the exact reaction he'd have to an underage girl getting bombed at his party.

"Let's not poke the bear."

The girls stay for the entire game but leave as soon as it's over. Another loss to a team that should have been an easy win.

My house is too quiet as soon as they're gone. I should go to bed, but I'm not really tired. It feels like all I've done this week is sleep and rest. Tomorrow I finally start physical therapy. I'm anxious to get to work. The sooner I can get back my full range of motion, the sooner I can get back on the ice and help my team.

CHAPTER EIGHT

Bridget

LIKE A KNIFE TO THE CHEST

As soon as I step outside of the hospital, I exhale and tip my head up to the sky. The sun is out and there's a hint of warmth seeping through the fall morning.

I survived another week of working the night shift. Only three classes stand between me and a weekend of sleep. Thank goodness. I'm dead tired.

Distracted by my overwhelming exhaustion, I don't see Ash until he's right in front of me.

My steps come to a halt and my backpack slides off my shoulder. A cocky smile tips up one side of his mouth. I feel my face heat as he stares at me.

"Hey."

"Hi," I reply slowly. Seeing Ash Kelly out in the world, walking around like he's a normal human, is incredibly strange. "What are you doing here?"

"I remembered you said you got off at seven."

"You're here to see me?" The question comes out squeaky, my voice high-pitched and full of surprise.

"Yeah, I'm sorry about our breakfast date last week."

"It wasn't a date," I say quickly.

"Good. I feel less like an ass for not showing then."

"I heard they'd taken you to imaging. I had to get to class anyway." Was I disappointed? Maybe.

He nods thoughtfully.

"How's the shoulder?" I motion toward the sling cradling his left arm.

"Better." He glances down at it, then turns his gaze back to me. "Are you headed to class now?"

"Home first."

"Time for coffee?"

"Oh...uh." I look around. No one else seems aware that Ash is... Ash, and they're just walking by like this incredibly hot, talented guy isn't standing here asking me out for the second time. It's bizarre. We're in bizarro land.

"Trying to come up with an excuse?" He chuckles softly. "It's just coffee."

I have a feeling nothing with Ash is *just* anything, but since my brain isn't functioning well enough to come up with an excuse, I lead him back inside. There's a coffee shop on the first floor next to the gift store. He orders black coffee with one sugar and a splash of cream. I get mine with lots of both.

With our drinks in hand, Ash and I find a small table out front.

"So..." His light brown hair is tucked behind his ears and he wears a playful smile that promises fun and flirting. I could probably use a little more of both in my life. "How've you been?"

"Fine." I blow lightly on my coffee and then take a sip. An awkwardness that I don't remember from the other night stretches out between us. "You?"

"Bored. Restless. I'm not used to sitting around so much."

"Have the doctors said how long you'll be out?" Medical talk, this I can do.

"Three more weeks minimum." His mouth is tight at the corners.

"I'm sorry."

His expression shifts and he veers us to another topic. "How's the apartment hunting coming?"

"I've barely looked," I tell him honestly, then add, "I'll find something."

"I know a couple girls who go to Whittaker. They live just off campus and one of them mentioned they were looking for a third roommate. If you want me to put you in contact with them, I'd be happy to."

"Oh wow. Thank you, but I think I prefer to live alone."

"Why? It's so boring."

I laugh. "I take it you live alone?"

"I had roommates until recently. Now my place feels so quiet and empty. I hate it." There's a whine to his voice that emphasizes just how much he hates it.

"I like the quiet. It's hard with my schedule too. I'm sleeping while everyone else is up."

"I never asked you the other night, what made you decide to be a nurse?" He rests his right hand on the table. His fingers are long and strong looking. His arms and chest are covered with a long-sleeved black shirt that stretches over his muscular frame. He's built exactly like you'd expect for a professional athlete.

"My cousin was born with a heart defect and spent a few years of middle school in and out of hospitals. She's fine now, but we were close, and I spent a lot of time visiting her when she was there. The experience stuck with me. It was different than I expected. The nurses were fun and happy. They played games with her and talked about pop culture and brought in books and magazines they thought she'd like. I don't know, maybe it doesn't sound like much, but they made all the difference in how she felt about missing school and time with friends. She keeps in contact with at least one still today."

"That's cool." The way he smiles at me like I just said something far more exciting than I did makes my stomach flip.

"Did you always want to be a hockey player?"

"Not always. For a while I wanted to be a firefighter."

"What made you change your mind?"

His smile gets shy, which is a very odd look for Ash Kelly, and I find myself leaning in, eager to hear his answer.

"I found out that not every firefighter gets their own Dalmatian. I was five and my kindergarten class went to the local fire station." He places his right hand over his heart. "Like a knife to the chest."

"The Dalmatian does really make the job."

"Right? They didn't have any dogs there. Major bummer." He grins. "And for a very brief time I thought I was going to be a rock star."

"Do you sing?"

"No." He gives his head a brief shake. "But I spent one ear-piercing week trying to learn guitar."

Laughter spills out of me at his admission. "A firefighter, a rock star, and a hockey player, huh?"

"I can't imagine it any different now."

"Me either."

His mouth curves. "Nurse Bridget. I still can't believe I had to get injured to find you again."

I run my thumb along the back of my ring on my middle finger, twisting the gold band around absently. "I'm sorry."

"It isn't how I would have scripted it, but shit happens." His gaze drops to my scrub top where my name badge hangs off the front pocket. "Being a nurse suits you."

"You don't even know me."

"I'm learning." After another sip of coffee, he asks, "Why'd you give up tennis?"

Why'd I do any number of the things I did over the past two years? Why'd I stop hanging out with friends or going home to see my family? Quitting tennis is just one more bad decision I made among many.

I go with, "It was hard to juggle it with school and work."

Not the complete truth, but it isn't a lie either.

"How long until you graduate?"

"May."

Speaking of school, I turn my wrist over to check the time. The minutes are flying by and I need to get home to shower and change before my first class.

"You need to go?" Ash asks.

"Yeah. I'm sorry. The professor for my morning class is a stickler for being on time."

"I get it. Plans this weekend? I'd love to take you out sometime. Drinks? Dinner?"

There's a part of me that wants to say yes, but even if I were ready to date again after Gabe—and I'm not, going out with Ash would be like signing up for a marathon without training. "Thank you, but I can't."

"Because you're busy." His brows lift in a playful, teasing expression.

"It's only been a month since my ex and I broke up and I'm not really in a place mentally or emotionally to get involved with anyone yet." It's honest, but I'm sure he thinks I'm blowing him off. A hint of sadness creeps in as I realize this is probably the last time I'll ever see him. "Thank you for the coffee and for asking me out. It's the nicest thing that's happened to me in a while."

"You deserve nice things," he says with such certainty that I wonder if he has any idea how hard the past month has been.

I clear my throat and swallow down my emotions. "I hope your shoulder heals quickly."

"Thanks." He pulls a napkin from the holder. "You got a pen?"

I hand him one from my backpack and watch as he scribbles on one side of the napkin and then turns it over and scribbles on the other side.

"That's my number," he says as he sets the pen down on top of it and slides it toward me. "If you change your mind, give me a call."

His name and number stare up at me in bold slanted letters. I flip it over and then look up at him quizzically.

"That is the name and number of the girl I was telling you about with the room for rent. In case you don't find another place. I told her about you. She's cool. I think you two would get along well."

I'm oddly touched by the gesture even if there's no way I'm calling some random girl that he probably slept with. I fold it and tuck it inside the front pocket of my backpack. "Thank you. Again."

His blue gaze holds mine. "You're welcome, Nurse Bridget."

Saturday morning, I pull the pillow over my head and groan. It's the third day in a row I've woken up to the sound of landscapers hard at work before sunrise. Chainsaws, leaf blowers, pressure washers, and today…some sort of weird, loud hissing noise?

I forgave the last two days because it was the middle of the day and I'm used to noise and distraction while I'm trying to sleep during normal work hours. I didn't even hold it against them (too much) when they left their tools on my front porch yesterday afternoon during their lunch break and I ran out for my afternoon classes and nearly ate concrete as I tripped and fell over a weed whacker.

The point is, I understand that people need to do their jobs and not everyone can work a traditional eight to five. Trust me, I get it. But it's the weekend and I had big plans of sleeping in.

Sitting up, I reach for my phone on the nightstand. Another groan slips out when I see it's just past six.

I stomp into the living area of the little guest house I've been renting for the past year and go directly to the coffee machine. Eyes only half open, I stand there and wait for it to brew, breathing in the smell and doing my best to block out the noise outside. I'm pretty sure they have a radio going too. That or I still have yesterday's heavy metal soundtrack playing in my head.

I'm a little less angry as soon as I take my first sip. They're just trying to do their job. It isn't their fault that Ms. Cole decided to do a complete overhaul of her landscaping before putting her house on the market. Although that thought has me slipping back into a bad mood because I have four weeks left to find a new place to live and so far, the best option is a tiny one-bedroom ten miles from campus and even farther from the hospital.

I take another sip, hoping the more caffeine I get into my system, the less cranky I'll be.

Saturday is my favorite day of the week. I usually sleep in and then go on a long walk in the nearby park. I listen to a podcast or audiobook and watch all the people with their cute dogs.

Slightly more awake, I take my mug over to the front window and pull back the curtain. I'm not at all prepared to come face to face with a man in a white-hooded jumpsuit. The only thing the jumpsuit doesn't cover is his face, but he has on a ventilation mask and goggles so there are just tiny splotches of skin exposed to confirm it's a man and not a robot.

I screech and spill my hot coffee down my bare legs and toes. The man doesn't startle at all, just lifts the fingers around the handle of the spray gun and continues painting the exterior of the house.

I wave back and then quickly pull the curtain back in place. A quick shower later, I pull on a pair of jeans and a sweatshirt. Then I grab my jacket and a hat to head out.

I only realize I've left my gloves when I arrive at the park. I go to the coffee cart and get another drink, wrapping my fingers around the cup to keep them warm, and start around the paved pathway that circles the park.

The park sits between campus and a cute downtown neighborhood that's popular with wealthy thirty-somethings. Today it's more of them than my fellow students. They're probably all still sleeping. Lucky them.

An adorable, but highly energetic, chocolate lab runs by. His owner, huffing as he's pulled along, waves and I think he says 'good morning,' but it's hard to tell since he's so out of breath. A couple with a gray Miniature Schnauzer stops to pick up a steaming pile of poo, and a girl about my age is pushing a tiny, little, very expensive-looking breed of some kind around in a stroller.

After a few laps around, I toss the empty coffee cup and sit on a bench. A guy with a Pug stops in front of me to tie his shoe. The Pug gives me a once-over, as if deciding if I'm friendly (or have treats), and ambles over.

"Hi," I say as I lean down. I glance up at the guy. "Is it okay if I pet her?"

"Yeah." He smiles. "She must like you. She doesn't usually go to strangers."

I slide my fingers through her short, tan coat. "I like her too."

I scratch around her green collar and twist it to read her name, "Pretty Girl."

Standing to his full height, the guy looks embarrassed as he says, "She was my grandmother's dog. I didn't name her."

Laughing softly, I coo at the dog. "Hi, Pretty Girl."

When I look back up, the guy is watching me instead of the dog. I sit straighter. "Thanks for letting me say hi to her."

"Any time. We were about to grab coffee and walk around the park. Would you want to join us?"

My gaze drops from his face to his green sweatshirt. A Wildcat sweatshirt. My thoughts instantly go to Ash, just as they have more times than I'd like to admit since we said goodbye in the hospital parking lot.

"I was just about to head out." I give the dog one more scratch, then stand. "Enjoy your Saturday. Bye, Pretty Girl."

When I get back home, I'm relieved to see they're done painting the guesthouse, but it's a short-lived relief when Ms. Cole comes out of the back door, waving and calling my name.

"Morning, Ms. Cole."

"Morning! Morning!" She's all smiles in her yoga pants and oversized T-shirt. "I'm glad I caught you. I'm so sorry about all the noise this week. My realtor wants everything in tip-top shape as soon as possible so she can take photos for the listing."

"It's okay," I reply, even as a yawn breaks free.

"Have you found a new place yet?" she asks in a hopeful tone. I know she feels at least a little bad about giving me the boot. Not bad enough to throw away her plans to sell and move to Florida, but normal, decent-human twinges of remorse.

"No. Not yet." I try my best to match her hopefulness, but I'm certain I fail when her smile falls into a pitying frown.

"If there's anything I can do, let me know. I can write a referral or ask my realtor if she knows of any one-bedroom rentals."

"Thank you. I appreciate it, but I'm sure something will come up."

She nods. "Okay. Let me know if you change your mind. And don't forget that on Monday they'll be coming by to get photos of the guesthouse."

"Got it." With one hand in the air in a wave, I hurry back to my guesthouse. Or at least it's mine for a few more weeks.

Shutting the door, I lean my back against it and blow out a breath. Looks like I'll be spending the rest of my day searching classifieds.

I grab my backpack and take it to the couch. Sitting cross-legged, I pull out my laptop and open it up. Nothing new has posted since the last time I searched so I go through the same few options. They're either way out of my price range or too far away from campus. Beggars can't be choosers at this point though. Looks like I'll be commuting in every day.

I unzip the front pocket of my backpack and dig around for a pen and paper to write down the contact information for the properties. A piece of paper flies out with the pen. I unfold it and stare at Ash's handwriting.

I'm not sure I believe in fate, but if I did, I'd say the universe is telling me there's another option. That or the universe thinks I'm an idiot for not agreeing to go out with him. Touché, universe.

CHAPTER NINE

Bridget

A GOOD FEELING

After two days of texting back and forth with Everly, I'm mostly certain of two things.

I'm not texting with Ash. I know, that may seem obvious, but it did occur to me that maybe he just gave me two different numbers for him and was gonna be like "Surprise! You can sleep in my bed." Cue, total ick. But it isn't him. Or at least I'm ninety-nine percent Everly is real.

Ash didn't lie. She's nice. Or at least polite via text.

The paper that Ash gave me with Everly's name and phone number is folded up and tucked into the back pocket of my jeans as I walk up to the adorable little yellow house.

The homes on either side are cute, but more rundown. Typical college housing, but this one looks brand new. The landscaping is meticulous with small plants and fresh mulch. It isn't anything I would have recognized before, but it has the same look as Ms. Cole's newly landscaped backyard.

Two steps lead up to a cute little porch that spans the entire front of the house with a white railing and two navy rocking chairs with a small side table between them. It's like something off the home improvement channels my mother watches.

I'm certain I've written down the address wrong when a girl with blonde hair and a huge smile steps out onto the porch. The screen door slams behind her.

"Hi!" Her voice is more tentative than the expression on her face. "Are you Bridget?"

"Yeah. And you must be Everly."

"That's me." She hooks her thumbs into the back pockets of her jeans. "Ash said you were pretty."

I open my mouth, then close it.

"Sorry." She scrunches up her face. "That was super weird. Forget I said that. Come in. Grace will be here soon. She had a study group on campus."

Everly turns and holds the door open for me to step in behind her.

My jaw falls open when I see the inside. It still has a new paint smell and the surfaces gleam. We're standing in the living room, but the kitchen and dining room are visible. The dining room has a rustic-looking table with yellow upholstered chairs around it. Textbooks are laid out all around the top.

"It's gorgeous," I say as I take a few more steps. I look back at the living room. A large, blue sectional takes up most of the space. The TV is on Spotify and I smile when I see the name of the station is Harry Styles radio.

"Thanks. Yeah, it's coming together."

"You did this?"

"Mhmm. Grace and I already had a few pieces, but the rest we did ourselves. We found those chairs at a flea market and I reupholstered them."

"I'm impressed."

"It's fun." She shrugs. "Do you want some coffee or tea?"

"Sure. Coffee would be great."

While she pours me a cup, she points out a few more things that she and Grace bought and Everly refinished. She's talented.

"What are you studying?"

"I haven't declared yet, but I'm thinking interior design."

"I should have known."

She hands me a mug and we sit together on stools in front of the kitchen counter. "Ash said you were a nurse. Is that what you're going to school for?"

"Yeah. I'm getting my BSN."

"That's so cool. I don't like the sight of blood, so I don't think I'd be very good at that."

"I don't think anyone does, but you get used to it."

We make small talk over coffee. I like Everly. She's not as overly sunshiney as I thought at first, but she wears her emotions on her face and speaks them freely.

I could picture her with Ash. She's beautiful and confident. Black winged eyeliner frames her hazel eyes. There are two different kinds of women: the ones who can perfect winged eyeliner and the rest of us.

Grace hasn't shown up by the time our mugs are empty, so she gives me a tour of the house. A nice-sized bathroom with a shower and soaking tub. Three bedrooms, two of which they've already claimed for themselves.

"This would be yours," she says.

I walk into the room. The walls are white, and the floor is the same medium-tone wood planks that cover the rest of the house. It should be drab and unoriginal, but the light that floods in through the window makes it warm and inviting. The room itself is bigger than mine at the guest house, but I'd be sharing a bathroom and living spaces.

But everything in this house is just…nicer.

"How is this still available?" I ask, unable to keep the question to myself.

"We haven't advertised it. We were still trying to decide if we were going to rent it or turn it into a closet for our shoes when Ash said you were looking for a place."

I am seconds away from being completely mortified. "Oh my gosh. You aren't renting this to me as a favor to him, are you?"

"No." Everly shakes her head adamantly. "We've been going back and forth on it, but honestly, I think we were just waiting for the right person to come along."

"And you think I'm that right person?" Disbelief creeps into my voice.

She tilts her head to the side, studying me. "I think you might be. I have a good feeling about you."

That blows my mind a little. And so does this house. I can't live here. Can I? I turn in a circle. The door handle is a cute little crystal flower looking thing with a place for one of those old skeleton keys. It probably doesn't even work, but it doesn't matter. Damn that adorable door handle. It does me in.

"This feels too good to be true. Rent is only three hundred dollars a month?"

She nods.

"And I don't have to sign a contract giving you my firstborn or something?"

"God, no. I'm not even sure I ever want kids of my own." She leans against the frame of the doorway. "My brother bought this place at a steal and then renovated it. Well, not him specifically. He's good with cars, but not so great with a hammer." She smiles and I can see the love and admiration she has for her brother. "Anyway, it's an investment property for him, so he's not charging me much to stay here."

"Wow. That's really nice of him."

"Yeah, Ty is pretty great."

I walk to the far wall and run my fingertips along the smooth wall. "How do you know Ash? Did you two…"

Her face blanches. "Oh my gosh, did you think he and I…" She shakes her head vehemently as she trails off. "We're just friends. My brother is Tyler Sharp. He plays hockey with Ash."

"Oh." Relief that she's not one of his hookups or ex-girlfriends washes over me, followed by a heavy dose of annoyance at myself because either way, I am so not going there. "Sorry. Ash didn't say how he knew you and I don't follow hockey."

I follow Everly back out into the hallway. Even the light switches are cute—each one is different and looks vintage.

"Do they stop by a lot?" I cringe a little at the awkward question, but I need to know what I'm getting into. Running into Ash all the time could be weird.

"Are you trying to ask if the Wildcats hang out here regularly?" Her gaze narrows slightly on me.

"I didn't mean…I'm not trying to use you to get more face time with your brother or his teammates. I meant what I said, I don't really follow hockey."

Her expression softens. "I didn't think so, but you don't grow up with a hot, talented brother and not have people pretend to like you just to hit on him or his friends."

"I'm so sorry. That has to be awful."

"Thanks. I always shut it down pretty fast when it happens. It helps now that Tyler is married. So are most of his friends now that I think about it." She brings one hand to her hip and loops her thumb in the waistband of her jeans, staring at me like she's trying to figure me out. "You're worried about Ash using us rooming together as a way to keep asking you out?"

"He told you about that?"

"Yeah, of course. We're friends. *Just* friends," she reiterates.

"Yeah, I guess I am," I admit and feel instantly ridiculous. Ash Kelly going to all this trouble to ask me out again? Yeah, probably not. But I still can't help but voice my fears just in case. "This was so nice of him, and you for considering it, but I'm really not interested in dating right now. It's a dumb thing to be concerned about, I know. He's probably already moved on, but I need you to know in case you were hoping to play matchmaker or something."

"I love Ash like a brother, so I know I'm biased, but he's a good guy. If you told him no, then he's going to respect that. And if it makes you feel better, I'll tell the entire team that they can't stop by without twenty-four hours' notice and a very good reason."

That makes me laugh. For some reason I can picture Everly doing just that. She's not afraid to speak her mind. I like that. And I think I trust her (as much as I trust anyone these days).

"And as for me playing matchmaker, my schedule is so busy this semester, you do not need to worry about that. If I find anyone a date, it's going to be me."

I feel like a weight has been lifted at her reassurance.

"Ev?" A voice calls from the living room.

"That's Grace," she says and motions with her head for me to follow her.

Grace is quieter than her roommate, but she gives me the same pleasant, friendly vibes as Everly. They finish each other's sentences and talk each other up to me. Grace tells me how amazing Everly is at picking out stuff for the house and putting together outfits for a night on the town, which I'd already pretty much gotten on my own by all the touches in the house. And Everly tells me how she's a terrible cook, but that Grace makes the best homemade muffins and pastries on the weekends.

The two of them remind me of my friends from freshman and sophomore year. There were three of us and we did everything together, including sharing a suite on campus, until junior year. I don't miss them exactly, but I miss having people I can count on. Not for the first time in the last month, I think to myself that I should text them to catch up. But I know I won't. Too much time has passed and we're different now. Or at least I am.

"So, what do you think?" Everly asks me when it's time for me to go. She walks me out, stepping out onto the porch and crossing her arms over her chest to brace against the wind. "Want to be roomies?"

And I guess I do because I say yes.

CHAPTER TEN

Ash

THE BEST LOVE IS SELF-LOVE

"**A**m I cleared for the game tonight?"

The doctor gives me a stern look, ignores the question, and sits down on the stool in front of me. "It's healing nicely. A couple more weeks and I think you'll be back to full mobility."

"So, I'm not cleared for tonight?"

"I know how much you want to be back out there, but this early in the season, your coaches don't want to risk you reinjuring it and being out for the playoffs."

I already knew he was going to say no, but I'm still frustrated as I let his words sink in. Another week watching the game instead of playing it.

"Can I at least start practicing again?" I'm dying to get back on the ice. To do something.

"Keep meeting with Shane and let's chat next week."

"So that's a no?" I ask, mumbling the question as I get to my feet.

He stands and cuffs me on my good shoulder. "Soon. I promise."

I thank him, stop by to let Shane know next week's schedule is the same for my physical therapy, and then head to the locker room. My teammates are just finishing up their morning skate.

Leo spots me first. His eyes are wide and hopeful, but when I shake my head, he lets his mouth fall into a straight line. "Sorry, man."

"Still not cleared?" Tyler asks as he tosses his gloves in the cubby above his locker.

"Another week sitting on my ass." I plop down in my stall and let my head fall back against the locker. "This fucking sucks."

"Ah, cheer up, buddy," Johnny Maverick calls. "I think I met the perfect girl for you."

Well, that has my attention. But I'm skeptical. "You met my perfect girl?"

An image of Bridget pops into my head. It's been more than two weeks since I gave her my number and I haven't heard from her. That's probably my sign to move on, as much as I don't want to.

"Yep." He runs a tattooed hand through his dark hair. Maybe I need some new ink. I've been wanting to get something on my forearm or maybe across the top of my hand.

"Who is she?" Leo asks. Like a good friend, he squares off with Mav to make sure he's not trying to set me up with some weird rando.

"She's Dakota's doula," he says, mentioning his wife. They're expecting their first baby.

"I'm sorry, a what?" I ask, even more skeptical.

"It's like a doctor who delivers babies," Mav says.

"That's an obstetrician or midwife," Leo clarifies. "A doula is more like a coach. They give emotional support during the pregnancy."

"Yeah, that sounds right." Mav snaps his fingers and points at

Leo. "Pregnancy coach. She sends Dakota these really supportive texts about listening to her body and eating nutritious food, which pisses Kota off, but I swear Harmony is magic because my wife does everything she says."

"Scarlett and I met with one of those when she was figuring out her birth plan, but they mostly just asked her how she was feeling and talked about her fears and shit."

The guys continue going back and forth. Even Declan pipes in at some point. What in the world is happening?

"Can we get back to me? Not that I don't want to hear about your wives shooting out babies and all that."

Mav laughs good-naturedly. "She's cool, pretty, single, and she's coming to Wild's after the game tonight. You're welcome."

Jack walks into the locker room, fresh off the ice, and takes a seat next to me. "Just heard, sorry, man."

"One more week," I say more to myself than him. Hopefully. And because I don't want to talk about my shoulder, I add, "And Maverick wants to set me up with his wife's pregnancy coach."

Jack's brows rise, then his gaze slides over to Maverick.

"It's a real job. She's cool. You'll all see tonight."

"Wait, wait. Tonight?" Jack asks, sitting forward.

"Yeah, she's coming to Wild's after the game. Is Meredith coming?"

"Yeah, and she's bringing her friend Kennedy for Ash."

"You both set him up on the same night?" Declan covers his smile with a fist over his mouth. "Oh man, and to think I was going to skip the bar after the game tonight."

I side-eye my buddy. "What in the hell?"

"She's really cool," Jack says. "She does PR for the Twins. And she doesn't know we're setting her up, so don't say anything."

"I don't need any help picking up girls."

"Says the guy that hasn't been out with one in…" Tyler trails off.

"I admit, it's been a bit, but I've been a little preoccupied."

Leo snickers. "And by preoccupied he means sitting around feeling sorry for himself while binge-watching Ted Lasso for the millionth time."

"It's the greatest show of our time!"

They all chuckle.

Something loosens in my chest, sitting here, going back and forth with my teammates. Fuck, I've missed this. Weeks of not traveling or practicing with them, and I'd forgotten how much this part of the game means to me. Playing hockey is my first love, but these guys are a close second.

"What are we going to do about Harmony and Kennedy?" Maverick asks.

"Harmony? You want to set him up with a girl named Harmony?" Jack scoffs.

"Didn't you date a girl named Denim a few months ago?" Declan asks him.

"One date." He cracks a smile. "And no, she did not wear denim on our date. In fact, she made it a point to let me know she never wears denim."

"Riveting stuff. Hard to imagine why you only went out once," Ty quips.

"I like the name Harmony," Maverick says. "It's very Zen. And Ash being all deep and shit, I thought he'd appreciate it."

"I don't care about names. Although admittedly I'd have a hard time telling people I was dating someone named Denim. But I can't go on a date with two girls at the same time."

"Meredith and Kennedy won't be at Wild's until eleven or so. They have some fashion event beforehand," Jack says.

"Meredith isn't coming to the game?" I ask him.

"Nah." He shakes his head like it's no big deal. Maybe it's too soon for that kind of thing, what do I know. I've only met Jack's newest girl once at the party he threw for her at his house. She seemed all right.

Mav crosses both tattooed arms over his chest. "Harmony already mentioned she had to get home early tonight for an early client meeting, so I think with some careful seating, we can pull this off."

"I don't know..." Even if I'm not the one that set up these meetings, it feels wrong to hang with two different women back-to-back.

"You gotta get back out there," Jack insists. "What's the harm in meeting one super cool chick and a random weird one that Maverick found for you?"

"She's not weird!" Mav calls over his shoulder as he heads to the showers. "You'll see."

I watch the game from the press box. Despite Jack having a good night and some sloppy mistakes from Boston, we still end up short. It's infuriating not being able to help my team out of this funk.

Wild's is a short walk from the arena. I leave my truck and head over with the girls. As soon as we arrive, Dakota pulls me over to the bar to introduce me to Harmony.

She's pretty. Long brown hair and big hazel eyes. I'm not sure what I expected her to be like exactly, but I know she's different. I offer to buy her a drink and then we go over to a quiet table in the corner to talk.

"I love your tattoo." She leans forward and touches the edge of my butterfly tattoo on my left bicep. "Does it have some special meaning?"

I hesitate and take a sip of my beer before responding, "Would you think less of me if I said no?"

"I have a random heart on my hip from spring break my freshman year of college, so I'm in no position to judge."

"Any other tattoos?" I ask as I scan her visible skin in the tank top and jeans she's wearing. I don't see any, but she proceeds to give me a rundown of a few that are out of sight and then I show her the only other one I have.

From tattoos, we talk star signs, where we grew up, and a dozen other topics.

Maverick walks slowly behind the booth, eavesdropping on us where Harmony can't see him, and gives me a thumbs up and a smile. Like I didn't already feel like a kid being chaperoned.

We talk about lots of stuff, but when Harmony glances at the time and says she needs to get going, I don't really feel like I know that much more about her than I did when we sat down.

That might be on me. I can tell she's cool, but I'm not sure I feel any type of connection with her, and I mostly answered her questions instead of asking my own. Basically, I was a terrible date. The team's in a funk and so am I.

"I enjoyed talking with you. I wasn't sure about being set up with one of Johnny's friends," she says.

"That's fair." I chuckle.

She takes a pen out of her purse, then grabs my hand. "I'm giving you my number. If you ever want to hang out again, give me a call."

I stare down at the red ink along the top of my right hand as she gets to her feet. "Let me walk you out."

She waits for me and the two of us make our way through the busy bar. I spot Jack and Meredith sitting at the bar, and a redhead with them that I can only assume is Kennedy. My buddy waves at me. His girl and her friend don't see me, and I wave awkwardly back, still tailing Harmony. This whole thing is beyond weird.

"You have a ride?" I ask as we step outside.

"Yeah. I think that's me right there," she says as a red car pulls up to the curb.

The driver rolls down the window. "Are you Harmony?"

"Yep. One second." She turns back to me and then steps forward. We exchange a nice, short hug that is incidentally the closest I've come to a girl in a really, really long time. My dick doesn't *not* notice. And it doesn't care how connected I feel to Harmony. It's ready to do this thing. For two seconds, I consider chasing the car and asking if she wants to come back to my place.

I don't, but only because it feels too pathetic and misleading. I stand outside a few moments longer. Fuck, I need to get laid. I need to do something, anything to stop moping around.

With that in mind, I head inside and go directly to Jack so I can meet Kennedy and get this night over with.

"Hey, you made it," he says like I just got here. Only the smirk on his lips gives him away. He turns to the girls. "This is my buddy, Ash."

"Hey." I tip my head to him in greeting and then let my gaze fall to the girls sitting beside him.

"Hey, Meredith," I say to the blonde sitting closest.

Her smile is friendly, if not a little practiced from all the on-camera work she does. "Hey, Ash. I heard you're still out with the injury. How long until you're back?"

"Uhh…"

"Sorry." She laughs and that fake ass smile is replaced with a real one. "Off the record, of course."

"It's doing good, but I'm not sure yet when I'll return." That's as much as I'd give anyone outside of my team, and I don't wait for a follow-up before I move on to Kennedy.

She looks up at me with dark green eyes framed with thick black lashes. Her mouth is pursed, lips wearing this almost humored expression I can't quite make out.

"Hey, I'm Ash," I say to her.

"Kennedy." She offers me her hand. The ring on her middle finger reminds me of Bridget and how she had on multiple that night of the game.

Kennedy already has a drink in her hand, so I ask the bartender for a water and take a seat to her right.

"We're going to play darts," Jack announces, sliding his arm around Meredith's waist as they both stand.

I shoot him a glare. He's deserting me and couldn't be more obvious about his intention to leave us alone together.

"You good, Kennedy?" Meredith asks her.

"Yeah." The word comes out with a quiet laugh. "I'm fine."

When they're gone, she shakes her head and says, "Being set up is the worst, right?"

"You knew this was a setup?"

"Please. They're not at all subtle. Jack must have slipped you into conversation a dozen times over the last hour before you just so happened to show up. I know more about you than the last three guys I went out with combined."

"Oh, good." A deep chuckle rumbles in my chest. "I don't have to worry about coming up with interesting and fun facts about myself then."

"Nope." She takes a sip of red wine and angles her body toward me.

She's in a tight green dress almost the exact shade of her eyes that molds to her curves.

"It seems I'm at a disadvantage. I barely know anything about you."

"I'll give you three questions."

"Only three?"

"The thing is, if I give you an unlimited number of questions, you'll ask a bunch of random things and we'll pass the night by going back and forth sharing random tidbits, but not really getting to know each other at all."

"You've done this before." One side of my mouth pulls up into a smile.

"Is that a question?"

"Shit. No. Let me think." I take a drink of water and then wipe the condensation off my hand by running my fingers over my thigh. "What is the last series you binge-watched on Netflix?"

Her expression shows her surprise at my question, but she thinks for a moment and then says, "Unsolved Mysteries. I watched like five episodes in a row and then couldn't sleep for a week without the light on."

"Do you live alone?"

"No, I have a roommate, but she travels for work a lot." She holds up a single finger. "One question left."

"I think I'll save it for later."

"Good, because I have one for you."

"Something you don't already know?"

She nods and then leans forward like she's telling me a secret. The angle gives me a clear shot down her dress before her long hair falls forward. She's beautiful, no doubt about it.

"Why are you still single?"

I laugh at the unexpectedly direct question.

She pulls back, smiling. "I mean, you're a rich, good-looking guy. So far, you seem to be able to hold a conversation and you've looked at my chest just the right amount."

Just the right amount? When my brows lift, she explains, "If you didn't look at all, I'd think you weren't interested in me. And if you looked too much, I'd think you were only interested in getting me naked. So, are you the kind of guy, like Jack, who isn't interested in more than casual dating or is there some other reason you're single? Waiting for the right girl? Pining over the last girl?"

"Uhhh..." I run a hand over my jaw and glance over to where Jack and Meredith are playing darts. He looks pretty happy with one hand resting on her hip possessively, but he does have a reputation for hopping from girl to girl. That's not me, but pining over the last one? My mind automatically goes to Bridget, but I can't even count her as the last girl. The last girl I seriously dated was Talia and that was more than a year ago. Aware I still haven't answered, I finally say, "Somewhere in between, I guess."

"Hmmm…" She studies me for a beat, then stands. "Look. This doesn't have to be more than tonight, or it can be, your call, but I think you should use your final question now and ask me to either go on a real date or go back to your place."

My brows shoot back up. I was not expecting that.

Her laugh chimes in the air again. She clearly enjoys catching me off guard. "I'm going to say goodbye to Meredith and give you time to think about it."

I watch her go, still in a state of shock as she sways her hips across the bar.

Goddamn. I turn back to the bar and chug the rest of my water.

"Sooo…" Mav slides into the chair that Kennedy just vacated. "What'd you think of Harmony? Are you going to call her?"

I glance down at her number still on my hand. "She was nice."

Jack's deep laughter announces his presence. "Nice? I told you he'd like Kennedy better."

They bicker back and forth for a minute before Jack nudges me. "Don't leave us in suspense, which one are you picking?"

"No pressure, but I am about to have a baby so I really need the money," Mav says in a loud whisper-voice.

Jack rolls his eyes. "Oh, please. I've seen the nursery. You couldn't fit another baby gadget in there if you tried."

"Better than the overpriced liquor you're likely to buy with it."

I rub my forehead with two fingers.

Of course, they bet on this. I'm not even surprised. I'm sure I would have done the same thing.

"So?" Mav asks me. "Which one is the perfect girl for you?"

"Perfect girl? I'm just trying to get my boy back in the game." I'm sure there's another eye roll with the snort that comes from Jack, but I spin in my seat and look toward the dartboard where Kennedy is standing with Meredith.

"Thank you both. I know you meant well, but—"

"You're still hung up on the nurse, even though she turned your ass down like a dozen times?" Jack asks with a smirk.

Mav has an equally annoying smirk on his face as he adds, "And the more time you spend with other girls, the more you realize that the connection you had with her was unique?"

Jack snorts again. "I so don't get that."

"You will someday," Mav tells him.

"No," Jack says, like he can keep himself from falling for someone that easily.

For a second, I get lost remembering Bridget's turquoise eyes and the dimples that are only present when she smiles for real. I've never been so emo about a chick before. I've always felt like if things didn't work out, then it was for the best. But I can't seem to shake off Bridget.

"First of all, she turned me down twice. Not a dozen times. And secondly, I don't know if what I felt for her was unique or if I'm just not in a good head space to date right now. Harmony and Kennedy were both cool and maybe I'll see them again, but tonight I am going home alone."

"Fair enough." Mav places a hand on my shoulder and gives it a reassuring squeeze. "The best love is self-love."

"But if you had to pick, which one did you like best?" Jack asks.

Laughing, I stand and watch as Kennedy heads toward me. "You two are idiots."

I walk Kennedy to her car and grab her number with a promise I'll text to make plans next week. I'm not sure about a lot right now, but I know that it's time I got myself out of this funk. Joking around with the guys today was the most fun I've had in weeks. I need to get back out there and stop sitting around feeling sorry for myself.

When I get in my truck, I start it up as a notification pings on my phone.

Little Sharpie: My new roomie is all moved in! Thanks for passing on my info to Bridget. She seems great. How's the shoulder? Any word on when you'll be able to play?

CHAPTER ELEVEN

Bridget

HOME

Snow is falling hard as I get home from work. Home. I shake my head as I turn off the engine and stare at the adorable yellow house where I now reside.

It's been almost two weeks since I moved in, and it still doesn't seem real.

Keeping my head down, I jog from the car up the front sidewalk and onto the porch. I stomp my feet on the outdoor rug and then push inside. Warmth greets me with the smell of coffee and sugar.

Everly looks up from the dining room table where she sits with her schoolwork laid out in front of her. "Morning. I just made coffee."

"Thanks. I grabbed some at the hospital before I left." I hold up the to-go cup in my right hand, then get out of my snowy coat and hat, and hang them to dry.

She nods and goes back to her schoolwork, and I head to my room. Grace is still sleeping. She's never up as early as Everly. With my schedule, I tend to only see each of them once or twice a day. Everly is usually up and out in the kitchen in the mornings when I get home from work, and Grace and I have the same lunch break.

They've both been so nice and welcoming. They're really close and spend most of their evenings together in the living room, watching TV. Sometimes Grace's boyfriend Lane comes over and sometimes the three of them all go out. If I'm around, they always do the polite thing and ask me to join them, but I try to give them space. The three of us don't have to be besties to live together, and I don't expect that from them.

By the time I shower and get ready for school, I can hear both of them in the kitchen. They walk to campus together in the mornings. Their first classes are farther away than mine, so I leave a few minutes later.

I'm checking to make sure I have everything I need in my backpack when there's a knock at the door followed by Grace's voice. "Bridget?"

"Uhh, yeah, come in."

She opens the door and sticks in her head. "Hi."

"Hey." I smile back at her.

"I know you like to walk by yourself usually, but it's really coming down out there. Do you want to walk with us today?"

"Oh." My brows furrow. Something about the way she said I like to walk by myself makes me pause. I guess from my actions that seems true, but really, I just don't want to impose on their friendship just because we're roommates now. "No. I'm okay. I still need to grab something to eat."

"Are you sure?" Her gray eyes widen and her eyebrows disappear under her dark bangs as she waits for my response.

"Yeah. I'm okay, but thanks. I'll see you at lunch."

She waits another beat before nodding and then closing the door as she leaves. A few seconds later I hear the front door shut with their departure. I bundle up again and grab my backpack and phone. A blueberry muffin sits on top of a yellow napkin on the counter with my name scribbled on it. With a twinge of sadness, I smile at the considerate gesture.

I wrap it up and stick it in my bag for later and then head out. The snow falls in white flakes so thick I can barely make out my car parked along the curb.

When I get to the sidewalk, a silver truck comes to a stop next to me. I think he's letting me cross and wave him to go ahead, but then he rolls down the passenger side window and leans over.

I met Everly's brother one other time when he stopped by to see her, but I'm surprised to see him at this time of day.

"Did Everly already leave?" he asks.

"Yeah. About two minutes ago."

He nods. "All right. She wasn't answering her phone."

"Do you need something? I could try to text her." I pull out my phone. Snow drops onto the screen as I unlock it.

"No, I was just on my way to the arena and thought I'd swing by and see if you all wanted a ride this morning. It's really coming down."

"Wow, that's so nice. I'll let Everly know I ran into you." I put my phone back in my pocket and brush a wet drop off my nose.

Tyler continues to stare at me through the thick blanket of snow. "Are you heading to class now? Do you want a lift?"

"Oh, no, that's okay. I don't mind the snow."

His mouth twists into an uncomfortable smile. "Are you sure? It's nuts out here and I'm going that way anyway."

I hesitate again as more snow covers my coat and hat. My feet are already icy. "A ride would be great. Thank you."

He leans over and opens the passenger door. I try to shake off as much snow as possible so I don't get it in his truck, but he waves me off. "You're fine. Don't worry about it."

"It still smells brand new." I glance around, and to my chagrin, it also looks brand new.

"I just got it last week."

"Oh my gosh. I am so sorry. I could walk, seriously." The only mess in the entire truck is the pool of water and dirt from my shoes on the floor mat.

"Really. It's fine." His tone sounds completely genuine, but I am horrified.

I relax back into the seat and do my best to ignore the mess I made in his immaculate new truck as Tyler drives slowly through the snow-covered roads toward campus.

"How's everything going?" Tyler asks. He and Everly don't look that much alike. His hair is dark and his features are sharper, but they've both been so nice to me.

"Good. Your sister and Grace have been so welcoming, and the house is beautiful. I can hardly believe how well things worked out if I'm honest."

He lifts his gaze from the road long enough to glance at me and nod. "Everly is really happy it worked out too. She doesn't let that many people into her inner circle, but she speaks highly of you."

"We have that in common," I tell him, then add, "I really like her too."

The snow doesn't let up all day. My afternoon classes are cancelled and instead of trudging home for lunch, I grab a salad and find a table in the student center to study while I eat.

I pull out my laptop and glance around. I'm not the only one who decided to hunker down on campus. There's something serene about sitting inside and watching the snow fall with the buzz of happy conversation and laughter all around.

Groups of friends and couples make up the majority of the tables. Not for the first time since my breakup with Gabe, I wonder how my life would be different if I'd never met him. Would I be here with my friends instead of sitting alone?

I don't even remember the last time I talked to any of the girls I used to hang out with. When I started seeing Gabe, I stopped going out with them. It wasn't intentional at first. I was excited about my new relationship and caught up in the excitement of it. Going to parties and bars didn't have the same appeal.

I guess we weren't as close as I thought because it didn't take much time for us to drift apart. By the time I realized what a mess my relationship was, I didn't feel like we were close enough that I could confide in them. And now? Well, I feel like a different person and not one that they'd understand.

My phone vibrates on the table in front of me, pulling me from my thoughts.

"Speak of the devil," I mutter quietly as Gabe's name stares back at me from the screen. Why the hell is he calling me? I'm not curious enough to answer. I send him to voicemail and focus back on my homework.

I'm fully engrossed in biopsychosocial dynamics when I feel his presence. I glance up as Gabe slides into the seat across from me. My pulse speeds up and my stomach clenches.

"What are you doing here?"

Relaxed and cool, Gabe drops one hand on the table. He's wearing a long dress coat over his suit. His hair is wet from the snow and his cheeks are ruddy. "You're still sharing your location with me."

A shot of panic races through me. Since we broke up, he's known how to find me at any moment. I swallow around the lump forming in my throat.

As if reading my thoughts, he says, "What? It's not a big deal. I tried to call, but clearly you're ignoring me." Anger flashes in his eyes but disappears quickly. "Anyway, I stopped by because I have news and I knew you'd want to hear it."

He's wrong. So wrong. I don't want to hear anything he has to say. "We broke up, Gabe. Go tell someone else. I'm studying."

"Don't be like that. I got a new job. It's big. Really big."

"I don't care." I close my laptop and shove my stuff into my backpack quickly. If he's not going to leave, I am.

"God, you can really be a bitch sometimes, Bridget. Things are happening for me and I want you by my side."

"Not happening."

"Are you really going to throw away the time we spent together over some stupid arguments? We had a good thing."

I wonder if he really believes the words he says. Does he really think that he wants to be with me? You don't treat someone like he treated me if you truly care about them. "You and I have a very different accounting of our relationship. It's not happening. Not now, not ever again."

"You don't mean that. You want to make me out as some kind of monster, but you know that's not me. We were great together. I messed up, but it doesn't change how I feel about you."

I stand, uneasy on my feet, and glance at the exit. I need to get away from him. I can't believe he's had access to my location all this time. "I mean it, Gabe. Don't contact me again."

"Are you fucking someone else? Is that what this is about?" He gets to his feet quickly and walks with me toward the exit. It amazes me how fast he can go from sweet and apologetic to bitter and angry.

"No. And if I was, it wouldn't be any of your business."

"You're wrong, Bridget," he says, holding the door open for me. "You'll always be my business."

I wake up from my late afternoon nap to a voicemail from work that says I'm not needed and should stay home. Whittaker closed campus tomorrow, too, so I have nothing to do for the next twenty-four hours.

Earlier I overheard Everly and Grace talking about watching movies tonight, so I throw on some sweats and a big T-shirt and head out to the living room. After seeing Gabe today, I don't feel like being alone with my thoughts.

"Hey," Everly says. She sits in the middle of the couch with a big bowl of popcorn next to her. "I thought you had work?"

"They called me off."

"You don't have to go in at all?" Grace asks.

"Nope." I shake my head and absently tug on the hem of my T-shirt.

"You have to join us for a movie marathon," Everly says, putting the bowl on her lap and scooting over.

"We just started Dirty Dancing," Grace adds. "I've never seen it and Everly thinks that's a travesty."

"Me neither," I admit. "Well, I've seen clips."

"It is a travesty!" Everly exclaims and pats the couch. "Both of you need to watch it. Classes are canceled tomorrow because of the snow, so it's the perfect night to stay up late and binge-watch old movies."

"I love a snow day," Grace says with a smile. "My psychology test was pushed back to next week."

"Lucky." Everly groans. "My philosophy professor sent extra homework by email. I swear the man is evil."

"Do you want the chair?" Grace asks, looking at me.

I still haven't moved from where I stand in the space between the hallway and living room. Are they asking me to join them because they feel obligated or do they really want me to join? I decide not to overthink it. They asked. If it sucks or I feel like a third wheel, I'll duck out after the first movie.

"No, the couch is good." I take a seat on the opposite side of the blue sectional from Everly. She offers me the popcorn bowl and I take a handful.

"All you've missed is Baby's family driving to the resort for vacation," Grace says, filling me in as she goes to the kitchen. "Soda, wine, water, or coffee?"

"Coffee with a splash of Bailey's," Everly yells, then they both look to me.

"Same."

"Oh, and grab the leftover muffins."

A few minutes later, the three of us have mugs of spiked coffee, popcorn, and muffins, and are fully engrossed in the movie.

I forget to feel uncomfortable with these two girls I don't really know that well. Grace likes to provide commentary on scenes, and Ev shushes her or tosses a pillow when she doesn't agree. And I smile as I truly relax for the first time with them.

At the end of Dirty Dancing, we're a little tipsy and highly caffeinated. The three of us open the front door and look out. The snow is still coming down, but not as fast. The roads haven't been plowed yet and it's all so still and quiet out.

"Hey, I forgot to tell you. Your brother stopped by this morning to give you a ride," I say to Everly as we close the front door and retreat back inside our warm house.

"I know. He told me. I wish I had still been here. My feet were so cold by the time I got to class and my jeans were basically soaked."

"You have to dress for the Minnesota winter," Grace tells her.

"I know. I know." Ev smiles. "But my leather boots are so much cuter than the winter ones."

"It's your toes."

As we settle back on the couch, Ev picks up her phone. "Speaking of Ty. He wants to know if we need anything? I swear he thinks I'm helpless without him.

"Pepperoni pizza, two bottles of wine, and a gallon of ice cream," she says aloud as she types what I assume are those very words to her brother.

"We should watch The Holiday next," Grace says.

Ev nods, still looking at her phone. "Yeah, I love that one. Bridget?"

"Sure," I say and then ask, "Is he really going to bring you those things?"

"No." She shakes her head. "I'm just messing with him."

"He would if she was serious," Grace clarifies. "Ty is the sweetest. Although not as sweet as Declan."

"Declan?"

"One of my brother's teammates."

"Oh, did you used to date him or something?"

"No. He just used to look out for me a lot." Everly looks to me. "I came to live with Tyler the second semester of my high school senior year after being expelled." Her face feigns innocence over what I'm guessing is a very interesting story.

"They all looked out for you," Grace says. "Still do, you just make it harder for them."

"Like you're any better with your dad."

"My dad thinks I'm an angel who never has and never will date or kiss boys. He's completely delusional about me growing up. At least Tyler and his teammates let you be you."

"Let me be me?" Ev scoffs. "Do you remember the time they rolled up into theater practice and threatened Jacob Matthews that he'd better be nice to me and spread the word?"

I don't cover my laugh in time. "Tyler did that?"

"All of them. Ty, Declan, Jack, and Ash."

My heart flutters at his name. True to Everly's word, she hasn't mentioned Ash or tried to play matchmaker since I moved in. Not that I've given her a lot of opportunities.

"It was so great. Hands down the coolest moment of senior year." Grace beams at the memory.

"I was mortified." Ev looks at me as she speaks. "It was bad enough being the new kid, but once people found out Ty was my brother and I was living with Ash, it was mayhem."

My brain snags on the last part of that sentence. "You lived with Ash?"

"Mhmm." She smiles and nods. "When I came to live with Tyler, he had this tiny little one-bedroom apartment and Ash offered to let us move in with him."

"That's really nice."

"It was. Ash is great."

Grace's phone starts ringing. "That's Lane. Five minutes. Don't start the movie without me." She hurries down the hallway as she answers.

A comfortable silence falls between me and Everly.

I break the quiet first. "Thank you for inviting me to hang tonight."

"Are you kidding? We're so glad you finally said yes."

"Really? I was afraid you were only asking because you felt like you should. It's been a while since I had roommates, or friends for that matter. I was dating this guy and sort of lost touch with all my girlfriends."

"Ah, yeah. Easy to do when you're in love."

I don't like thinking about Gabe and love in the same thought. If that was love, I don't ever want it again.

"What happened with the guy?"

"We broke up a couple of months ago. Right after I met Ash at the game."

"Because of Ash?"

"No, no, no. Things hadn't been that great for a while." I clear my throat and avoid eye contact. "How's his shoulder? Is he back to playing?"

Everly's smile widens. "I'm not sure I can say."

At my confusion, she adds, "When he asked me about you, I told him I wasn't going to give him any details and that he should ask you himself."

"He asked about me?"

"Yeah, I saw him last night after the game." Her head bounces from side to side, the blonde locks catching on the light. "And since it's public knowledge, I guess I can tell you that he hasn't been cleared to play yet, but he is practicing with the team again."

"That's good. I'm glad."

She studies me a little too long. "You should come to a game with us sometime. There's one this weekend. Saturday night. I have good seats, and Tyler always hooks us up with drink and food tickets."

"I'm back. Sorry." Grace drops onto the chair. "What'd I miss?"

"I'm trying to convince Bridget that she should come with us to the game this weekend."

"Oh yeah. The games are so fun."

"I'm not sure," I say, biting at the corner of my lip.

"Worried about running into Ash?"

"No," I say too quickly, then amend my answer. "I guess a little."

"He'll probably be playing Saturday anyway, so the only way he'll see you is if he looks up from the ice and spots you in the crowd."

They both laugh, but Ash spotting me in a crowd is exactly how this all started.

CHAPTER TWELVE

Ash

LOST CAUSE

"Quit eyeing me like that, Kelly," Declan says as he shifts his weight from skate to skate.

"I can't help it. I want to rip off your clothes and skates, put them on, and go out there." I'm standing in the tunnel with the guys as they get ready to head out for the game. I want to play so badly. This should be the last time I have to sit out, but it doesn't make it any less painful.

"Whoa, buddy. You want to rip his clothes off?" Leo arches a brow. "That is, uhh...well, it's something."

Declan's dark brows rise. "You're looking at me like Jade looks at me when I—"

"Okay, yeah, no need to finish that sentence," Tyler interrupts, then looks to me. "I thought you were going to ask Kennedy out?"

"I did, but then she had to travel for work and then when she got back, she was sick." I shrug. To be honest, I'm not all that disappointed it hasn't happened yet.

Not as disappointed as I am to be standing here in jeans and a T-shirt. I clench my fingers at my side. "I want to be out there more than I want to breathe. More than I want sex."

"Shit. He's a lost cause, boys." Jack walks past me to get the team razzed up. He offers some fist bumps and others a few encouraging words. When he circles back to me, he bumps me in the stomach with the end of his stick. "I think that's the guy they're hiring to replace Richard."

He jerks his head up to indicate behind me and I open my stance to check out our new assistant GM. We got the news yesterday from Coach at practice. Not totally surprising, we'd been hearing rumblings that Richard was going to be let go for misconduct. Which usually means someone did something sketchy and they don't want the details to get out. That combined with our shit-tastic start to the season and none of us were that surprised.

I keep staring at the guy, scoping him out. An assistant GM has less pull than the GM, but they still have a say in which players come and go. And with this being a contract year, I have to care a whole lot about those types of things. "That's the same guy that was with Jim at the Vegas game."

He nods. "Yeah. He brought each of the guys they interviewed in for a game."

I scan the guy again, certain I've seen him before. Something about him puts me on edge, but a change in personnel mid-season never feels good. "What else do you know about him?"

"Not much. He's pretty green. Youngest assistant GM in Wildcat history. Coach said he was a scout for a minor team in Iowa and then most recently the Penguin junior hockey team." Jack shrugs it off. I'm still staring at the guy, trying to get a good take on him when Jack asks, "Do you want to meet up in the morning and do some drills?"

"I can't tomorrow. My family is in town."

"Momma Kelly," he says, letting his voice go soft.

"Her last name is George now." She got remarried four years ago and this isn't the first time (or even the third) I've corrected him.

"I know, but you get this crazy eye thing going on when I call her Momma Kelly." He keeps on grinning. "How is she?"

"Good. She's here tonight. So are my aunts, sisters, and my dad and his new family."

He opens his mouth, but before whatever wisecrack he has in store, I add, "Stay away from my mom and my sisters. Aunts too for that matter."

Biting his lip, he wanders off to keep pumping up the team. I know he'd never really make a move on a teammate's family member, but he likes to fuck with me just to be annoying.

Every minute that ticks down, the guys get quieter, more amped-up. I get more frustrated.

I lean against the wall and will my body to chill the fuck out. Tyler paces in front of me. I have each of these guys' routines memorized as well as I know my own. It's just one of those things that comes from spending so much time together and he's acting strange.

"Everything okay?" I ask him.

He walks by again, side-eyeing me, as he holds his stick in one hand.

Now I'm doubly concerned. He's been having a rough start to the season. He was our number two scorer last year, but the past few months, he's struggled to find the net. It happens. I've gone weeks with everything being just a hair off. It's infuriating. I try to think what people said to me during those times, and what made a difference.

I go with, "Just keeping firing. Any chance you get. Eventually your head will stop trying to compensate and you'll find that rhythm again."

He pauses, gives me another strange look, then nods. "Thanks, I appreciate it."

But then the dude keeps pacing. So much for my rousing words of wisdom.

On approximately the fiftieth pass by me, he stops. "I'm trying to decide if I should tell you something or not."

"Well, now you have to." I push off the wall.

He glances up and works his jaw side to side like he's really considering how to say whatever it is.

"You're freaking me out. What the hell is going on?" The only time I've ever seen him this agitated is when something is going on with his sister. *Oh, shit.* "Is Everly okay?"

I haven't checked in on her much since I heard Bridget moved in. She made it very clear that she was not going to give me any information about her new roommate. Maddening, but I respect it.

"Yeah," he says automatically. "She's good."

My body relaxes.

"She's coming to the game tonight."

"O-kay." She comes to most home games to support her brother. "You want me to check on her? Where's she sitting? Usual spot?"

He sighs, acting all annoyed because I can't read minds and didn't correctly guess whatever the hell he's trying to tell me. "She brought her roommate*s*."

The S at the end of the last word hangs in the air while my brain connects the dots. Roommates. More than one. Roommate*sssss*. Plural.

Both of them.

My heart skitters to a stop. Hell yeah.

Bridget is here.

CHAPTER THIRTEEN

Bridget

HELLO, MR. KELLY

I am a bundle of nerves when we arrive at the arena Saturday night. It's been so long since I had a night out with girlfriends. I forgot about the hours of getting ready together and all the fun, happy conversation that I once loved just as much as whatever plans came later.

After we load up on food and drinks from the snack bar, Everly leads us to our seats. Grace sits between me and Ev and there's an empty seat on the end of the aisle. I'm thankful for a quick escape route in case I need to go throw up. I keep telling myself it's stupid to be nervous. Everly told me a dozen times that Ash has no idea I'm coming and that he'd be too focused on the game to be searching for me. I believe her but my anxiety does not.

We're about halfway up in the lower section between the net and the team's bench. Both teams are on the ice warming up. A player I don't recognize is across the ice, handing a stick over the glass to a fan.

The back of his jersey says Sato. He doesn't take off his shirt or stop to flirt with any unsuspecting women, but nonetheless it transports me right back to the last time I was here.

Everly cranes her neck to see every single player as they stretch or shoot pucks into the net. Grace is looking down at her phone, texting Lane. She told me before we left that she doesn't really care that much about hockey, she comes for the snacks and to watch Everly get all mouthy and riled up—something, admittedly, I'm also excited to witness.

"Nachos?" Grace offers by inching the plate toward me.

My stomach is in knots. "No thanks."

With a shrug, she takes another for herself and goes back to texting.

At first, I don't look for Ash at all. I watch the jumbotron advertisements and chat with Everly and Grace over the loud music pumping into the arena. But the more time that passes without me seeing him, the more paranoid I get. Is he here? Has he spotted me? And most ridiculously, can he feel me here freaking out?

I set two rules for myself tonight (don't ask about Ash and don't drool over Ash), and I broke the first one before warmups were over. Leaning over Grace, I shout at Everly, "Is Ash playing tonight?"

A small smile curves her lips, but she smooths it out and then stands to get a better look at the players on the ice. "I don't see him."

Disappointment hits me so unexpectedly that I don't hide the frown on my face in time and Grace catches it. She doesn't call me on it, simply offers a solution. "If he's not playing, he'll probably watch the game from the press box."

She points toward the sky boxes. Without binoculars, or staring really hard, it's impossible to make out the people sitting and standing around for the start of the game. But like any good friends would do, Everly and Grace help me look all around the arena for a missing hockey player.

"I'm sorry, Bridge," Ev says. She's started calling me that for short. "I don't see him. Do you want me to text him?"

"God, no," I reply. The last thing I want is to draw attention to the fact I'm here or that I'm searching for his whereabouts. I'd never hear the end of it from him, cocky bastard.

The players head to their benches and the pre-game show begins. The arena goes dark, making it impossible to see.

"We'll keep looking," Grace reassures me. "He's here somewhere."

Everyone gets to their feet to cheer as the announcer on the starters for the Wildcats. A man steps up next to me, standing in front of the vacant seat. He leans over me, throwing his voice to be heard over the noise in the arena, "Who are you looking for?"

He's wearing a Wildcat hat low over his eyes, but I recognize the low timber of his voice and the way my entire body lights up in his presence. Not to mention the smell of him. Groan. Why is soap and laundry detergent mixed with his cologne the sexiest thing ever?

"Oh my gosh!" Everly squeals when she sees him. "A—"

He puts a finger to his lips.

She ducks her head and lowers her voice a tad. "Hi! We were just looking for you."

I widen my eyes at her. Sellout. Heat creeps up my neck when a knowing smirk plays over his lips. My roommate reaches over and hugs Ash. Then her smile falls. "I'm sorry."

His lips press into a straight line as he tips his head. "I should be cleared for Monday."

Everly moves back to her seat. Ash nods his head in greeting to

Grace and then all his attention focuses in on me. I was not prepared. Not the first time when he gave me the puck, or the second when he tried to intervene with Gabe, or at the hospital, over coffee, and certainly not now.

He's standing so close that we're nearly touching. I forgot how tall he is. And how good-looking. No, that's a lie. I didn't forget that last part. But I had hoped I'd exaggerated it with the time that's passed. Nope. No such luck. Ash is easily the hottest guy I've ever seen.

"Are you sitting there?" I point at the seat behind him.

He glances back at it before replying, "No, I'm meeting someone. Ty told me Everly was coming to the game, so I thought I'd pop over quick and say hi."

"Oh." Of course. He and Everly are tight. Then the beginning of that reply sinks in and it dawns on me then what he's saying. "Oooooh. Right. You're meeting a girl. Err…a woman. Congratulations!" My voice is way too high and cheery. Some weird feeling takes over my body that I refuse to acknowledge as jealousy.

Congratulations?! If he weren't watching me with that gorgeous and annoying smirk, I'd be giving myself the world's biggest head palm.

"Thanks. I mean, it's just my mom and a few other family members but I'm pretty stoked."

His mom. If I had been jealous, and I definitely was not, I'd probably feel relief about now.

Luckily, I'm saved from responding because the national anthem begins, and we fall silent with the rest of the crowd. Ash removes his hat, but keeps his chin tucked low. I wonder how many people would freak out right now if they realized Ash Kelly was standing right by them.

"How've you been? How's school and everything?" He steps closer to me and whispers the words.

I can feel the heat of his body and I get another whiff of his cologne. Warm, cedar, with just a hint of spice.

"Good. You?"

"Not been the best month of my life, but it's looking up."

I mistakenly glance up and over, directly into his eyes. Can he hear how loud my heart is beating?

"Looks like things with Everly and Grace worked out well." His gaze briefly flicks over my roommates before concentrating back on me.

"They're really great. Thanks for that."

"Happy to help." He puts his white hat back on and tucks his long hair behind his ears as everyone claps through the end of the national anthem.

"Where are you sitting?" Everly asks him as we take our seats.

"My family is in town, so I got a box."

Everly's eyes widen and Ash chuckles. "You want to come up?"

"I mean, can we?" Everly asks with a hopeful smile.

"Sure. If you want. My box is your box."

"Really?" Everly looks from me to Grace. "Do you guys want to go? The view is incredible up there."

"Whatever." Grace already has her purse on her shoulder and her snacks gathered.

What am I going to say except, "Sure."

The private box is pretty much exactly what I expected. Gabe took me to a Vikings game once and we sat in one that was similar. Better seats, more space, quieter, and free food and drinks.

When the four of us step into the packed suite, Ash is rushed by two tall, pretty young women I assume are his sisters. They take turns hugging him, then Ash introduces us.

"Jess and Leigh, meet my friends Everly, Grace, and Bridget." Hearing him say my name does funny things to my insides. "These are my sisters."

Next up, we meet his dad, stepmom, and two younger siblings—Harper, who is five, and Hunter, who is three. Then his mom and two aunts.

Everly, Grace, and I make our excuses so he can catch up with his family.

"I feel like we're imposing," Grace says as we take our seats. "It's like a family reunion in here."

Everly glances over her shoulder where Ash and his family members are all gathered in a circle still. "Nah. Ash is one of those 'the more the merrier' people. He likes having a lot of people around."

"I'm proud of myself, I made eye contact for the first time since this summer and didn't want to die of embarrassment." Grace shoves a large chip covered in cheese and jalapenos into her mouth.

"Why would you want to die of embarrassment?" I ask, sneaking another peek at Ash. He's got Harper clinging to one side of him and he's holding Hunter. They're both wearing little miniature versions of his jersey and it's just about the cutest thing I've ever seen.

"It's only weird if you make it weird," Everly tells her and then offers a sympathetic smile.

I'm still clueless.

"I had this stupid crush on Ash earlier this year," Grace starts to explain. "And then this summer we were all over at Leo and Scarlett's place hanging out…" She squeezes her eyes closed. "And I tried to kiss him."

I have a physical reaction to her words. Heat courses through me as a visual of the two of them together flashes before me.

She keeps one eye still closed and peeks out the other.

Everly shoves her shoulder lightly. "It was not that big of a deal."

"Nothing happened." Grace turns to me and says it like she's clarifying for my benefit. "But it was humiliating. He pulled me into a hug and told me how cool a chick I was."

"That doesn't sound so bad. You are gorgeous and I could see you two together." It's true. I could. Grace is stunning. Dark hair, eyes that are this storm blue that's almost gray, and a smile that transforms her from sweet and pretty to vibrant and stunning. But it's not just her looks. Grace's father played professional baseball in the nineties, so she fits into Ash's world in a way I don't. They make sense.

"Maybe he just didn't want to get involved because you're friends," I say.

"We were never really friends. I tagged along with Ev to a few team parties. Ash and I would make small talk. He was always friendly and made me feel welcome. Sometimes I'd think he was checking me out, but you know Ash, he's got a way of making everyone feel important. It's hard to tell what's going on in that big, handsome head."

I nod like I know, but the truth is I know very little about Ash and how he is with other people.

"Anyway, it all worked out because I met Lane and he's the best." The blush on her face as she smiles makes me incredibly happy for her.

The game is good. Everly's brother, Tyler, gets the first goal of the game. Grace was right about our roommate being super entertaining to watch. She barely takes her eyes off the ice, but somehow manages to stay in conversation, never missing a beat while also calling out to the players like they can hear her.

Ash comes over during the first intermission with Harper and asks if we need anything.

"Define anything," Ev says. "Because I could use a cute guy or a million dollars or—"

"They have cotton candy." Harper holds up hers to show us. It's almost as big as her head.

"Ooooh. I might need some of that." Grace stands.

Harper leads the way.

Everly looks between me and Ash. "You know what? Me too. Maybe I'll find a cute boy out in the halls."

"Having fun?" Ash asks when we're alone. It feels weird to sit at the front of the box all alone, so I get up and the two of us slowly walk back to where the bar is set up.

"Yeah. I am. Thank you for letting us crash. Your family seems great."

Ash's sisters walk by with their heads together, whispering. If I'm not mistaken, they give me a thorough once-over with nosy, prying expressions.

"They are. Mostly." He chuckles. "My sisters are trying to figure out which one of you is my girlfriend and I think you just became the front-runner."

I dip my head to hide my blush.

"I told them it wasn't like that, but they refuse to believe anything I say about girls since the tenth grade when I lied about kissing

Catherine Thomas at a birthday party, and then the next day there was photographic evidence of said kiss being shared around the school." One side of his mouth pulls up into a boyish half-smile. "Do you want something to drink or eat?"

"No. I'm good," I say as his little brother runs a circle around us and then darts off in the same direction he came. "Does your family come to a lot of games?"

"No, not really. Once a season they come here, and they make it to all the games we play in Boston. That's where they all live."

"Tonight is the one game of the season they all came here?" I ask, finally realizing that his entire family is here and he's not even playing. I guess I assumed they came often, or maybe I was too distracted by Ash to think anything.

"Yeah. Perfect timing to get hurt, huh? I didn't know until about a few hours before the game that I was for sure not going to be out there. They'd all already made plans to come in for the weekend." He shrugs. "I guess at least this way I get to spend more time with them."

"I'm sorry. I can't imagine how much you wish you were out there."

"You have no idea. I'm ready to trade my left arm for a robot arm."

Laughter slips from my mouth and Ash's smile gets bigger. "What about you? How's everything going for real?"

"Good," I answer with the same canned response I gave him the last time he asked.

He looks at me like he's waiting for more, so I add, "Nothing new to report. School, work, home, repeat."

"Still *busy* then?"

"Yeah. Still busy."

He chuckles softly. "All right. I can take a hint."

"You can?" I ask, in mock surprise.

"Smart ass." He bumps his good shoulder against mine.

His mom passes by us and waves. She's tall, striking like her son, with the same dark blue eyes. She's dressed in a pantsuit with heels that I'm not sure I could walk in. She is the picture of a power boss.

"What do your parents do?" I ask him.

"My mom owns a storage solutions company." He glances over in the direction of his mom. "She started designing shelving and storage for sporting goods and athletic equipment when I was in high school. Our garage was first, then she did a few family friends' closets and spaces, and now she does it for companies and organizations. And she runs a non-profit for youth athletic programs."

"Wow. Your mom is way cooler than you."

"Oh, definitely. I'm not even offended, though I know that was the intent."

We both smile and my stomach dips. God, what is it about him? Bantering with him feels like foreplay.

Everly and Grace move back past us with their cotton candy to the front of the box when the teams are back from intermission. There's a large TV up here where you can see the game as it's televised.

"Seriously, though, your family seems great. And your mom really does seem awesome. I have a feeling her shoe collection is impressive."

"Yeah, it's a trip. Most of my childhood, she stayed home with me and my sisters. I have this vision of her in jeans and my dad's baggy T-shirts. She's the one who'd go outside with us and throw the ball or put on pads and a mask and let me shoot pucks at her."

"That sounds dangerous." I still stand by my statement; his mom is way cool.

He laughs quietly, grinning all boyish and filled with mischief. "She only did that once."

I'm enthralled listening to him talk and seeing the way he smiles like he's picturing it in his mind.

"What about your dad?"

"He's an engineer. Or was. When they got divorced, he decided to go back to school to teach high school history."

"It's really nice that they're both here. Are you all still close?"

"I guess so." Ash shrugs and finally glances down at the ice as the game is about to restart. "He got remarried quickly, so it was weird at first. But then when Harper and Hunter came along, things seemed to be okay. Different, obviously, but I think it forced us all to get over it faster or something."

"Bridge!" Ev calls my name, snapping me out of the moment.

I look up to see my roommates waving me over to join them.

"I should probably…" I tip my head in that direction but don't move just yet.

"Yeah. Me too. Gotta make sure everyone has a good time. Hunter's the hardest sell. He told me earlier that hockey was dumb. Think he'd be more impressed by a visit from Wenzel the Wildcat or signed merch? Probably Wenzel, huh?"

"Go with merch. I mean, a high five from the team mascot is cool, but something signed by Ash Kelly, that's far rarer. Well, unless you're a girl in the crowd before a game."

His lips pull apart, flashing his teeth and a panty-melting smile. "I'll have you know, I'd never done that before."

"No?" I ask, my tone full of sarcasm. "I don't think I believe you."

"It's true," he insists. His blue eyes lose all playfulness. A serious, almost pleading expression takes over his handsome face. *Hello, Mr. Kelly.* I feel that look everywhere. And I do mean everywhere. "Sure, I've signed all kinds of things for fans—women included, but I have never used it as a tactic to ask out someone. I can't explain it. I don't even remember deciding to approach you. Then all of a sudden, there I was without a plan or any clue what to say next."

"I think what you said was 'Wanna puck?'"

He rubs the back of his neck with one hand. "Yeah, not my best opening line."

"Do you have good opening lines? Because that's not the word on the street."

"I don't regret it. Even if you thought I was the biggest chump to ever hit on you, it was worth it." He bumps my shoulder again. I really like when he does that. "Here we are."

Here we are indeed.

Ash's family leaves before the game is over. First his dad and stepmom with a snoozing Hunter and heavy-lidded Harper in tow. Then his mom and aunts say their goodbyes. His sisters are the last to go a few minutes before the end of the third period.

The Wildcats are up by four goals, but Everly is still glued to the action like it's a nail-biter of a game. There'll be no getting her out of here early.

When the final buzzer sounds, the four of us stand. We thank Ash again for letting us hang out and watch the game with his family, which he waves off.

Everly and Grace are chatting with Ash about his weekend plans, and I excuse myself to go to the bathroom. It's down the hall just a few feet from the private area where we've been watching the game.

Tonight was fun. And even though it was a little awkward at first,

I'm glad that I saw Ash. We're bound to run into each other from time to time and I don't want it to be weird. Although weird might be preferable because it's difficult to be around him and not wonder what could happen if I let my guard down for him.

On my way out, I spot Ash leaning against the wall. When he sees me, he pushes off the wall.

"Hey," he says. "I wanted to catch you before you left. I'm glad you came. It was good to see you."

"Thanks. I'm glad I did too." Strangely, as the night went on, I relaxed. I did it. I saw Ash, which was inevitable living with Everly, and I survived. We even talked. It was fine. No big deal.

He lifts the jersey in his right hand, then uses the other to unfold it and show me the back. It's just like the one Harper and Hunter were wearing, except this one is signed in the middle of the giant three. "I didn't want you to leave empty-handed."

"Thanks," I say, oddly touched by the gesture and most certainly blushing.

He leans closer and asks, "Better than a high five from Wenzel?"

"Yes. Much better." My heart feels like it's in my throat. "But then again, I think mascots are a little creepy, so the bar is low."

He chuckles. "Good to know."

I pull it on over my head. "How's it look?"

His scan is slow and appreciative, and even though he doesn't answer, I get that he likes it very much. I do too. I swear it smells like him, which is probably my imagination.

My lips curve up and my heart patters along happily. "Are Everly and Grace still…"

"Yeah. They're waiting for you."

"Thank you for everything. It was really good to see you, Ash."

He dips his head in a parting nod.

I take a step when someone calls my name. My smile slips, but it's several seconds before I fully place the voice calling my name.

"Bridget?" he asks again.

I turn with a mixture of anxiety and fear. Gabe's dark brows are raised in surprise. His black hair is gelled to perfection and his suit tailored for his tall and wide frame. He takes me in, gaze lingering on the jersey I'm wearing and then flicking up to Ash, who's moved to stand beside me.

"I thought that was you," he says. "I was going to ask what you're doing here, but I think that's pretty obvious. He's why you're too busy to take my calls?"

I blocked him and stopped sharing my location after I saw him last, but instead of correcting his assumption that I'm here with Ash, I ask the only question banging around in my head. "What are *you* doing here?"

"I tried to tell you. Now that I know you're fucking him, I'm glad I didn't ruin the surprise." He looks at Ash, way too pleased with himself, and dread washes over me.

Ash curses under his breath.

"Do you want to tell her, Kelly, or should I?"

A moment passes where Ash does nothing but keep his stony expression aimed forward at Gabe.

"You're looking at the new assistant GM." He puffs out his chest and his slimy smile widens.

"Wait, what? You got a job here? With the Wildcats?" I look from Gabe to Ash. The latter's expression confirms my questions.

"So, you've heard?" Gabe asks Ash.

Ash looks at me apologetically. "I saw him earlier, but I didn't piece it together until now."

Gabe takes another step forward and I tense. Ash moves farther in front of me.

That stops Gabe, but he huffs an amused laugh. "It's best if you stay out of my way, Kelly, and keep away from things that belong to me."

Belong to him? Surely he doesn't mean me. Because hell no. I'm not property. Certainly not his.

Ash's body goes rigid in front of me, back muscles straining against his shirt, but he doesn't say anything as Gabe gives me a parting look that's filled with the promise, *this isn't over*.

"Guess I'll be seeing you both around." He turns and takes a step, and then pauses and glances back at Ash with a slimy smile. "I was sorry to hear about your shoulder. And during a contract season. That's a tough break." He sucks in air through his teeth. "I look forward to seeing you back on the ice. The team needs help with scoring right now or we're going to have to make some painful adjustments."

CHAPTER FOURTEEN

Ash

HARD AND PISSED

Bridget left in a hurry after we ran into Gabe. What a fucking prick. A prick that I now have to work with.

I catch Jack downstairs as he's coming out of the media room.

"Hey," he says as he turns his hat backward. "Wanna grab a drink at Wild's?"

"We have a problem." I lean forward and whisper the bare minimum info to fill him in.

His expression morphs instantly from relaxed to on edge. He's a good captain. He's always led by example first, but he's also the first guy ready to jump in and solve any obstacle in the way. Personal and professional, because with a job like ours, it all sort of bleeds together. In a fight, there's no one I'd rather have my back.

"Give me five to grab my stuff."

While he does that, I congratulate Tyler on his two goals tonight.

"Thanks for the advice," he says. "It helped."

"I didn't do anything. That was all you." I lift my fist and he bumps his against it.

"Can't wait to have you back on Monday." Leo shoulders his bag. I know he's eager to get home to his wife and baby, so I don't tell him about Gabe for now.

It only takes Jack two minutes and then we're heading out. I follow him in my truck to our neighborhood and then his house.

He's pouring two glasses of whiskey, some expensive shit he saves for the good nights and for the bad.

I take a seat on the barstool in front of the giant island in the middle of his kitchen. I wrap my fingers around the glass but don't sip yet. "How bad is it?"

"That depends."

"On?" I ask, finally taking a drink. It's rich and strong and burns my throat as I swallow.

"If you're planning on staying the hell away from Bridget or not." He leans back against the counter, crosses one ankle over the other and regards me seriously.

I think back on the night. If she hadn't already turned me down twice before, my answer might be different. No matter how much of a connection I feel, I'm not sure she's in the same place as me. I shake my head. "She's made it very clear that she's not interested in dating me."

"Then I don't see any reason for this to be a problem."

His words don't reassure me like I'd hoped they would.

"You should have heard him. The way he talked to her. She held her own with him, but I could tell she was rattled."

"Repeat after me, 'It's none of my business.'"

"If some asshole talked to a girl like that in front of you, you'd be able to just let it go?" I know he wouldn't.

He doesn't reply, though. He finishes what's left of his drink in one long gulp.

"What if it'd been Everly?"

"Everly is different," he says, eyes narrowing. "She's a teammate's sister. If anyone in the organization did that to a player's family, they'd be tossed out."

He isn't wrong, but it shouldn't be okay that he talks to anyone like that. Especially Bridget.

I stay for one more drink. My mom planned a big breakfast out tomorrow before everyone heads back home and I don't want to show up hungover.

"Thanks," I tell Jack as he walks me to the front door.

"Any time. You know that."

"I do." I walk backward down the sidewalk toward my truck. "Just out of curiosity, if I'd said I wasn't going to stay away from her, then what?"

He doesn't miss a beat. "Then you better make sure as fuck that you come back Monday night and prove to everyone how much we need you. Guys have been traded for a lot less than sleeping with a GM's girlfriend."

"*Ex*-girlfriend," I bite out, but I get his point.

When I get home, I pull out my phone. I fire off a text to Everly, letting her know it was good to see her and making sure they got home okay.

Her response is exactly what I should have expected: *Home safe and sound! It was good to see you too. X*

"I know. I know," I mutter under my breath. "You're not going to share any info on your roommate."

Which is why I'm shocked when another text comes in a few seconds later.

Everly: Sharing Bridget's number with you. She knows I'm giving it to you, but don't make me regret it. She seems pretty shook up. Is her douche ex really the new assistant GM?

I save Bridget's contact information, thank Everly, then sit there, thumb tapping against the side of my phone as I think about what I want to say. Sorry your ex-boyfriend is a giant asshole? Sorry I gave you my jersey, you put it on and then your ex walked up at the least convenient time. No, fuck that. I'm not sorry about that at all. That image is going to stay with me for a very long time. I never thought I'd be one of those guys so turned on by seeing a girl wear my name and number on her back. But here we are. Hard and pissed and ready to burn down the world.

Me: Hey. It's Ash. I'm sorry tonight ended the way it did. It was really good to see you.

I wait, even though I don't expect her to reply. I can't get the way she looked so anxious when Gabe walked up out of my head. I've had enough awkward encounters with ex-girlfriends to know that some of that is expected. But he was just awful, and she didn't seem that surprised. She didn't flinch or yell or do any of the things I'd have expected from someone who is used to being treated with love and respect.

Fucking Gabe. I knew that first night when he was yelling at her outside of Wild's that he was a piece of shit. No, you know what? I knew before that. The very first time I laid eyes on Bridget and saw him sitting next to her not giving her a bit of attention.

Relationships aren't always rainbows and sunshine, I know that. But there's a difference in sitting quietly beside someone and not talking and existing in the same space.

Nurse Bridget: It was good to see you too. Good luck with the rest of the season.

Me: Guess you won't be coming to any more games, huh?

Nurse Bridget: Probably not. Everly will keep me updated though.

Me: Bummer, but I get it. You're okay though? Gabe was kind of intense.

Nurse Bridget: Yeah, I'm fine.

I'm not sure I believe her, but what am I going to do? Demand she lay her wounds out for me? We barely know each other. It should be said, I want her to. I really do. I'd hold them with the care they deserve. But that's not the kind of shit you say to a girl you're most definitely not pursuing.

She starts typing again. Those three little dots go on so long I think it's a mistake until her next message pops up.

Nurse Bridget: If I've made things complicated for you with Gabe, I'm so sorry. I had no idea he was interviewing with the Wildcats. We didn't end things on the best of terms, but you shouldn't be punished for that. I sent him a text tonight and told him there was nothing going on between us.

Nothing going on between us. I read the words a dozen times, hating them a little more each time.

I did wonder if she'd known that Gabe was up for the job. Not that it'd matter now. What's done is done. And I don't regret any of it. Well, maybe one thing. I wish I'd punched the guy like I wanted to outside of Wild's. I could have gotten away with it then, but not now. From here on out I need to play nice, whether I like it or not.

CHAPTER FIFTEEN

Bridget

CLUB MIDNIGHT

"Come in," I say after a knock on my door Sunday evening.

Everly pokes her head in tentatively and smiles. "Are you busy?"

"No, just finishing up." I take off my glasses and sit up straight on the bed where I've been hunched over my notes from class for the past...shit, three hours.

My roommate comes in and shuts the door, then takes a seat on the edge of the bed. "I haven't seen you all day."

"Yeah, I know. I've been studying for finals and catching up on homework all day. Every one of my professors doubled homework after Friday's snow day."

"I know. Like it was our fault that we got two feet of snow." She laughs softly and I join in. "So that's the only reason, then?" she asks with concerned eyes.

Crap. I don't want to lie to her, but I'm not sure how to explain everything she'll want to know if we start talking about Gabe and what happened last night either.

"I promise it's nothing you guys did."

"You seemed really upset last night after running into your ex. I'm not going to pry, but if you ever want to talk, I'm here. I know a thing or two about shitty ex-boyfriends."

My throat constricts at her words. It's the most perfect thing she could have said. It's been so long since I've had a friend offer that up. A sympathetic ear and the consideration and space to process things by myself first. I know some of that's my fault for letting those friendships slip away, but I won't take it for granted again. I won't lie, though, it's hard to think about confiding in anyone. Gabe is an asshole, but I'm still afraid that people will hear the whole story and think I was being silly or blowing things out of proportion. I never want anyone to take Gabe's side over mine. So it's easier not to give them a chance to take mine either.

"Thank you. That means a lot."

She reaches over and squeezes my hand. "Lane's over. We're going to watch a movie. Join us and save me from being the third wheel?"

"I wish I could." I chuckle softly, loosening the anxiety that's sat on my chest all day. "I'm going to finish up and then go to sleep early. Another night."

"Okay." She stands and goes to the door. "We're going out for my birthday on Friday. I know you usually use Friday night to catch up on sleep, but I'd love it if you came with us."

"Where are you going?"

"Club Midnight. Have you heard of it?"

"Yeah, of course." The new dance club opened a few weeks ago and everyone has been talking about it.

"Is anyone else coming?" I fidget with the edge of my notebook so I don't have to look Everly in the eye while she replies.

"Don't worry. I didn't invite the guys. It's girls only. Me, Grace, and hopefully you."

"Not even Lane or Tyler?"

"Especially not them. Grace would be off making out in the corner all night, and Tyler, well I love him, but I'd love to have one night out where people in this town aren't fawning over him like he's the greatest thing ever."

"Okay, yeah. I get that."

"So, you'll think about it?"

"I don't need to think about it. Of course, I'll come."

The giant smile on her face makes me glad I said yes. She's a good friend. Or at least I think she could be if I let her.

Friday night I wake up from a nap to voices in the living room. Last night's shift at the hospital was awful. The quiet shifts are always the worst and last night there were no surgeries, no new patients, nothing to occupy my time or keep my thoughts off the run-in with Gabe and the texts with Ash. Classes are done for the semester, so I didn't even have homework to busy myself. Staying awake all night was torture. But tonight, we're celebrating Everly's birthday and tomorrow I'm driving home to spend a couple of relaxing weeks with my family for Christmas break.

I get up and throw on a sweatshirt over my tank and shorts, then head out to the kitchen. My eyes are bleary and half-closed when I come up short.

"Hey!" Everly exclaims. "They didn't wake you up, did they?"

My gaze scans over the five men standing in our small kitchen. Tyler, Leo, Declan, Jack, and Ash all look at me. Five hot hockey players in my house looking at me expectantly. I raise a hand in greeting.

"It's fine. It was time for me to get up anyway." I shuffle over to Grace, intending to hide in solidarity with her, another mere mortal in this small space of ridiculously beautiful people, but the joke's on me. "Wow. You look stunning."

"Thanks." She smiles bashfully. She's in a tiny black dress that shows off her long legs and perky boobs. Her hair is all done in big waves and her makeup somehow makes her eyes three times as big.

And I look like I just rolled out of bed. Because I did.

Now that I get a good look at Everly, she's already dressed up for tonight too. Her dress is red, and her hair is pulled up in a high ponytail. She has on less makeup than Grace but some eyeliner and red lipstick perfect the look.

I'm second-guessing the club tonight. I'd planned to wear jeans and a cute shirt.

"Sorry about waking you," Tyler says to me, then wraps an arm around his sister's shoulders. "This one wouldn't let me throw her a party tonight, so I had to drop by to give my little sister her birthday present."

"That explains the giant basket of candy and liquor on the counter," I say. And wow, it really is giant. So many different kinds of goodies.

Everly pulls out a bottle of champagne and points to the label. Nonalcoholic. I fight a grin as she rolls her eyes.

"You guys know I drink sometimes. There's literally wine in our fridge right now. I'm twenty, not twelve. I can handle myself."

"Three hundred and sixty-five more days and we'll stop giving you shit about it. Hell, I might even buy you a shot or two," Ash says, finally forcing me to look at him. I'd been doing a really excellent job of avoiding his presence until now.

Like the other guys, he's in some version of athletic leisure. Gray sweatpants and a black zip-up jacket that matches his all-black sneakers. He looks good in dark colors, something about the way his light brown hair contrasts against it. Today those long locks are tied back in a bun. I didn't think I had a thing for long hair, but Ash's is this great length. It's long enough to pull back into a small bun but too short to do anything else. It suits him.

"I'm going to hold you to that," Ev tells him. "You are throwing me the most epic party when I turn twenty-one."

Jack is standing with his back against the wall, arms crossed over his impressive chest. Grace showed me this advertisement he did for some suit company. He's super intimidating but undeniably one of the hottest guys I've ever seen in real life. "I'll be skipping that one. Nothing says fun like a twenty-one-year-old getting alcohol poisoning," he says dryly.

"You're not invited," Everly snaps back.

"And I think that's our cue to get out of here." Tyler steps forward and hugs his sister. "Happy birthday."

"Thank you." She rests her head against his chest and wraps her arms around him. Their relationship makes me long for that closeness with someone. A friend, a family member, a partner. I've pushed away so many people that my circle is depressingly small. And the truth is I feel too old to form those kinds of relationships again. When you reach a certain age, people have already found their people. It's not like high school where friend groups change weekly.

The guys each hug Everly and wish her a happy birthday. Tyler and Ash hang back as the others file out the front door.

Grace and I walk in the space between the rooms, standing between the two groups.

"Be careful tonight, and call me if you need anything," Tyler says. "Don't take drinks from strangers. Are you driving?"

"We're taking an Uber," Everly tells him. "And we'll be fine. Tell your wife and the rest of the girls if they need a night out, to come find us."

"Have fun, Little Sharpie," Ash says. "Make terrible decisions and text me later to tell me all about it."

Tyler cuts him a glare, which Ash just laughs off. Then those blue eyes find me and he winks. He winks at me in my faded high school sweatshirt and shorts that date back just as far. Do I own nicer things? Yes. But they're not nearly as comfortable.

While Tyler is giving Everly more instructions, Ash walks by me slowly and whispers, "Text me later with embarrassing pictures of Ev dancing in the club?" He says the last word in a deep, mocking voice.

"Absolutely not."

"Boo. You're no fun." He winks again and nudges me lightly with his elbow as he heads out.

Once Tyler is through the door, Everly closes it and turns with a huge smile on her face. "Who's ready to party?"

She and Grace squeal together.

I glance down at my sleepwear. "Uhhh. I think I need to change first."

They both look at me and laugh.

"Yeah," Grace says. "Though with legs like that, they'd probably let you in regardless."

"Are jeans okay?"

Grace's brows rise, but she says nothing.

Everly pauses but then says, "Sure. Jeans would be fine."

I'm going to stick out with these two. And not in the way I'd like. Sure, it's Everly's birthday and all the attention should be on her, but I'd like to look just slightly less hot than her for my first night out at a club with my new friends.

"I don't have anything like that." I motion to their outfits. "I have a knee-length dress I wore to Gabe's company party last year that might work."

My roommates exchange another look that I can't comprehend, then they both walk toward me.

"Don't worry. We've got you covered."

CHAPTER SIXTEEN

Bridget

EWWW

"**S**top fidgeting. You look gorgeous." Everly glances over her shoulder at me as the line moves up another step.

The thing is, I believe her. I feel gorgeous, but I still can't stop pulling on the hem of the very small blue dress. One of at least twenty that my roommates made me try on until they found the perfect one. It was fun. Their closets are much more adventurous than mine. Between school and work, and a long relationship where I didn't go out very often, my clothes need a serious overhaul for this new phase of my life. Oh, and jeans… yeah, they would not have been fine. I've not seen a single scrap of denim.

She and Grace also did my makeup. I have on more eyeliner and mascara than usual and they did some contouring magic that makes me look like I have a more excellent bone structure than I do. I've always liked playing around with makeup, but never been that great at it. My mom hardly wore it when I was growing up, and playing tennis,

I didn't worry about it because I'd just sweat it off.

Ev tried to put red lipstick on me, but I talked her down to some gloss. I didn't want to worry about getting it all over my face. My hair is down and curly like usual. I've always loved my hair. Well, okay, not always. There was a short period in middle school where I desperately wanted to have straight hair like all my friends. But I came to terms with it at some point. I can get it straight, but it requires an awful lot of effort, and at the first blip of humidity or sweat, it would have all been for nothing.

That's too much to worry about. Tonight I want to dance and have fun with my friends.

"I wonder how much longer." Ev steps out of line to check the front door, where security is letting people in. We've been inching forward for the past thirty minutes. Heaters are set up along the sidewalk – a nice touch since none of the women are dressed to be standing outside in late December.

Apparently, there's a limit to how many people can be inside or something. Which is bullshit because I've seen several people walk right up and get in.

She sticks her bottom lip out in a pout as she comes to stand back in front of me. "Maybe we should have just gone to a bar or invited people over to the house."

"What? No way. We're getting in," Grace says. "Come on."

She grabs both me and Everly and drags us with her to the man dressed in all black blocking the entrance. He's an intimidating dude. He doesn't even speak and I want to run back to our spot in line. But not Grace. She gives him her sweetest smile.

"Hi. I'm Grace, this is Everly and Bridget."

He glances down at his clipboard, which I can now see is a list of names. I try to read them upside down.

"We're not on your list, but it's her birthday." Grace looks back at Everly as the guy takes in the three of us standing with pleading eyes in front of him.

Everly raises a hand and flashes a smile that's more like a grimace. "So, if you could—"

He moves out of the way and unclips the black rope to get into the club. "Have fun, ladies."

The three of us are frozen in place for several seconds where we share a surprised smile, then hustle into the club. *Holy shit, that actually worked?*

The music is louder with each step. We could hear it outside, but in here I can feel it. Another bouncer checks our IDs before we're allowed onto the main floor. Everly and Grace get yellow bands since they're underage.

The club is three floors. The second floor is the one we're on now. There's a large bar on the right side and seating on the left. The center of the room is open, creating a circle walkway that looks down to the first floor, where the DJ is set up and people are dancing. The top floor looks like private rooms. It's too dark to make out details, but it has that sleek and clean look of a new business.

The three of us huddle together.

"You are amazing!" Everly hugs Grace. "Thank you."

"Very impressive," I add, basically screaming over the bass thumping.

"I was so scared I thought I was gonna pee." Grace laughs. "Let's get a drink and walk around. This place is huge."

We start for the bar, but a woman cuts us off. She looks to be a little older than us and has on a dress that's more business than club.

She's still rocking it, but she has an air of authority about her that makes us all pause.

"Are you Everly?" she asks, looking directly at the woman standing between me and Grace.

"Yeah," Ev answers with more than a little defensiveness in her stance.

"If you'll follow me." She smiles so sweetly. The three of us share a confused look, but decide to go after her anyway.

She leads us up a small staircase. The third floor is similar to the second in that it's open and you can look down on the floors below, but this area is less crowded.

Leather couches and chairs are set up in groups and there are two bars, one on each side. People watch us as we follow her to a section of furniture that's empty. She motions with one hand. "Rachel is your private bartender for the night. Anything you need, let her know."

And with that, the woman turns on her heel and leaves us.

Rachel is there in a flash with a bottle of nonalcoholic champagne, a lot like the one Tyler gave Everly earlier, sitting in ice with three flutes. She pours us each a glass, asks us if she can get us anything else from the bar, and then leaves us with the rest of the bottle.

"How?" Grace asks in a hushed voice like she's afraid someone will overhear and kick us out. It's quieter up here and easier to talk.

"It had to have been Tyler. I'm going to kill him." Everly rolls her eyes and pulls out her phone.

While she texts, Grace says, "But you didn't tell him where you were going."

She makes a good point. But I guess it's not that hard to figure out where three girls would go for a birthday out on the town.

"Did you tell Ash?" Ev asks me after she slides her phone back into the small black purse in her lap.

"What? No way. I've barely talked to him. I would never do that to you."

"Okay." Ev smiles and rests a reassuring hand on my arm. "I believe you. But just so you know, if you had, I wouldn't be mad. I know how good he is at getting information out of people."

"He is charming," Grace says as she brings the champagne to her lips again. "The way he was looking at you tonight. He'd die if he saw you right now."

"What? No." I shake my head. "If he was looking at anyone, it was you two. I was in a ratty old sweatshirt and shorts."

"Eww." Everly makes a face of disgust. "He's like my brother."

"I don't think he was looking at your clothes," Grace mumbles and then laughs. Everly joins in.

My cheeks are warm, which I'm absolutely blaming on the two sips of fake booze and all the bodies in this club.

"I promise you, he wasn't looking at me like that. We're just... friends." That feels like the wrong word, but we're more than acquaintances at this point.

"Uh-huh. Sure." Grace smiles at me, hiding behind her glass.

"I'm not interested in dating. The run-in with Gabe reminded me exactly why I am on a hiatus from men."

Everly gives me a sympathetic smile. "Understandable. After my last relationship, I didn't go out with anyone for like two months. It was very cathartic." She finishes her drink and then stands and holds out a hand to me. "You aren't interested in dating hot guys, but tell me, how do you feel about heading downstairs and dancing with some?"

I take one more sip and then place my hand in hers. "I feel great about it."

We dance for hours, going back to our VIP section occasionally to cool off and get another drink.

Everly somehow manages to sneak several drinks bought for her by a group of guys that overhear it's her birthday. The security watching for that kind of thing is a little more lax up in VIP, but if she gets us kicked out, it'll at least be a good story. Grace isn't drinking at all and I'm sipping on my third vodka and Sprite.

I'm so happy I don't even need the alcohol to feel tipsy, though it's certainly helping. Tonight has been so much fun and I feel so lucky that I've found these two people after the worst year of my life. If we weren't dancing and laughing so much, I'd probably do something embarrassing like cry.

We're taking a breather now, sitting on the comfy leather couches. Grace is texting with Lane, and Ev with her brother.

"Tyler swears it wasn't him," she says. "Or I think that's what this says."

She hands me the phone and I read through their texts. Her replies are filled with typos and too many exclamation points. But she's right. "Maybe it was the guy at the door?"

Ev shrugs. "Whoever it was, thank you!" She screams the last two words and we get a few looks from a group of guys nearby.

A new song starts and Grace gasps and looks to Everly, who has the same wide-eyed, excited expression.

"I love this song!" they say in unison.

"We have to dance."

"You two go ahead," I tell them. "My feet are killing me."

"No way!" They each grab one of my hands and pull me up.

I'm dragged behind them to the first floor. Every hour more people have piled into this space. We only make it to the edge of the dance floor before there's a wall of bodies too thick to move farther.

The two of them sing along with the lyrics, basically shouting them at me until they realize I don't know them. It's some catchy pop song. I've heard it a dozen times but never really listened to the lyrics. I don't register them now either. My heart is so happy and I feel so light and free. It's probably that last drink talking, but I don't care. Tonight feels like a tiny baby step to getting my life back.

We're in our own little bubble, dancing with each other and a little drunk, so at the first shout, none of us react. I look up, but I can't see anything but more happy people dancing around us.

It's not until someone knocks into the back of Grace and pushes her into me that we realize something isn't right, and then it's too late. We're all pushed again and then there are screams. It's eerie because we can't see anything. The path to leave the dance floor is blocked and suddenly everyone is rushing toward us, all trying to leave at the same time.

I grab on to both Everly and Grace and hold tight as we try to keep from being trampled. Staying upright is hard, but I'm so scared if one of us falls we'll be seriously hurt. We huddle together as close as we can get. None of us speak.

It's not long before security is everywhere and light floods the building. We're escorted outside with everyone else. Police cars line the street and the three of us hurry with others until we're far enough away that it feels safe.

My heart is hammering so hard in my chest. I'm still squeezing Everly and Grace's hands.

"What the hell happened?" Everly asks, looking back toward the club where people are still pouring out.

"I don't know." Grace looks the most spooked and winces as she finally inspects her foot. She's bleeding from where she got stepped on during the chaos.

"We should get out of here," Ev says.

We're all in agreement. The only problem is everyone else has the same idea. Everly's teeth start chattering as we wait for the Uber.

"Maybe we should call Tyler," Grace suggests.

I'm relieved not to be the first one to say it.

"No way. He'll just use it as an excuse to tell me he should have been there with me."

"I don't know, Ev. I think he'll just be glad you're okay." I check my phone again to get an update on our estimated wait. "And who knows how long until we can get a ride."

She sighs and pulls out her phone. "Okay."

As she brings the device up to her ear, a flashy Mercedes SUV comes speeding down the road, the black paint gleaming against the night and catching my eye seconds before the tires screech and the vehicle stops in front of us. All three of us jump back startled and still on edge from the club.

Jack rolls down the window, a murderous look on his face. I just barely register Tyler in the passenger seat before Jack says, "Get in the car."

CHAPTER SEVENTEEN

Bridget

YOU'RE SO HOT YOU CAUSED A BAR FIGHT

The three of us pile in the back of Jack's G-Wagon and he pulls away from the police-lined streets.

"Is everybody okay?" Tyler turns in the passenger seat to look us over.

"Yeah. We're fine," Grace answers. "What's going on?"

"There was a fight," Tyler says. "Couple of guys got into it and then their friends jumped in. Turned into a brawl in a hurry."

"How did you find out what was going on before us?" Ev sits forward, staring between her brother and Jack. "And how did you get here so quickly?"

Tyler glances at Jack, who says nothing, before replying, "Jack heard it from a friend."

"A friend?" Everly's voice is full of suspicion.

"I know the guy that runs the place." He keeps driving while Grace, Ev, and I relax into the back seat.

My heartbeat slows, but I'm still antsy. So is Grace, if the death grip she has on her seat belt is any indication.

"Are you okay?" I ask Everly quietly.

"Yeah," she says, not at all convincing, then lets out a long breath. "Yeah. That was nuts. I'm totally sober now and going to be home before midnight."

"You got drunk at Club Midnight?" Jack asks, glaring back from the rearview mirror.

"Tipsy."

"How? You're underage."

"Yeah, well, I'm sneaky. It was only a few shots."

Jack curses under his breath.

Tyler turns around again and before he can say anything, Everly holds up her hand. "Don't say it."

"What?" her brother asks defensively, fighting a smile.

"If you're about to scold me for underage drinking or tell me I should have let you throw me a party and this wouldn't have happened—"

"That's not what I was going to say at all." The expression on his face is full of sincerity. "I'm sure I would have tried to sneak drinks at the club when I was twenty too."

Jack pulls into a gas station and parks in front of the storefront. "Be right back."

"I'm sorry your night got ruined, Ev," Tyler says. "That majorly sucks. I'm glad you're okay."

Her shoulders relax. "Thanks for coming to get us. Were you really asleep?"

"Yeah, I passed out early."

"You're the oldest twenty-five-year-old I know," Ev teases him. "I should have invited Piper to come out with us."

"Yeah, about that."

Jack returns with a tray of to-go coffees in one hand and a brown paper bag tucked under the other. He opens the back and sets it all inside, except the coffees, which he passes up to us.

"What's this for?" Ev asks him.

"It'll help you sober up. Try not to spill it all over my back seat."

"God. Just when I think you're being nice, you ruin it by opening your mouth." Ev takes the coffee with a huff.

He shuts the back without another word, but then two seconds later, he opens Everly's door and tosses a sweatshirt at her. "And put that on. I can't focus with your teeth chattering in my ear."

She opens her mouth to talk back, but the door closes again.

Tyler clears his throat and hides a laugh. "Like I was saying, I feel bad your night out got ruined and I know it isn't what you wanted, but as soon as Piper heard, she called everyone and they're waiting back at our house to help make it up to you."

"At your place?"

He nods.

"Define everyone," Grace says.

"The team and anyone else in her contacts she could get a hold of for a last-minute party."

No one says anything else. Everly looks at me and I shrug. Grace does the same.

Ty sounds sincere when he says, "If you're not up for it, then we'll take you home. Your call. I just want to make sure you have the best birthday possible."

I think it's sweet, but keep that to myself. I can't pretend to know what it's like to have a famous brother that you feel overshadowed by.

"Yeah, fine, let's do it." Everly sets the coffee between her legs and pulls on Jack's sweatshirt. "But no hovering around me and acting all protective. I'm twenty now. I can take care of myself."

Jack snorts from the driver's seat and Tyler shoots him a glare before saying, "Deal."

Tyler and Piper's house is filled with people when we get there. There are even balloons and streamers hung up. Piper comes running forward to greet us at the door. She pulls Everly into a hug and then steps back to look the three of us over. "I'm so glad no one was hurt."

"How did you get so many people here this fast?" Everly asks, cocking her head to the side and giving her sister-in-law an endearing smile.

"All I had to do was ask. Everyone adores you and were more than happy to come help you celebrate."

"You threatened them, didn't you?" Everly smirks and raises one brow.

"Little bit." She grins. "Come on. There's cake."

Everly and Grace know everyone already, so I feel a little like the odd man out as we walk around the party. They introduce me and everyone is nice, but it isn't until I spot Ash in the kitchen that I feel my lips pull into a real smile.

He walks over, two beers stacked in one hand—one on top of the other. He's changed into jeans and a white sweater since I saw him earlier. His hair is down and tucked behind one ear.

"You're alive." His gaze travels down the length of me, holding on my legs for a fraction longer than necessary before slowly dragging up. "And I'm dead. I suddenly understand why there was a brawl at the club."

My insides light up even if I want to roll my eyes at him a little. "Wow. That was bad even for you."

"I thought it was clever. Maybe you just didn't get it the first time. You're so hot, you caused a bar fight." He grins proudly. God, he's too much.

"It was a club."

"Same difference." He holds up the beer in his hand. "Want something to drink?"

"Uhhh. Yeah."

He tips his head and motions for me to follow him farther into the kitchen. Soda and liquor bottles line the counter, along with snacks and a cake.

Ash grabs a cup, flips it into the air with a wink, and then pours several different types of alcohol and mixers into it before handing it over.

"What is it?"

"A little of this and a little of that. It's good. Trust me. I'm great at mixing drinks."

I take a tentative sip and then cough. Holy mother of... "I think my throat is on fire. That's terrible."

Like he doesn't believe me, he takes the cup from me and drinks. His face is impassive for a few moments and then he nods. "You're right. It's terrible."

"I think I'll stick with beer." Laughing, I take the unopened beer he was carrying and pop the top.

I turn and glance around for Everly and Grace. They're in a conversation with a few women I recognize as Wildcat players' wives, so I stay put with Ash in the kitchen.

He leans back against the counter. "Did you have fun tonight? You know, before shit went down."

"Yeah, I did actually."

"You seem surprised."

"No. I mean yes, but it's not what you think. Everly and Grace are great and hanging with them is always fun. I just forgot how much I missed having friends to do stuff like that with." I'm a little embarrassed to have admitted that out loud, but Ash doesn't laugh or make me feel like a loser for being a friendless twenty-two-year-old. "And I feel really bad the night got cut short. Everly would have closed that place down on the dance floor."

"I'll bet." Ash's eyes sparkle with happiness. He picks up his beer and the mixed drink he made me. "Come on. I want to show you something."

Ash opens a door to a stairwell and then leads me down to the basement. What I assume was a living room has been cleared out and the furniture is pushed to one side. No one else is down here, but music is playing from speakers hanging on the wall and the lights are dimmed.

"What do you think?" Ash asks, raising his hands out to his sides. "As good as Club Midnight?"

"Not bad," I say, smiling at the thoughtfulness. I don't know if it was his or Piper's idea, but I love that they made a space for Everly to keep dancing the night away. "It's missing all the cute boys, but close enough."

He narrows his gaze playfully. Freaking hell, he's hot even when he's not smiling. He's the hottest guy in every room and that would have been true at Club Midnight too. He knows it too, even if he acts all offended by my comment.

He sets both of his drinks on top of a bookshelf, then takes mine and does the same.

"But they don't have my sick dance moves." His long, strong fingers take hold of my hand and he tugs me into the center of the room.

When he lets go, my skin tingles. Ash is all smiles as he starts dancing in front of me.

I don't join in and it just makes him dance bigger and wilder. He steps closer and takes my hands again, forcing me to sway to the beat.

I finally crack a smile and that just eggs him on more.

"You're as bad of a dancer as you are a drink maker," I say.

Does that deter him? Absolutely not. He lifts our joined hands and makes me do a twirl. Then he does one of those moves where he brings me in close with an arm wrapped around me and then uncoils and stretches to send me spinning out with our arms outstretched.

"That is not how we were dancing."

"No?" His stare holds on my mouth and then he steps back and sweeps a hand in front of him. "Show me how it's done then."

I hesitate, but backing down feels like admitting that I care what he thinks of me.

I move just a little at first. Hips swaying, arms flowing at my sides. Ash falls into step with me, closing some of the distance between us as he dances in front of me.

He doesn't touch me, but he's so close that I can feel him all around me. Ash is a good dancer when he's not trying to get a laugh, which I guess shouldn't come as any surprise. He doesn't break out any amazing skills; he's just intuitive and playful. He makes funny faces like he's really into it, nodding his head as he sings along with the chorus. Even acting silly, though, he never takes his eyes off me.

The song ends and we both come to a stop. Tipping my head back, I glance up at him. The next song has a slower beat. I'm about to step back and suggest we go back upstairs when he holds his hand out to me. "One more song?"

I place my hand in his and he tugs me closer. My chest brushes up against his and then long fingers caress my hip, sending a shot of warmth zipping through me. The three of us shooed away any guys who tried to get all up on us at the club. Despite our joking about it, tonight wasn't about dancing with cute boys. But if Ash had been there, maybe it would have been.

There's something about him that puts me at ease and makes my heart feel like it's going to explode all at once.

Every brush of contact makes me dizzy and warm. My pulse races. If he can hear how fast my heart is beating, he doesn't comment on it. I should stop this. There are so many reasons why it's a terrible idea, but I'm tired of pushing people away. Everything in me craves more of this—more fun, more connection, more heart flutters.

"We didn't dance like this," I say, a little breathless. *Do not fall for this man. Do not fall for this man.*

"No?"

I shake my head.

"Their loss."

CHAPTER EIGHTEEN

Ash

OUT OF YOUR SYSTEM

The sound of feet coming down the stairs barely registers, but Bridget can't get away from me fast enough when she glances up to see Everly and Grace at the bottom of the stairs looking at us.

"What do you think of your dance floor?" I ask Everly, pushing the last few minutes dancing with Bridget out of my mind for the moment and smoothing over the awkwardness that she's obviously feeling. I don't know why. We were just dancing, but the why isn't important. I don't ever want to be responsible for making her feel anything but good.

"This is incredible." Everly walks out to join us. Grace is right behind her with three shot glasses in her hand. She gives one to Bridget, then Everly.

"What is it?" Bridget asks.

"Tequila."

She scrunches up her face.

"If it's the stuff Jack brought then don't worry. It's good tequila."

"Good and tequila don't belong in the same sentence."

I lean over and whisper, "Can't be worse than the concoction I made."

"True," she says with a little laugh.

"You're not going to give me a lecture about underage drinking?" Everly asks as she brings the shot to her lips.

"Would it do any good?"

Her smile widens. "No."

"To Everly. Happy birthday!" Grace lifts her glass.

"Happy birthday!" Bridget reluctantly pushes hers into the air.

Ev clinks her shot glass against the other two girls' and then all three of them toss back the tequila.

Bridget only drinks about half of hers, grimacing as she holds the glass away from her. I take it from her and swallow the rest.

She watches me like she's waiting for me to make a face. "I don't know how you took that so easily."

"Lots of practice," I say as Grace and Everly start dancing together. Bridget sticks by me.

"What's your favorite kind of shot?" I ask her.

"I don't know…a lemon drop."

"So sweet drinks?"

"Only in shots. I don't like super sweet cocktails. You?"

"Tequila?"

She laughs. "Figures."

"I don't have a go-to shot, I guess. I usually stick to beer, sometimes whiskey, sometimes wine. Basically, whatever is available."

"So, you're easy?"

Her teasing me is so unexpected that my brows shoot up in

surprise. That just makes her smile widen. Fuck, she's gorgeous.

The dress she's wearing hugs her curves and shows off long legs and toned arms. And that hair. I'm a total goner for her hair. All those blonde curls framing her face and hanging down her back.

"Ash?" she asks, snapping me out of a haze I didn't realize I was in. She laughs again.

"Sorry, what?"

"I said I'm sorry about Gabe."

"Nothing to be sorry for." I bite down on my back molars at the thought of her asshole ex. He came by practice this week with Jim to introduce himself but otherwise I've been able to avoid him. His threat still hangs over my head, though.

Even so, he's the last thing I want to think about right now.

"I texted him and let him know that nothing was going on between us, then I blocked him."

"I'm sure it'll all be fine," I tell her.

"Okay." She smiles again, then Everly comes over and takes her arm and pulls her over where Grace is dancing. A few more people have come downstairs and join them.

Nothing going on between us. Accurate, but I still don't like the sound of it.

Jack comes to stand next to me, holding a half-empty bottle of water in hand. A lot of the party has moved downstairs since that's where the birthday girl has stayed. Some of our teammates are making asses of themselves on the makeshift dance floor, others are sitting around. It's been a long week and partying wasn't on most people's agenda for the weekend. We have three days before our next game, then a short break for the holiday. After that it's madness until the end of the season.

"I thought you were going out with Meredith tonight?" I ask him.

"I did."

"Funny, I don't see her." I turn in a circle, pretending like I'm looking for the gorgeous blonde that's been out with Jack the last few weeks. It's possibly the longest amount of time I've known him to spend with one woman.

"I dropped her off when I got the call from Midnight."

"Everything end up okay with that?"

"Nothing that won't blow over." He clears his throat. "Speaking of Midnight, can we keep that between us."

"You haven't told anyone else that you're—?"

He gives his head a small shake before I finish the sentence. "Only you and Declan know."

Jack owns the place, though his involvement isn't public knowledge. It's just one of many investments he's made, so I'm surprised he's kept it private.

"Sure, but why?"

"Just until I'm sure I'm not going to sell. If I do, then it won't matter, and if I don't, then I'll tell everyone."

I nod my agreement.

"Meredith said you've been blowing off Kennedy since you started playing again."

"I'm not blowing her off." As soon as I say the words, I wonder if they're true. Fuck, maybe I have been. "I'll text her tomorrow. I don't think it's going to work. It shouldn't be this complicated to just set up a single date, you know?"

"It's only complicated if you make it that way. She's home tonight. Call her now." He turns to face me. "Unless there's some other reason you haven't called."

Slowly, his gaze roams around the room and lands on Bridget.

"Fuck you."

He chuckles. "Thinking of blowing up your career and making a move?"

The reminder of what's at risk has me gripping the can in my hand a little tighter. "No."

Both of his dark brows rise like he isn't buying it.

"No," I repeat with more force. "But she reminds me of what it could feel like. Excited, hopeful, a little crazed but in a good way, you know? When's the last time you felt that way about someone? Do you feel that with Meredith?"

"Insane? You're asking me if I feel insane when I'm with Meredith?" He shoots me a disbelieving look then shakes his head.

"In a good way," I emphasize again.

"Feeling insane is a good thing?"

"Yeah. It's like everything inside of you is on fire and at the same time you're so aware of every thrum of your pulse in a way that you usually don't notice."

"You *sound* crazy, I'll give you that. Whatever floats your boat. Just make sure Gabe doesn't find out."

"She's not interested anyway, so it doesn't matter."

"You sure about that?"

When I look over to where she's dancing with Everly and Grace, she's staring this way. A hint of a smile pulls up her gorgeous lips and then she looks away.

Jack claps me on the shoulder. "I'm out of here. I'll see you in the morning. And uh, try to get the crazy out of your system before then."

Jack heads out and I linger back a few minutes longer. Get her out of my system? I don't think that's possible. Not sure I even want to. I've dated enough to know that what I feel for her isn't common. If there's a chance that she feels it too, then I don't want to ignore whatever this is between us. We can figure out the shit with Gabe if it gets to that point, right? He's an asshole but it isn't like they're together anymore.

Slowly, I make my way across the room toward her.

Everly is hanging on Grace, nearly taking her friend down. Maybe I should have given her that lecture on drinking after all.

"I think it's time for some water," Grace says.

"Ash!" Everly lights up when she sees me, then frowns adorably. "Why aren't you out here dancing with us?"

"I'm here now."

"Grace is making me take a break." She glares playfully at her best friend.

"Seems like a good idea."

"I'm fine," she insists, then stumbles.

I step up on the other side to steady her. "You all right, Little Sharpie?"

"Totes fine." She shrugs away from me. "Stay here and keep Bridget company."

"I'm coming with you," Bridget says.

Everly, not so discreetly, looks between us, but whatever she wants to say, she refrains. The four of us go upstairs. I get Ev water and Grace makes her a plate of food.

"I wonder if we should get her home," Bridget says quietly, where only I can hear.

"Piper already made up the guest rooms here. She thought you three might want to crash."

"Oh." She gets this cute little wrinkle between her eyes as she squints.

"Problem?"

"No. It's just that everyone is so nice. It keeps throwing me off."

"You're not used to people being nice to you?" I immediately think of Gabe. Fucker.

She must realize that's what I'm thinking because she flushes and then her gaze drops.

"Want something else to drink?" I ask.

"Sure." She still doesn't quite meet my gaze.

I grab two more beers and then make another mixed drink while the girls get some food and water in their system.

"Is the firepit going outside?" Ev asks.

"I'm not sure. Let's check." I head outside with them behind me.

"It's so cold," Grace protests when we step onto the patio.

The firepit isn't on but I get it going while the girls huddle up together. It's not long before heat is coming out of it, warming the space and cutting the bite of the frigid winter night.

"I'm going to grab some blankets." Everly starts for the door.

"I'll come with you." Grace follows.

When they're gone, I set my drinks down and move over to a plastic bench seat and lift it up. As expected, there are blankets in here. I hold them up and Bridget laughs.

"You seem to know your way around this place pretty well."

"Jack owned this house before Tyler and Piper. I spent a lot of nights out here rookie year." I drop one blanket onto a chair for Grace and Ev, and then take the other and unfold it before carefully wrapping it around Bridget's shoulders.

"Thanks." Her hand comes up to pull it tighter around her, brushing against my fingers in the process.

Next, I pull out my phone and connect to the speakers out here to get some music going. Bridget takes a seat in one of the chairs next to the firepit. She leans forward, cupping the beer can with both hands.

"Here." I offer her the mixed drink I brought out with us. "Try this."

She hesitates.

"This one is good. Promise."

She brings the cup to her lips and takes a small sip, then smiles. "Lemon drop?"

I nod. "Technically it's a lemon drop cocktail but if you only take a sip at a time, it's a shot."

She takes another sip and then hands it back.

I take a seat in the chair next to her.

"Wanna share?" she asks, taking the blanket off her shoulders and holding out half to me.

I drag my chair closer to hers. The scrape of metal against the concrete drowns out the voice in my head—Jack's voice, warning me that this is a terrible idea.

Her knee knocks against mine as we place the blanket over both of our legs. Bridget leans forward so the top of the fabric also covers her bare arms and shoulders.

"Everyone should be nice to you," I say, still thinking about our conversation inside.

"Well, that's not life. Is everyone nice to you?"

"No, but everyone that matters is."

"It's over. Gabe and I are so over."

"I'm sorry."

"You're sorry? For what?"

"That he was a dick to you. That I didn't hit him that night outside of Wild's bar."

"I can take care of myself."

"I know, but you should have people that look out for you too. Like Everly and Grace."

The wind blows her hair into her face so I can't see her lips. I reach forward and capture the long, blonde strands. The pads of my fingers drag along her smooth skin as I tuck it behind her ear. "I want to be one of those people for you."

"Why? You don't even really know me."

"I guess not, but that's not how it feels when I'm around you."

She glances down at my mouth and then angles away from me, staring into the fire. "Why weren't you into Grace?"

"Grace?" I'm thrown by the change in topic, but I guess I'm not totally surprised she knows about the brief time period in which I considered what it might be like to date Everly's best friend.

"Yeah. I know that she liked you last summer."

I nod and roll my bottom lip behind my teeth.

"She's smart and beautiful and really nice. I could see you two together."

"Grace is great."

"But?" she asks, laughing at my obvious attempt to divert.

"But nothing. I just didn't feel that way about her." I could tell her the same lie I told myself, that I thought Grace was too young and that we were at different places in our lives. Those things are true, but I know now it isn't the whole story. Maybe it's part of it, but we didn't have the same spark I feel when I'm with Bridget.

She looks at me, unblinking, like what I've said doesn't make any sense.

"You want me to be into Grace?"

The reaction is quick and gone before I can get too excited, but it's there. The flicker of jealousy. "She's with Lane now."

"It wouldn't change anything if she wasn't." And because I don't want to walk away from here tonight with Bridget having any doubts on how I'm feeling, I add, "I like you. I know that I don't know everything there is about you, but it's still true."

"We can't. Gabe—"

"Isn't here."

"Everly is my friend."

"She's mine too." I shift so more of my leg is resting against hers under the blanket.

"I know. Which is why us getting involved is complicated."

I remember what Jack said earlier. "It's only as complicated as we make it."

The wind blows her hair into her face again and I capture it, lingering with my fingers caressing her face. Her breath catches.

"I should go inside and find Everly and Grace. Let them know we found blankets," she says but doesn't move. Her stare bounces between my lips and eyes like she's deciding on something.

Everything inside of me screams to close the space between us, but I don't move until she does.

Bridget leans forward the tiniest amount and then wets her lips. "Can I have more of the lemon drop?"

Without tearing my gaze from hers, I lift the cup to my mouth and take a sip.

"I thought you made that for me." She smirks, then tracks the movement, her gaze darting to my lips and then to my throat as I swallow. Instead of handing over the cup, I press my mouth to hers.

Adrenaline zaps through me at the small contact. Her soft lips gently mold to mine. I let some of the liquid trickle from my mouth.

She giggles, clearly not expecting it.

"That isn't what I had in mind," she says, not pulling away as the sticky, sweet liquid drips down her chin.

"No?"

"No." She still doesn't move. We're breathing each other in and it's fucking intoxicating.

"Something more like this then?" I bring a hand to the back of her head as I crash my lips back down on hers. I don't waste any time before deepening the kiss. I'm usually patient, but the weeks I've thought about this moment has me rushing. My tongue sweeps in, tasting her with the sugary liquid. A soft moan escapes her lips and goes straight to my dick.

I don't want to stop, but scaring her off would be worse, so I pull back with a strangled groan.

"Better?"

CHAPTER NINETEEN

Bridget

AM I GOING TO HAVE TO KICK YOUR ASS?

"**G**ood morning!" Everly pokes her head into my room.

When I groan and throw an arm over my eyes to block out the light, she laughs and comes to sit on the end of the bed. The three of us insisted on coming home last night to sleep in our own beds, which I'm thankful for now. My head pounds and my stomach is queasy.

I peek out at her. "How are you not hungover?"

"Oh, I was, but Grace made muffins and I ate like five of them. Soaked the alcohol right up." She holds up a large muffin on a napkin. "I saved you some and I made fresh coffee."

"I don't want food or caffeine. I want sleep."

"Nooo," she whines. "You promised to tell me everything that happened with you and Ash this morning. I'm dying. I let you sleep until noon."

"It's noon?"

"Yes."

I groan and sit up. "I don't think I promised that I'd tell you everything."

"You did. I'm almost certain."

"Like you remember anything. You almost fell in the hot tub."

"Yeah. That last shot was not a great idea."

My eyes feel like sandpaper and my head aches. "I can't believe I have to drive home today."

She hands over the muffin. "Then don't. Stay an extra night with me. Grace is staying with Lane tonight. We can go out or stay in. I'm sure Ash won't mind."

"I knew I was going to regret telling you we kissed." I tear off a hunk of blueberry muffin and stuff it into my mouth. "I was tipsy, he was tipsy. It wasn't a big thing."

I'm not sure I believe the words even as I say them.

"Uh-huh. That's not what it looked like to me."

Everly and Grace walked outside right after the kiss that will forever live rent-free in my head. Damn can he kiss. If they hadn't interrupted us, I'm not sure I could have stopped.

The night as I remember it after that was filled with a lot more dancing and fun with Grace and Everly. Ash and I didn't have any more moments alone, and I'm trying to decide if I'm thankful or sad about that.

Thankful. Definitely thankful. That kiss was incredible, but it would be dumb to get involved.

It was a one-time thing that I will replay for eternity.

"I have to go back today, anyway. I promised my mom I'd go shopping with her this afternoon."

"What time do you have to leave?"

"Soon. I probably should be on the road already."

"Well you have to eat, so that's enough time to tell me everything."

I flop back onto my mattress. "I don't know what happened. We were outside talking and then…he kissed me."

She lets out a little squeal.

"Are you really excited about this?" Her reaction surprises me. Ash is like a brother to her and she knows my relationship with Gabe was messy. Even if my ex weren't working with the Wildcats, there are a lot of reasons she might not be on board with me getting involved with someone she cares about.

"Of course. I love you and I love Ash."

"Yeah, but isn't it weird or something?"

"No." She laughs. "Why would it be weird?"

"He's your brother's teammate."

She doesn't blink, totally unfazed.

"Grace liked him."

"Months ago. And, I don't really think he's even her type. We were just spending so much time with him that it was easy and convenient. Plus, Ash is so damn charming it's hard not to crush on him."

"I thought you said he was like a brother."

"To me, yeah, but I see how girls are around him." She pulls on my arm to make me sit up. "Tell me what's really worrying you. Do you not like him? Are you going to break his heart? Am I going to have to kick your ass?"

"Me break his heart? You're not serious. He's…Ash Kelly."

"He's just a stinky boy who happens to play hockey really well."

"And kiss really well," I mutter under my breath.

She catches it and smiles. "So you do like him?"

"Yes. Maybe. I don't know. I liked kissing him."

"So your lips like him. That seems promising."

"Every part of me likes him," I say honestly. "But it was one kiss. He knows it's as bad of an idea as I do."

"You're not a bad idea. He likes you too."

I don't know what to think. But I'm going to be gone for a couple of weeks, so I don't have to figure anything out today.

I put the rest of the muffin on my nightstand. "I should shower and pack. What are you going to do all break?"

"Sleep in, hang with Grace until she goes to Hawaii, go to some hockey games. My mom is coming up on Christmas Day and then I might go with Ty and Piper to visit her family the day after. When will you be back?"

"I'm not sure. I'm scheduled to work on the third, so I'll be back by then."

Everly scrambles to her feet. "Be right back."

While she's gone, I swing my feet over the side of the bed and get up. Ugh. I need a shower.

Last night was fun. Next time I need to drink less and remember to do my skincare routine before bed, but nonetheless, I'm really happy I went out with Everly and Grace.

I missed this so much. Going out with friends and then spending the next day talking about it and laughing at all the dumb stuff we did. Except the dumb stuff in my past was never quite as exciting as kissing a hot hockey player.

Everly comes back into my room as I'm pulling out my suitcase from the closet. She's carrying a red giftbag with white ribbons hanging off the handle.

"Merry Christmas."

The back of my eyes sting with the threat of tears as she hands over the present. In true Everly fashion, the outside of the present is picture-perfect. "You didn't need to get me anything."

"I know. I wanted to. Open it."

I remove the white tissue paper until I pull out a flat, rectangular wrapped item. "You could be a professional gift wrapper."

She snorts. "I'm a bit of a perfectionist."

I tear the smooth paper and unfold it until I reveal a wooden picture frame. Me, Grace, and Everly have our faces squished together. The Wildcat hockey arena is the background. I barely remember taking the photo at the game we went to last week because I was nervous about seeing Ash. But despite that, I look happy. I *am* happy.

I run my finger over the bottom of the frame. Our names and the date are painted in pretty lettering. "Did you make this?"

"I bought the frame, but yeah, I painted it."

"I love it." I hold it to my chest. "Seriously. Thank you."

"You're welcome."

"I have a little something for you too." I set the picture down on my nightstand and open the first drawer where I stashed Everly and Grace's gifts. I wasn't sure if we'd do this. I had just planned on leaving them on the kitchen counter before I left for home.

"It's just something silly."

She tears into the present with more excitement than it deserves. When she sees what's inside, she looks up and smiles. "Oh my gosh. Bridge, this is beautiful."

She pulls out the snow globe and shakes it.

"It reminded me of the night we were snowed in and watched movies."

"The first night we all really hung out together." She smiles at me and then stares at the fake snow falling inside the little globe. "I love it so much. It's perfect."

The doorbell rings as she hugs me.

"I wonder who that is," she says.

"You're not expecting anyone?"

"No."

She hurries out of my room to get the door. I stay put and start to look through my clothes to figure out what I want to take home for a week or more of lounging around my parents' house.

"Bridge!" Ev yells. "It's for you."

"For me?" I swipe under both eyes like that's going to make me presentable. I need a very long shower, but apparently don't have time for it.

When I get into the living room, Everly is holding out a black box with a red bow, grinning like a fool.

"It's for you," she says.

"From who?"

"Look and see."

I flip open the small card on top of the box without taking the present from her. *Bridget, I owe you a drink. – Ash*

I'm certain I'm blushing as I move to open the box. Inside are four small bottles of vodka, triple sec, simple syrup, and fresh lemon juice. Each one has a little red bow on top. Laughter bubbles up inside me. He got me the ingredients for lemon drops.

Everly moves closer to look inside.

"It's what we were drinking," I say by way of explaining the contents of the gift.

"Damn, Kelly. I'm impressed," she says more to herself than me. She turns those knowing hazel eyes on me. "Still think it was just one kiss?"

It's late before I'm able to hide away in my old bedroom at my parents' house. I spent all afternoon shopping with my mom before she and my dad went to a work party.

I have a text waiting for me from Ash. It came in while I was in the car with my mom. I could have looked at it before now, but there was something exciting about knowing it was there. Anticipation and giddiness that I wanted to last as long as possible.

I sent him a thank you for the present earlier this afternoon and his text is a reply to that.

Ash: You're welcome. Have any plans tonight? Want to have a drink with me?

And a little later when I hadn't replied yet.

Ash: I knew I should have gone with roses.

Me: The gift was perfect. Sorry, I was shopping with my mom. I drove home this afternoon for the holiday break.
Ash: Where's home?
Me: Rockview. It's about two hours north.
Ash: Well shit. How long do you think roses will last?
Me: Umm a week maybe. Why?
Ash: I panicked and sent roses to your house about twenty minutes ago.
Me: You did not.
Ash: Oh, I absolutely did.

I smile at the screen as I crawl under the covers with my phone.

Ash: When will you be back?
Me: I'm not sure. I work on the third, so maybe the first or second of January. Do you get to see your family for Christmas?

Ash doesn't reply right away. I'm conflicted. Being around him is fun and that kiss was incredible. The gift and the texting are so sweet, and I can't deny how happy it all makes me, but pretending like it's perfectly fine as long as Gabe doesn't know we're talking seems incredibly naïve. Then again, it's not like Ash is proposing we get married and have babies.

So maybe we can kiss a little more.

As happy as I am to be texting him, my eyelids are heavy from lack of sleep last night. I'm so looking forward to sleeping in while I'm home. My phone is resting on my chest and my eyes are closed when it pings with his response.

Ash: Sorry. I was trying to text and hold a crying baby at the same time. Do not recommend. I'm flying to Boston on Christmas Eve and staying for two nights.

He sends a picture of him with a cute little baby snuggled up against his chest. Wow. It's a good look for him.

Me: Cute!
Ash: I try.
Me: I obviously meant the baby.

Ash: Was it obvious though? 😊 Meet Callum, Leo's little guy. I'm his favorite uncle.

Me: I have no doubt.

Ash: January 2nd, huh?

Me: Yeah.

Ash: All right. That's twelve days from now.

Me: Good math-ing.

Ash: I graduated college and everything. So in twelve days, wanna hang out?

My stomach flips as I read the message three times before responding.

Me: Sure.

Ash: Sure? Wow, don't sound too excited.

Me: YES!!!!

Ash: Muuuuch better 😎

CHAPTER TWENTY

Ash

COPY AND PASTE

Nurse Bridget: Good morning. Did you get drunk and accidentally copy and paste all of Google to me?

Ash: Afternoon, sunshine. I did not get drunk and copy Google. At least not ALL of it. I was thinking about what you said, how I don't know that much about you. So I found a few questions to help with that.

Nurse Bridget: A few. This looks like more than a few.

Ash: Thirty-six. And there's a lot I don't know about you.

Nurse Bridget: You want me to answer all these now? I haven't even had coffee yet.

Ash: Thirty-six questions in twelve days, that's only three a day. And I'll answer too.

Nurse Bridget: Your math skills continue to impress me.

Chuckling, I glance up from my phone to find Leo watching me with an amused expression.

"What?" I ask.

"Nothing." He holds Callum on his lap. The little guy is wearing a snowman onesie and it's just about the most adorable thing ever, even if he has drool hanging from his tiny little lips. "You've just got this big smile on your face. Which is surprising since practice this morning was shit."

The smile drops from my face. "It was brutal. I thought Coach's eyes were going to bug out of his head."

"He's feeling the pressure. I overheard him talking to Jim yesterday. They want to make some more changes in the new year."

"What kind of changes?" Panic squeezes my chest.

"As far as I know, your name hasn't come up. My guess is they'll send a couple of the rookies down and try to grab someone after the trade freeze."

The trade freeze keeps teams from making any changes during the Christmas holiday. So at least for another week I can relax.

My four-year contract with the Wildcats ends after the season is over. When I signed it, my agent didn't think a long contract was the way to go because my value would likely go up as I got more experience. He was right about that, but something I didn't foresee was how much the team would mean to me.

All the teams I've been a part of have meant something. I spent four years in Vermont going to college and playing hockey. From there, I went to New Jersey for two years, then a year in Pittsburgh before I was traded to the Wildcats. I didn't care where I went, I just wanted to play hockey as long as I could. I thought it'd always be like that, at least until I got married and had kids. That all seemed so far away and not like something I needed to worry about.

Which is why I didn't balk at not having a no-trade clause in my contract. Instead, I have a limited trade clause that specifies which teams I cannot be traded to. It's not a long list, just eight teams based mostly on location.

I had no idea how much I'd grow to love the Wildcat organization. How it would feel more like family and home than anywhere I've ever played before. Anywhere I've lived period. I don't want to go anywhere else. I don't want to start over with new guys. Even if my career was over tomorrow, I'd want to be right here.

"How's Bridget?" My buddy glances at the phone still in my hand.

"Good. Sleeping in, enjoying break."

"I remember those days," he says with a smile. "When does she get back?"

"Not until after the new year. If I'm even still here."

"I really don't think you have anything to worry about."

"I'm still not back to where I was." I sink back into the couch cushions.

"Is the shoulder bothering you?"

"No, not at all. But I'm out of sorts since Coach moved me to the second line. Now he's talking about putting me at center." Coach Miller loves to mix things up, especially when we're struggling. I never minded it until now.

"No matter where you play, you'll make a difference. You had a month off, give it time."

Time that I might not have. The truth is I'm not Leo or Jack or even Declan. They all make up crucial components of the team. Jack is a leader through and through. He looks out for everyone and he's been one of the top scorers for the team every year I've been here.

Leo is quieter than Jack, but he's the guy people go to when Jack is unavailable. Plus, he's got this uncanny ability to jump from line to line and mesh with players of all caliber and game style. He's a difference maker.

And Declan is our top defender. Maybe the top defender in all the league.

I'm not minimizing my contribution. I work fucking hard, and I put up good numbers every year, but the league is full of guys like me.

"So…" My buddy grins at me. "You really like this girl, huh?"

A chuckle slips from my mouth at his not-so-smooth change of topic. "Yeah, I do."

"And Gabe? Do you really think he'd try something dirty if he knew you two were talking?"

"I don't know, but he doesn't give me the warm fuzzies."

"What are you going to do?"

"Nothing. Bridget and I are just getting to know each other. It isn't like we're going out and flaunting it in his face. You don't need to worry."

"I'm not," he says. "We've all got your back."

"I appreciate it, but let's hope it doesn't come to that."

My phone pings with a text as I'm walking back to my house from Leo's.

Nurse Bridget: Knocking out an easy one before I force myself to get out of bed and do something productive. I'm a Virgo. My birthday is September 3. You?

I don't hate the image that I have of her lying in bed, smiling at the screen while she texts me.

Me: Aries. March 26. What are your plans for your first day of vacation?

Nurse Bridget: Showering, eating, watching many hours of TV. Not necessarily in that order.

Me: Wow. Busy day. You're making me look bad. I'll probably only get in one or two hours of TV time today.

Nurse Bridget: Total slacker.

Me: What are you going to watch?

Nurse Bridget: I don't know. It's been a while since I watched anything. Speaking of... question two for the day: I don't have a favorite TV show because I rarely have time to watch anything during the semester. You?

Me: Ted Lasso. Hands down. It's ruined me.

Bridget: Never watched it.

Me: Unacceptable. Not sure I can associate with someone with such bad taste in TV.

Nurse Bridget: Hmmm. I should probably be offended but I'm just so relieved I don't have to answer the rest of these questions.

Me: 🙂

Me: Watch it. Episode one at least. Then report back.

I don't hear back from Bridget while I pack and get ready for our game in California. But I go through my normal routine, trying to find some calm and rest up. I need to have a good game. If nothing else, it'll be peace of mind that I've done all I can. Teams will always make the best decision for themselves, so I just need to keep proving that the best place for me is right here where I am.

We leave late this afternoon for a one-night trip, playing tomorrow and then back. I fly out to Boston hours after we return so I make sure I have everything packed for that trip too.

By the time I step onto the team jet, I'm feeling relaxed and ready to go. I take my normal seat next to Leo. He's got his headphones on so I give him a nod and take out my phone and place it along with my coffee on the table in front of me.

The missed text notification catches my eye and I unlock the screen.

Nurse Bridget: I just finished season one. I haven't moved in five hours. Honestly I was prepared to hate it. Why is it so good?

Me: And to think you doubted me. Season two is even better.

Nurse Bridget: I'm skeptical, but plan to find out right after I shower and feed myself.

I'm tapping out a reply when my gaze snags on the people stepping onto the jet. My stomach drops. No fucking way. Gabe scans the jet before dropping his bag onto the seat at the front across from Jim. The last assistant GM rarely traveled with the team. What the hell is he doing here?

As if he can feel me glaring at him, he looks my way and juts his chin toward me. A hint of a smirk plays on his lips, but his eyes are filled with loathing.

I refuse to be the first to break eye contact. So what if I kissed his ex-girlfriend or was just texting her. There's no way he could know that or should even care. The only thing he needs to worry about is my performance on the ice.

I need to make sure I'm playing the best I can. The rest doesn't concern him.

CHAPTER TWENTY-ONE

Bridget

BEST KISS

Me: I was fifteen and it was during a game of spin the bottle. I know, super original. You?

Ash: Same. I was fifteen and it was at a school dance.

I grab another sugar cookie from the plate on the coffee table and tap out another text.

Me: Thanks to you showing me your mad dance skills the other night, I'm struggling to picture a girl kissing you after that.

Ash: You mean like you did?

Me: Oh right. Ha! Well, I was tipsy. And you kissed me.

Ash: Uh huh.

Me: What did you ask Santa for? Hockey sticks and skates?

Ash: Nah. I get those for free.

Me: lol of course, what was I thinking?

Ash: You forgot to answer the second half of the last question.

For the past three days, Ash and I have been texting basically nonstop. I've learned that he loves all sports movies, TV shows, and documentaries (no big surprise there) and that he prefers salty food over sweet. He hasn't cut his hair in two years but he's thinking about it after the season is over. He has a house on Lake Laurie and that's where he spends all summer. And his last relationship was more than a year ago and it ended because 'they wanted different things.' I didn't push too hard on that last one. Does that mean she wanted it to be serious and he didn't? It fits with everything I know about him, but I still don't like the idea that whatever we're doing has an expiration. It does, of course it does.

I'm focusing on that and not the question I'm avoiding answering: best kiss.

It's him. It's obviously him. But if I tell him that, I'm either going to be horrified when he replies that his was with some other person or I'm going to send his ego rocketing to outer space.

I'm trying to play it cool. Or as cool as I can while texting him all day. Yeah, yeah, I know. That ship has sailed. But it's easier over text and being however many miles away.

Ash: How about I go first?

Me: Sure. If you want.

Ash: The best kiss I ever had was with this smoking hot girl I met at work.

Yep. Yep. That's jealousy making the sugar cookie turn bitter in my mouth.

Me: Wow. At work? Scandalous. I guess mine was probably this guy I dated briefly my freshman year of college.
Ash: Jesus, woman. I meant you. I met you at work. Brb, gonna go jump off a cliff.

A huge smile breaks out on my face, and I type back quickly.

Me: Oops. Sorry. That went right by me. To be fair, I've eaten like a dozen sugar cookies today, so I think my brain is shutting down.
Ash: Sure, sure. I'm not at all disappointed that some shmuck three years ago was your best kiss.
Me: I'm sure you'll survive.
Ash: Barely.
Me: If I'd said you, would your ego have launched you to space?
Ash: Fuck yeah it would have.

I smile harder at his honesty.

Ash: Heading out to dinner with my family. Talk later?
Me: Yeah, I should go too. My parents and I are going to the movie theater. Bring on the popcorn!
Ash: Have fun.

And then a second later, he sends another.

Ash: Am I at least the second best?

By Christmas Eve, I've binged so much TV that the couch has a permanent indent of my butt in my favorite spot. I've also eaten dozens of homemade sugar cookies, done festive things with the family, and slept in nearly every single day. It's been glorious, but now I'm bored.

My parents are both busy—Mom is wrapping presents and baking for dinner at my grandparents' house tonight and my dad left early this morning, probably to finally buy his presents.

I've had to navigate a few awkward conversations about Gabe. My ex and I dated for over a year and my parents really liked him. Last year, he even came home with me for the holidays.

I shake off the reminder as I sit on my bed in my room. It's exactly the same as when I left to go to college. Same teal walls with fairy lights and pictures above my bed, tennis trophies and awards scattered around with high school memorabilia.

My dad threatens to turn it into an office every time I'm home, but it's reassuring in a way to come back and have things be just the way I remember them.

When peak boredom hits, I decide to clean out my closet. I pull out everything and lay it on my bed. Old prom dresses, tennis skirts, visors, shoes—so many shoes, and jeans that don't fit anymore.

I'm trying on a dress that I think I wore to a junior Homecoming party when my phone starts ringing from somewhere underneath the pile of discarded clothes.

On the fourth ring, I manage to find it. Ash's name flashes on the screen with a FaceTime call. I don't have long to consider whether to answer before it goes to voicemail, so I press accept.

My pulse kicks up a notch when his face appears. That playful and sexy smile of his widens as his gaze roams over me.

"Hey."

"Uhh. Hi." I can see myself in the small frame on the bottom right-hand side of the screen. I showered this morning and then threw my hair up into a ponytail. I'm not a troll under the bridge, but this is not how I would have chosen to look if I'd known he was going to video call me.

I do my best to push away any insecurity about how I look. If he wants the kind of girl who sits around at home wearing a full face of makeup with perfect hair, FaceTime-ready at any moment, then he should just know that's not me.

"I've got about ten minutes before my mom finds me and makes me help decorate the tree. Thought I'd call instead of text." He leans back against a wooden headboard.

"You're avoiding your family already?"

"Not my family. Decorating the tree."

"I thought everyone loved doing that."

"Not me. My mom and sisters say they want me to be a part of it, but then they go behind me and move every ornament to a different spot."

Laughing, I push some clothes out of the way to make a spot for me to sit on my bed. "Do you have a tree at your house?"

"Yeah, but my housekeeper decorates it." He looks a little sheepish at the admission. "What are you up to?"

"I made a very big mistake," I say and then move the phone to show him my messy bed.

His eyes widen.

"I thought I'd clean out my old closet, but it sucked me in."

That easy smile returns and his gaze dips to what he can see of my outfit. "Are you trying on all your old clothes?"

"Maybe."

He shifts on the bed he's sitting on and props one arm behind his head. "I'm intrigued. Show me more."

"You must really hate hanging ornaments."

"Or really like looking at you."

My face flushes but I get up and go to the full-length mirror attached to the back of my closet door.

I flip the camera so he can see the dress I'm wearing. "Don't laugh. It barely fits anymore, but I love it."

"I like it," he says. "Blue is a good color for you. What else you got?"

For the next half hour, I try on various pieces from my closet and Ash helps me decide whether to keep them. Or he tries. He doesn't put a single thing in the throwaway pile.

I draw the line at an old tube top that is so tight across my chest it hurts my boobs.

"No way. It barely fits anymore. I was a few sizes smaller then." I pull at the top.

"From what I can tell, it fits perfectly."

I laugh. "You're no help."

"I can't help it if everything you put on looks good."

"You're full of crap."

"Nope. Straight facts. You're a ten. Own it."

"Do you hear the things that come out of your mouth?"

He laughs, but it's interrupted by someone talking to him. I only catch part of the encounter, but when he looks back to the screen, he says, "Busted. I've been summoned."

"Poor you. I hope you'll survive."

"Thanks. I'm sure it'll be a battle. Me against the Kelly women. And they are fierce." He stands, carrying me with him as he walks. "By the way, I meant to ask, any chance you could come back a day or two early?"

Before I can reply, he adds, "Jack is having a New Year's Eve party. We play at home that afternoon. You could come to the game and then we could go to the party together after."

My stomach flutters with excitement and nerves. We made vague plans to hang out when I got back, but having something more concrete makes it seem more real.

"I'd love to hang out, but do you think that's a good idea? What if I run into Gabe again?"

"I'll make sure your seat is as far away from him as possible."

I chew on the side of my lip.

"Think about it. Even if you don't want to come to the game, I hope you'll come for the party. You can wear that sexy blue dress."

Everly: Merry Christmas! Miss my roomies.

Grace: Aloha from Hawaii! Merry Christmas!

Me: Merry Christmas!

Everly: I'm so jealous you're in Hawaii, Grace. It's so cold outside I had to wear my "real" winter boots. I was so bored yesterday I cleaned out the refrigerator.

Grace: Oh thank god. The veggie drawer was disgusting.

Everly: Yes, yes it was.

Me: I cleaned out my closet this week.

Everly: How do you think I'd look with bangs?

Grace: Put the scissors down, Everly Rose!

Everly: Just some cute little fringe ones, maybe?

Grace: Don't do it. I'm going to be growing mine out forever.

Bridget: You could definitely make bangs work, but maybe sleep on it?

Everly: Ugh. Fine. I need something to do. Campus is dead, everyone is still gone for break, and Ty had a game in Seattle.

Grace: Go out and meet new friends.

Grace: And by friends I mean cute boys. I bet Mike's is busy tonight.

By the end of the first week home, our group text thread is basically a running commentary of our days. Grace is still in Hawaii, so she pops in and out to share gorgeous photos. Everly and I are commiserating in our boredom. We've buddy cleaned out our email inboxes, learned a TikTok dance together, and did an eight-hour read-a-thon where we FaceTimed and read the same book.

So when she video calls me as I'm flipping through Netflix looking for something new to watch, I'm not surprised.

"Hey," I answer, setting the phone down and scrolling the romantic movie section.

"So, I did a thing." She's in her car so I can't see her that well.

"Uh-oh. You didn't cut bangs, did you?"

"No." She laughs. "I'm outside."

"Outside of where?"

"Your house." She grins at me through the screen. "I know, total creeper vibes, but you were bored and I was bored... we can be bored together. I brought wine."

An hour later, half the bottle is gone, and Ev and I are sitting on my couch with the TV muted.

"I can't believe you're here."

"Well, to be honest. It's not just because I was bored and missed your face." She traces the rim of the glass with a finger. "You sounded a little bummed the past couple of days. Is everything okay?"

"What? Bummed?" I shake my head. "Just bored."

"Where are your parents tonight?"

"They went out to dinner."

"And you stayed in?"

"Yeah..." I trail off as I try to figure out how to explain my relationship with my parents. "We've done all the obligatory family activities. I played racquetball with my dad yesterday and helped my mom make sugar cookies."

"So you are close with them?"

"Yes." I sigh. "Things have been a little weird over the last year."

She waits for me to say more. I'm not sure how to put it all in words.

"Has anyone ever told you that you're incredibly hard to get to know?"

"Yeah." My shoulders slump.

Ev laughs and hugs me with one arm. "Why are things weird with your parents?"

"Because they keep asking about Gabe. *Where is he? What happened? He seemed like such a nice, young man.*" I roll my eyes. "They really liked him, and they can't understand why I'd break up with him."

"Ugh. That's the worst. Why'd they like him so much? Everything I've heard about the guy is less than flattering."

"I think it's because before I started dating Gabe, I was going out and partying a lot and my grades had started to slide. I've always had to work hard at school, and my friends at the time either didn't need to study to keep up or didn't care as long as they squeaked by with a passing grade."

"I feel that. Grace is so smart that I want to strangle her sometimes."

I smile. It's true. Out of the three of us, she spends the least amount of time on homework and studying and is still getting straight As.

"Then I met Gabe and things were different. He was older and already had a job. Before the Wildcats, he was a scout for a junior hockey team. Anyway, my lifestyle changed when we got serious. We went out some, but during the week he was pretty strict about his routine. I stopped going out too. At first it was because I just didn't want to, I wanted to spend my time with him. Then it was because he didn't really like it when I went out with my friends without him. In hindsight, that should have been the first red flag."

Ev squeezes my hand, and I summon the courage to continue.

"However shitty the circumstances, the result was that I went out less and studied more. My parents were thrilled that I was settling down and taking things more seriously. They credited it all to Gabe, who they loved. He has a way of charming people."

"The biggest assholes always do."

"Anyway, since we've broken up, my parents just keep asking about him." I scrunch up my face in disgust. "When my dad found out that he was working with the Wildcats, he called Gabe to congratulate him."

Ev offers me a sympathetic smile.

"I know they mean well, but I can tell they're so bummed that we broke up and hoping we'll get back together. Three times already they've managed to drop his name into conversation." I lower my voice to mimic my dad. "'Remember last year when Gabe got us all those matching Christmas pajamas?'"

"He bought your family matching pajamas?" She snorts a short laugh.

"I can't even blame them for wishing I was still with him because as far as they know, he was the perfect boyfriend." Guilt washes over me. "I let everyone think that and now..."

Now I can't tell them how truly awful he was to me. They'd never believe it.

"Can I ask you something?"

I nod, then take a sip of wine.

"What really happened with you and Gabe?"

My heart beats rapidly and I let out a slow breath as I decide how much to share. I trust Everly, but what if she thinks I'm being dramatic or making too big of a deal out of what happened?

"At first, he was great. I'd been hanging out and hooking up with guys from school and you know how romantic and considerate they can be."

She snorts again.

"So, when Gabe planned actual dates and bought me presents, I thought it meant he really liked me. Maybe he did, I don't know. I've had a lot of time to think about it and I still don't truly understand what happened and what part I played in it."

"Whatever happened, it wasn't your fault."

"About six months in, maybe a little sooner than that, he changed. Little things at first. He'd get really upset with me if I made plans that didn't include him. Why didn't I want to spend time with him? Was I cheating on him? I'd basically abandoned my friends for him at that point anyway, so I just quit accepting their invites for parties or going out to bars altogether. Some part of me felt like what he was asking was reasonable, I guess. I thought this is what a real relationship is like. But then he just found more things to be annoyed about. I was dressing too sexy or not sexy enough. Nothing I did was right. I'd given up so much already, so I found myself giving in more and more until I finally realized whatever we had wasn't love. He was only happy if he could control every action I made."

I take another breath. "We got in this cycle where we'd fight, and I'd be ready to leave and then he'd apologize and go back to the charming and sweet guy I fell for. It was confusing. He played the part of a doting and loyal boyfriend so well. But it never lasted. God, he could be so mean and hurtful and then flip it so fast my head spun. Things got bad. *Really* bad."

I fiddle with the ring on my pointer finger. "It got to a point where I knew I had to leave. So, I ended things. Since then, he's been calling and texting, trying to get me back, promising me things will be different. For the life of me I can't figure out how he could possibly think what we had was good."

I'm ashamed it took so long to realize just how much he manipulated me. The more time that passes, the clearer I can see it.

"He sounds like a real asshole. You deserve so much better than that." She sets her wine on the coffee table and then leans in and hugs me tight against her. "I'm so sorry you went through that."

"Thank you. I can't tell you how good it feels to say some of that stuff out loud."

"You can always tell me anything."

"You know what's the most humiliating part?"

"What?"

"He treated me so bad, but I still cried when I ended things."

"You spent a year of your life with someone. You cared about him. You're human, babe."

"Yeah. Anyway. It's been over for a few months now and I'm still picking up the pieces. I lost all my friends and my relationship with my parents is awkward. I never told them, or anyone else, about the yelling or fighting. I made it seem like we were the perfect couple, and after I couldn't figure out how to explain all of that to anyone. I never felt more alone in my life before I met you and Grace. You two are the real deal. Thank you for driving up here to check on me. I'm really glad to have you in my life."

"And I'm not going anywhere." She grabs her glass and clinks it against mine.

CHAPTER TWENTY-TWO

Bridget

MY HEART JUST STOPPED

Everly stays the night, and the next morning she folds the clothes in my donation pile from my closet cleanout. "I didn't get a chance last night to ask you about New Year's Eve."

"What about it?" I'm busy hanging up all the keep items, coordinating by season and color.

"Ash told me that he asked you to come to Jack's party. But you haven't mentioned it. So, you're either not going or holding out on me."

"I'm not holding out on you."

"I figured." She smiles. "Why aren't you going?"

"I won't be back. I had planned to stay here until the second, remember?"

"Because you're having such a great time avoiding your parents?"

I glare at her from across the room.

"Look, I totally get it. I have my own tricky relationship with my parents, but if things are weird, why aren't you jumping at the chance to head back a couple of days early, hang with me, and kiss a cute boy at midnight?"

I won't lie, the thought of kissing Ash again does funny things to my stomach.

"I'm not sure it's a good idea." No, scratch that, I know it isn't a good idea.

"Why not?"

"He works with my psycho ex."

"Who you broke up with."

"Regardless, it's messy."

"Life is messy."

"And then there's you."

"Me?" She looks absolutely horrified. "There is nothing going on between me and Ash. I swear to you."

"No. I know. I believe you. But he's a big part of your life and if things were to go bad between me and him…"

"You think that if things with you and Ash don't work out, I'd take his side and stop being friends with you?"

"I wouldn't even blame you. We've only known each other for a short time. You and Ash have history."

"Okay. I'm not saying that there wouldn't be some situations that'd be tricky if you two hated each other or something, but I'm not going to stop being friends with you over something like that. You're stuck with me. I promise, okay?"

I nod and swallow down the lump in my throat. I want to believe her. Everly has been so lovely to me, but I know her connection with Ash is stronger.

She stands and comes over to hug me. "So will you come back

with me or are we going to have to organize our bookshelves over FaceTime tonight?"

"I actually should organize my bookshelf." I glance over at it. It's full of mostly books I read in middle school and didn't want to part with. I should probably donate them at this point. "But yes, I will come."

"Yay." She jumps up and down in front of me. "Jack's parties are huge. Ahhh! We're going to have so much fun."

On New Year's Eve, Everly and I watch the Wildcats game in our living room while getting ready. Grace calls from Hawaii to give us input on our outfits and catch us up on all the fun things she's been doing on vacation. She comes back tomorrow, and I can't wait to see her. It's really nice having friends again.

Every time Ash comes on the screen, my stomach flutters with nerves. Our texting slowed the past few days. After his short Christmas break, the team had two games on the road. Yesterday they were off, but I spent it with Everly shopping for dresses.

I keep telling myself that it's just a party. He'll be there, I'll be there, but so will a bunch of other people, so there's no reason to get all freaked out like it's a date.

But when Everly and I walk into the party, that all goes to hell. Ash is standing in the living room. He sees us immediately and his blue eyes widen as he walks over to greet us.

"Fucking hell," he mutters, stopping in front of me. He slowly brings his stare up to my face. "My heart just stopped for a second. I forgot how gorgeous you are. Damn, it's good to see you."

He wraps me in a quick hug, then pulls back and continues to look at me in disbelief.

"Congrats on the game." Everly breaks the tension while holding back a laugh at Ash's stunned stare still on me.

He clears his throat and then steps over to hug her too. "Thanks, Little Sharpie."

"Who needs a drink?" Everly asks.

Ash's gaze flicks to me and he blows out a breath that makes his cheeks puff out. "Can I have a second with Bridget?"

The smile Everly was fighting stretches across her face. "Yeah. I see Ty. I'm going to congratulate him and then pick out a cute boy to kiss at midnight."

"Gonna pretend I didn't hear that last part," Ash says with one brow quirked.

"Oh, please. I kiss boys. Get over it." Ev waves her fingers at me and then disappears into the crowd of people standing around Jack's living room.

The atmosphere between me and Ash shifts as soon as we're alone. I'm a bundle of nerves. I twist the ring on my first finger around and around.

He looks too good to be real in jeans and a black sweater. His hair is still slightly damp and he has on cologne that is warm and spicy.

I like him. I've always been attracted to him, but the texting over break made me realize it's more than just a crush on a super-hot guy. He makes me feel excited and hopeful in a way that I haven't been since Gabe, and wasn't sure I'd ever feel again.

Maybe he was right. It doesn't have to be complicated. We can hang out and kiss and keep things casual. I could use some no strings attached fun. And this way there's nothing to get back to Gabe and no reason that it'll be weird between me and Everly when it's over. We'll be like him and Grace. They had a moment, or an almost moment, and they can be around each other with no problem.

I'm going over it and over it, solidifying it all in my mind, that I only realize Ash is pulling me away from the party when he steps into a dark room and closes the door behind us.

Ash backs me up against the wall and rests a hand above me. "Hey."

"Hi," I say a little too brightly. Did it suddenly get very warm in here? "Everything okay?"

"Yeah. I just couldn't go another second without doing this." His hand drops to the nape of my neck and he pulls me toward him.

His mouth covers mine and his fingers splay out over my collarbone. Unlike last time, there's no hesitation. He kisses me like he's done it a thousand times before and like he can't get enough. It's an intoxicating combination.

He pulls back too soon and rests his forehead against mine. "I've been thinking about that for ten days."

"You and your math-ing."

The backs of his fingers glide over my skin next to the strap of my pink dress. "I've got a whole lot more math I'd like to do, but eventually I think Ev would come looking for you."

"Probably so."

"Ready to meet some people?"

I don't feel nearly as certain as the definitive nod I give him.

Ash leads me back out to the party. The massive house is filled with people, many I recognize but a lot I don't. Everyone knows Ash. People call out to him—guys and girls. He waves or offers a head tip in acknowledgment, but he doesn't stop until we reach the kitchen.

Everly is in here talking to Piper and some of the other players' wives. She gives me a knowing look but doesn't interrupt as Ash leans down and asks me what I want to drink.

I go with a hard seltzer and Ash gets himself a beer.

The man of the house walks in as we're taking our first sips. I don't miss the way he takes me in standing next to his friend before settling his attention on Ash. "We need one more for darts, you in?" He smiles at me. "Good to see you again, Bridget."

"You too. Your house is beautiful."

"Thanks." He opens a cabinet and pulls down a bottle of whiskey.

"Breaking out the good stuff?" Ash asks. "Good or bad night?"

"That remains to be seen."

Ash gets a weird expression on his face. "Everything all right?"

"Just peachy."

"Where's Meredith?"

Jack's gaze moves past us. "She and Kennedy are coming later."

When Ash doesn't reply, Jack asks, "You cool with that? I invited her before..." His gaze flicks to me and back to Ash.

"Yeah, of course." Ash plays it off, but the two guys are having a stare down, silently communicating something.

I look away to give them privacy, but a second later, Jack is saying he needs to get back to darts, and Ash and I are alone.

"I'm sorry about that," Ash says.

"About what?"

He grimaces like he isn't sure what to say. "Jack and his girlfriend Meredith tried to set me up with Meredith's friend, Kennedy. She's going to be here later."

"Oh. Is that weird?"

"No. We only hung out once, nothing happened."

I laugh a little at the bizarre conversation. Of course, Ash has dated other women. He's young and hot and charming. "It's okay."

"Are you sure? I feel kind of like a dick now. I didn't think about her being here."

"It's absolutely fine. You've dated other people. I've dated other people. We're not even together. We're just...whatever. We've kissed twice. I don't have any claim over you and even if I did, I wouldn't care."

Maybe it isn't the same thing as Gabe keeping me from hanging with my friends because he was jealous, but it's too close to ever be something I'd ask of someone.

He wears an amused expression as I finish talking. I take a large gulp of my drink to keep myself from rambling on any longer.

"It'd be okay if you wanted to have a little claim over me." He winks, then rests a hand on my lower back. "Come on. I want to introduce you to some more people."

CHAPTER TWENTY-THREE

Ash

WORKED THEN AND WORKS NOW

Hanging with Bridget at the party is fun. If not a little bit torturous. I'm not usually the kind of guy to want to go all caveman and throw a woman over my shoulder (unless it's in the bedroom), but every time I introduce her to one of my teammates and their eyes linger a little too long, I'm ready to hightail it out of here with her in tow.

I keep reminding myself that this is our first date. It's funny, I sent her all those questions because I wanted her to feel like we knew each other better, not because I thought we needed to know each other better. I thought I knew plenty about her before, but it solidified my feelings in a way I didn't realize was missing.

I like her. I like the way she thinks and texts and talks and makes me feel when she smiles at me, like she's doing right now. We didn't make it all the way through the list of questions since she came back early, so we're doing that now.

Who is your celebrity crush? Me—Florence Pugh. Bridget—some young prick I'd never heard of but now hate.

Where would you live if you could live anywhere? Me—the lake house. Bridget—undecided because she hasn't been to enough places to choose.

"What's your house like?" she asks, angling her body to face me. That long, blonde hair hangs over one shoulder and her eyes lock on me instead of roaming around to take in all the people here. Jack has a lot of friends. Hockey players, baseball players, a couple of actors, lots of models. People fly in for his New Year's Eve party every year. The man knows how to throw a party.

"Want to find out? I could show you easier than I could try to describe it." I waggle my eyebrows playfully and tighten my grip around my beer bottle to keep from touching her. She agreed to come out tonight, but her body language is timid. I don't want to scare her off.

She laughs, dimples flashing on either side of her beautiful smile, and then sidesteps the question by firing off more of her own. "Is it a one-story or two? What's your favorite room? What's the backyard like?"

"Two-story. The master is downstairs, which I really like. I hardly go upstairs at all, so I guess it's kind of a waste, but when I've had roommates that's been nice. I spend the most time in the living room. I guess that's my favorite. The backyard has a pool, but honestly it doesn't get used that much because I spend so much of the summer at the lake."

She's still staring at me, focused on each word. That guy that stars in *Euphoria* just walked by and she didn't even give him a cursory glance.

"When we were texting over break, I kept trying to picture you sitting around at home doing normal things and couldn't."

"Well, I don't do normal things. I do awesome things."

She shakes her head at me.

"I'll show you sometime. Give you a tour. Might even let you sit in my favorite spot in the living room."

There is only one question left on the list. When I pulled the list from Google, there were only thirty-five, so I added one of my own. A question that I'd been avoiding asking but that has plagued me since we met. How did you meet your last boyfriend/girlfriend? I cleverly concealed it by not naming him, but I know he's the last person she dated.

"All right. Final question. How'd you and Gabe meet?"

Her demeanor shifts instantly, and I really want to kick myself for bringing him up. I just need to know how a girl like Bridget could fall for that jerk. It doesn't make any sense to me.

"At a bar." She laughs. "Real original, right?"

"There are worse places."

"Like prison?" Her eyes get a little twinkle back as she jokes.

"Exactly."

She laughs again, then grows quiet.

"Sorry. If you don't want to talk about him, we don't have to."

"I get it. How could I date someone that's so awful?"

"Basically."

"He wasn't awful to me. Not at the beginning."

My body tenses at the implication of those words. Not at the beginning means he was awful to her later. I knew that. Hell, I witnessed it. Still pisses me off.

"What about you? How'd you meet your last girlfriend?"

"At a party. One of Jack's parties, actually."

"How long were you together?"

"Eh…" I run a hand along my jaw. "It was kind of on and off."

"You broke up and got back together a lot?"

"No." Shit, I hadn't really thought it through that I'd have to talk about my relationships too. Talia was beautiful and we had fun, but it only worked because we didn't expect much from each other. We were together when she was in town, but otherwise, we were both free to do whatever we wanted. "We weren't exclusive."

"Oh." The surprise on Bridget's face makes me wince inwardly.

"We both traveled a lot."

"You don't have to explain," Bridget says and shakes her head. "I get it. It makes a lot of sense. It must be hard to have relationships with your schedule." She waves a hand. "Not to mention, you're always surrounded by beautiful women. I think I saw that girl over there on the cover of a magazine last month."

"With the right one, I don't think it'd be that hard. Most of my buddies are settled down now and they make it work."

She nods thoughtfully. "Do your friends know about me and Gabe?"

"Just that you dated and he's a giant prick."

She snorts a surprised laugh. "I worried a little about coming tonight. I don't want to cause any problems for you."

"You're not. And no one here will run to him and say anything. I promise. They have my back and that means they have yours too."

"That's going to take some getting used to."

"People having your back?"

She nods, then blushes like the admission makes her uncomfortable. I hate that for her, but it makes me that much more determined to be someone she can count on.

A little before midnight, Bridget and I are sitting outside with some of the other couples. Shit, am I part of a couple? The thought has me grinning.

Scarlett, Jade, and Piper pulled Bridget into conversation with them and I'm pretending to care about the card game the guys and I are playing.

I've got one hand resting on Bridget's thigh under the table and every few minutes she looks over at me and smiles.

Some of her earlier hesitation seems to be gone. Thank fuck.

And I'm feeling more at ease than I have in weeks. I played my ass off the past few games. The team is still struggling a little, but we've found ways to win.

"It's almost time," Scarlett says as Declan wins another hand of rummy.

Leo checks the time. "She's right. Five minutes. We should head in."

"Why are we heading in?" Bridget asks me as the others stand.

"Jack makes a big toast right before the new year. It's a whole thing. The man loves being the center of attention."

I get both Bridget and me a fresh drink and then find a wall to lean against as Jack takes his spot in the middle of the living room. Kennedy and Meredith are nearby. Somehow, we've managed not to bump into them all night. Maybe they just got here. I haven't been looking anywhere but at the girl next to me.

"Hey, Ash." Meredith waves and she and Kennedy come closer.

"It's good to see you."

"You too." I nod to Kennedy. "Hey. How've you been?"

"Pretty good." She steps forward and hugs me. "I was hoping I'd run into you tonight."

Bridget stiffens beside me and tries to take a step away. I take her hand as Kennedy pulls back.

"Have you met Bridget?" I ask her. "Bridget, this is Kennedy and Meredith."

Kennedy's gaze finally slides to the woman next to me and understanding dawns.

"Hi," she and Meredith both say politely, then Kennedy glances at me with a somewhat disappointed smile.

"Hi." Bridget's smile is small as she replies. She looks like she might be thinking about running off.

"Good to see you both," I say, pulling Bridget with me away from them.

I don't stop until we're out of earshot. Bridget turns to face me with an amused smirk. "She's pretty."

"Probably."

"Probably?"

"Yeah. I was too busy checking you out to notice."

"Oh my god. That was bad even for you."

"Even for me?"

"The things that come out of your mouth remind me of the boys in junior high."

"Worked then and works now."

"You wish." She laughs again.

I tug her to me and drop my mouth over hers. It might not be midnight yet, but I'm too impatient to wait.

She giggles but melts into me, hooking her arms around my neck. When she pulls back, she glances around like she's checking to see if anyone is watching us.

"Come on." Holding her hand in mine, I weave to the back of the room where we're less likely to be spotted.

"I want to thank everyone for coming tonight," Jack says.

I wrap my arms around Bridget's waist and pull her back against me as I listen to my buddy give his annual toast. He does what any good man and team captain would do—he lets the people in his life know he appreciates them, shares a few favorite memories from the last year, and fills us with hope for everything that's coming in the next.

I move Bridget's hair away from one side of her neck and drop my mouth to the soft skin. She shivers into me. I continue, grazing my lips from her shoulder to the sensitive column of her neck. My hands around her waist drop to the hem of her dress, teasing the skin.

Her breaths quicken and she turns to face me.

I slide my fingers through her hair and tug gently so her head tilts to the side and gives me better access. I place soft kisses on every inch, then bury my face into the crook of her neck and suck until she lets out a little whimper.

No one is paying any attention to us. Jack is a damn good speaker. Somehow the man always manages to time it just perfect so as soon as he finishes, we drink, and then the ten-second countdown begins.

And that's my cue that it's almost time. The people around us start chanting. Ten, nine, eight...

I stand tall and look down at Bridget. Her blue-green eyes are bright, cheeks flushed, and her chest rises and falls with her rapid breathing.

Have I had someone to kiss at every New Year's Eve party? Yeah, probably. I don't really remember. But I know that tonight, kissing Bridget is going to be a memory that lasts.

We're locked in a stare-off until the clock strikes midnight, then slowly I cover her mouth with mine.

Her fingers grip the front of my sweater and I use an arm around her back to crush her against me as my tongue explores her mouth.

Someone bumps into me, forcing me to break the kiss.

I don't want to be here anymore. I want to be anywhere else as long as it's alone with Bridget.

"Come back to my house."

"Now?"

I nod, heated gaze boring into her. "Yeah, now. Right fucking now. I can't wait a second longer."

Her cheeks flush pinker. "I should find Everly and tell her."

"I'll text her."

Bridget wears a knowing smile.

"It could take a while to find her and those are minutes I don't want to waste." I pull her tighter against me so she can feel how hard I am. "She has a key and knows she can always crash at my place."

"You want me to stay the night?"

I'm probably jumping about fifteen steps, but I'm finding it hard to slow down. "I've wanted that since the night we met. Is that something you want?"

She wets her lips. "Yes."

CHAPTER TWENTY-FOUR

Bridget

THAT'S KIND OF A LOT

Ash's hands frame my face and his mouth covers mine as soon as we're inside his house. He kicks the door shut and we fumble around, walking through his dark house.

"I'll give you the full house tour later," he says, sweeping my hair away from my neck and kissing the sensitive spot above my collarbone.

Goosebumps race down my arms. His hands return to my face and he captures my mouth again. The man can kiss.

A throbbing started between my legs hours ago. Everything about him. His touch. His words. The way he spent all night acting like no one else mattered but me. His attention is all-consuming.

I slide my hands under his sweater and flatten my palms against his warm, toned stomach and then up over his chest and around to his back. Hard planes of skin and sculpted muscle. Chiseled and lean, strong.

He's doing his own exploration. His hands roam all over my body.

From cradling my face to pulling my hair to squeezing my ass and teasing the skin just under the hem of my dress.

I let out a whimper when his fingers graze the inside of my thigh.

"I don't usually do this," I say, knowing I'm such a cliché.

"Do you want to stop?"

"God, no."

He chuckles, then moves his hand up over the curve of my ass. He hooks his thumb around the back of my thong and pulls so the material tightens around my core. My entire body trembles and I react by sinking my nails into his skin.

He lets out a low groan. Long fingers splay out over my ass cheeks. He pulls back and looks down at me with my dress bunched up around my hips and my panties wedged between my slickness.

"Goddamn, Bridge."

Flames dance over my skin. I pull his sweater up and he helps me remove it. My eyes adjust to the dark and I admire his tattoos. I trace the butterfly tattoo with a finger and read the script over his chest. *Collect moments.* It seems appropriate because this moment right now, I don't ever want to forget it.

Slowly, I let my hands drop back over his six-pack abs and v-cut to the top of his jeans. He's patient, letting me have a moment to take him in. But his jaw is tight, and his muscles are coiled taut.

He flips on a light, revealing his living room when I flick the button open and then slide the zipper down.

He goes back to kissing my neck and collarbone as I glide my hand down the front of his open jeans, under his boxers, until I can wrap my fingers around his hard length. He's thick and long. He rocks into my touch and I swipe my thumb over the tip.

I'm rewarded with his teeth scraping along my skin and his hands squeezing my ass so hard it almost hurts. He shifts, sliding one leg between mine. My sensitive pussy jolts at the contact.

"Wait," I say, pulling away only enough to get out the word. "This…us. Is this just tonight?"

He freezes immediately, but his dick twitches against my stomach in protest. "Definitely not."

"But it's just casual, right?"

His gaze narrows a fraction. "Is that what you want?"

"Yes." I swallow. "We should keep it casual. It works with your schedule and I'm not ready to do another relationship. Plus, who knows what Gabe would do if he thought we were together, and I don't want to do anything that could come between me and Everly."

"That's a lot of reasons."

"I've thought about it a lot."

He clicks his tongue and nods, fighting a smile at my admission. I've thought about us together and now he knows it. "We can do this however you want."

"Casual," I repeat. "We'll see each other when we both want but no labels, or going out together in public, and when it's over, we'll be friendly or at least civil when our paths cross."

"Already talking about the end and I haven't been inside you yet." Ash chuckles, then groans again as he finally moves his fingers to my clit. It feels too good to do anything but rub against him. I need more.

"I just want to make sure we have a plan," I say. What I mean is that without one, I think this man could crush my heart into a million pieces.

"Got it." His voice is gruff. "Do you want to sit down?"

"Sit down? Why? Do you want to stop?"

"Fuck no." He takes my bottom lip between his teeth and lets out a low growl. "I want to keep kissing you, but I think we'd both be a lot happier if you were riding my dick while I did it."

My body shudders. "We agree on something."

I push his jeans and boxers down while we walk over to the couch, and Ash frees me of my panties.

He takes a seat, dick jutting up strong and proud. I swallow thickly as he hooks one arm around my back and pulls me down onto him.

We lunge for each other, kissing like it's been days instead of seconds since his lips were on mine last.

While he devours my mouth, he pulls the fabric of my dress up. He breaks the kiss to pull it over my head, then tosses it on the couch beside us as his stare locks on my chest. A bra didn't work with this dress, and damn am I grateful.

His movements are slow as he brings both hands up to cover my breasts. Calloused fingers stroke and squeeze. He leans in to taste me. Licking, then taking a nipple between his teeth.

His cock stirs underneath me.

"Condom?" I ask.

He doesn't remove his face from between my breasts as he answers, "In my wallet."

I lean down to get his jeans off the floor. They're just out of reach so I bend farther, arching away from him. He holds on to my hips and keeps me from falling back onto the ground as I grab his jeans.

I basically do a sit-up to get back on his lap. Hello, ab workout. I hold them up over my head like a prize. "Got 'em."

He takes them, pulls out his wallet from the front pocket and opens it to get the condom. He tosses everything except the rubber back onto the floor.

I gawk a little as he tears it open and covers himself. He's bigger than anyone I've been with before. It all seemed normal and proportional until I thought about putting it inside me.

"Wow," I say. "Umm…that's kind of a lot."

His body shakes with silent laughter.

"No, really. Are you above average or has it been too long since I've seen a penis in real life?"

In one sweeping motion, he has me on my back on the couch and he hovers over me. "Let's just say we need to make sure you're ready for me."

My eyes widen, but any trepidation is quickly replaced by pleasure as he slides down my body and buries his face between my legs.

Heat pools in my stomach as pleasure jolts my hips up. Ash pins me in place, devouring me until I'm squirming and whimpering.

"Ash." His name comes out raspy and quiet.

"Ready for me, babe?" He places a soft kiss on my inner thigh and then chases it with a bite.

I am *so* ready. If I have to wait another second, I might die. I'm unable to form the words, so I nod.

I'm more than a little nervous as the head of his dick nudges my entrance. He pushes in slowly, inch by thick, long inch.

"Still okay?" he asks.

I let out a shaky breath and look up at him. His beautiful face is tense but painted with pleasure.

"I'm great."

"You feel so damn good squeezing my dick. So beautiful. So tight. So perfect."

His words feed the frenzy of emotions bouncing around inside me. I've had casual sex before, but I don't remember it feeling like this.

When he starts to move, pleasure rolls through me so fast I'm a little embarrassed at how quickly he's going to be able to get me off. I'm not usually so fast to orgasm. But Ash. Oh god, Ash.

I accidentally say that last part out loud and he gets a wicked gleam in his eyes. His pace is slow and lazy like he's in no hurry.

Still, every thrust takes my breath away and makes my limbs liquify. I'm putty in his very big and capable hands.

"I like it when you say my name," he says as his lips sweep over mine.

"Ash," I say again as he licks my neck and then sucks.

"Been dreaming about this since the first time I saw you," he admits, pausing with his dick buried inside me. He wraps an arm around my back and pulls me back to a sitting position on his lap.

The new angle is bliss. Stars explode behind my eyes and my head falls forward and rests against his shoulder.

"You're close," he says.

"I think it's the alcohol."

"I think it's my dick."

I laugh and the movement makes me clench around him again. We both groan.

Ash starts to move underneath me, raising his hips to push himself deeper and using the arm around my waist to hold me in place.

It only takes a few more pumps before I'm coming apart around him so hard that I see stars. It's the best thing I've ever felt but it still somehow doesn't quell the ache between my legs. He follows a few seconds later, threading his fingers through my hair and sucking hard on my neck as he groans through his release.

We collapse against each other, breathless and panting.

"Damn. That was hot. Your pussy is still clenched so tight, I don't wanna pull out."

Laughing softly, I move off him with all the grace my jelly legs will allow. Ash removes the condom and gets rid of it while I look for my panties. I'm pulling them on when he comes back into the living room.

His body is insane. And his dick—wow. I don't know how that thing was inside me. He arches one brow with a cocky smirk. "Where do you think you're going?"

"Umm…I'm not sure. Home maybe. I know you said I could stay over, but Everly is probably still at the party and I can grab a ride home with her. This was fun."

I have no idea how to act after casual sex that felt very *not* casual. I should have laid that out in the plan. We had sex. Now what? Am I supposed to stay and chat or get the hell out of here?

"Fun, huh?" He walks over to me and places both hands at my waist. Those long fingers caress my skin and my core throbs.

"It was fantastic, okay?" I roll my eyes at the ego on this man. "But there's no need for me to stay the night."

"I disagree," he says, lifting me into his arms. I wrap my legs around his waist instinctually. "I'm not done with you yet."

I wake up in Ash's bed with his muscular arm wrapped around my waist. My body feels like I ran a marathon or climbed Mount Everest. Sex with Ash was a workout.

I carefully wiggle out of his hold and get up. He offered me a T-shirt and sweats to sleep in, then proceeded to strip me out of them again once we got into bed. I find both discarded items and put them on before padding out of the room in search of my phone.

I think I left it in the living room. Or maybe the entryway.

"Good morning." Everly scares the crap out of me. She's standing in the kitchen and wears a pleased smirk as she leans against the counter, cradling a mug in both hands.

I squeak my surprise and place a hand over my now racing heart. "Holy crap."

She laughs wickedly. Bless her, she hands me a cup of coffee before she says, "Looks like someone had fun last night."

I bring a hand up to my messy hair. "I'm sure I have no idea what you're talking about."

"Must have been some night. Ash never sleeps this late."

I don't tell her that he only stopped giving me orgasms about two hours ago.

"Morning." Ash ambles out, eyes still half closed, wearing only a pair of loose sweats that are dangerously low on his hips. He aims a sleepy smile at me as he rubs the back of his neck. God help me, I glance down at his crotch like I could possibly have any more sex right now. I'm going to be sore for a week. "Morning, Little Sharpie."

"Hey. Thanks for letting me crash last night. It felt like old times." She looks at me. "Well, almost."

"You're always welcome to crash here. You know that." He pours a cup of coffee before joining me on the other side of the counter. He brushes his lips over mine in a kiss so quick I don't have time to freak out. Okay, not too much time. "You're always welcome to crash here too."

"Yeah, I bet she is," Everly mutters.

"What are your plans today?" Ash asks us.

"Food and then a nap. By the way, Leo and Declan stopped by about five minutes ago to see if you wanted to go on a run. And Ty texted me to get a hold of you. He and Maverick were going to play on the outdoor rink behind Mav's house. I told all of them that you were occupied."

My face heats. I'm not embarrassed that his friends know we spent the night together, but it all feels very not casual.

"We should get going," I say to Everly.

She shoots me a surprised, wide-eyed look, but nods. "Sure. I'm starving. Want to see if Grace will pick us up and we can find somewhere for brunch? Her flight got in about an hour ago."

"That sounds great."

Everly nods and picks up her phone.

"I can take you guys home," Ash says as he brings his coffee up to his lips. He looks real good shirtless, and those sweats should be criminal. Another inch and I could see his dick.

"Already on her way." Ev's fingers tap quickly over the screen. "She'll be here in ten minutes."

Ten minutes? I snap out of my trance. I don't even know where my panties are. I glance down, then up to find Ash smirking at me like he knows exactly what I'm thinking.

"I'm going to get my stuff together," I say and hurry away.

My clothes are all over the place. I finally get a good look at his house. It's cozier than I expected. In the living room is the big, gray sectional we had sex on last night. My stomach does a cartwheel at the memory. There's also a chair and smaller couch on either side of the room. I bet half his team could comfortably sit in here.

A huge TV takes up the other wall, but there isn't much else in terms of art. Still, it's impressive and I can picture Ash in here with his friends.

Once I find all my clothes, I scurry back to Ash's room as he continues to chat with Everly in the kitchen. I'm slipping back into last night's dress when he comes in and wraps his arms around me.

"Running away?" he asks, voice still a little gruff from sleep.

Definitely. I slept with Ash. *Many* times. And, wow, I'm going to need a minute to freak out. Ash Kelly blew my mind. Instead of saying all that, I go with, "You have things to do. Your friends are looking for you."

"They're not as pretty as you. Stay and hang out. I'll feed you and then we can chill. I don't have anywhere I need to be until late this afternoon."

"I can't."

"Fine," he huffs playfully. "What about tomorrow? We leave for St. Louis around four, but I'm free after practice in the morning."

My first instinct is to say no, even though I want to spend more time with him. I'm hesitant about jumping into a new relationship, even a casual one. But Ash has agreed to everything I've asked. He's nice and funny, and I lost track of the number of times he made me come last night.

"Yeah, that sounds good."

A smile takes over his face. "I'll swing by and pick you up after practice."

CHAPTER TWENTY-FIVE

Bridget

NOT MY BEST WORK

I check my phone as I walk out of a patient's room. The night has been slow, and I haven't heard from Ash since earlier today before the game.

For the past week, we've been texting and hanging out when we can. His schedule is hectic, and they've been on the road more than home, so the hanging out has been limited.

But tonight he should be on his way back and the next two games are here. I never thought I'd be following a sport's team's schedule so closely. It's all so fun right now and I want to soak up all the giddy and happy feelings.

I'm hoping he'll text when the jet lands. I'll be glad for him to be in the same state again, even if I'm stuck at work for the next seven hours. Maybe I can swing by and see him tomorrow after classes.

Sliding my phone back into my scrub pants pocket, I walk through the quiet hall and come up short when the man occupying my thoughts stands at the nurses' station. He leans casually against the desk, one ankle crossed over the other as he talks to Hannah.

My heart skips a beat and the emotions bubbling to the surface play out on my face in a way that there's no playing it cool.

"What are you doing here?" I ask as I close the distance between us. I want to throw my arms around him and kiss the crap out of him.

He's wearing black athletic pants and a long coat over a Wildcat T-shirt. He pulls off athleisure so well it's scary.

"We just got back and I thought I'd stop by and see if you've taken your break yet."

"She has not," Hannah says giving me a pointed stare. I'm going to have a lot of explaining to do later. Maybe I should have told her, but since it's casual, I didn't want to oversell what's happening. Plus, it's not something I want to get out with Gabe working for the Wildcats.

My coworker tips her head toward the elevators. "Go. I'll cover you."

"Thank you."

She watches with a knowing smile as Ash threads his fingers through mine and pulls me away.

He bypasses the elevator and drags me to the first empty room on the VIP wing. I'm laughing when he brings his mouth down onto mine.

No one should come down here tonight, but I guide us back out in the hallway and across to the on-call room just in case. It's small and almost never used. The hospital added on much nicer ones downstairs in the surgery center, but this one has a bed and that's all I need.

"I was going to bring you lunch, but I got sidetracked trying to get here as fast as I could." He mumbles the words against my lips and then kisses me again.

"It's okay. I usually just grab a protein bar or something."

"I'll bring food next time."

Next time. The promise makes my heart flutter. I press my mouth harder against his to block out the war of emotions. It feels like too much, too fast, but I can't seem to make myself slow down.

"I missed you."

I grab a fistful of his T-shirt and guide us toward the bed. He chuckles in my ear as I sit on the creaky mattress and try to pull him down with me. "I take it you missed me too."

I don't know why I hold on to the words so closely. It's obvious to him I did, but instead of saying the words, I slide his coat off.

His playful smile darkens when I reach for his pants.

"Fuck, really?"

I nod.

He grabs a condom from his wallet while I take him out of his pants. I still can't get over how big he is.

He covers himself and then pulls the ties on my scrub pants. "Turn over."

As I flip onto my stomach, Ash tugs my pants and panties down to my knees. "Your ass in these scrubs will be the death of me."

One large hand settles on my lower back as he teases my entrance with the head of his cock. He doesn't need to worry about me being ready for him. I was soaked the second he kissed me. But he still works me over until I'm desperate for him.

I push back against him, taking him deeper.

"Oh, fuck, baby. I'm not going to be able to last long. Been dreaming about this pussy for three days." His words make a shiver roll down my spine.

I cry out as he fills me completely. Ash stills and lets out a groan before he moves again. Every thrust is torture and bliss. My orgasm is on a hair trigger, released when he whispers my name against my neck.

"Ash," I call out in reply, hoping that he understands in that one word all the things I'm not saying. I missed him. I really like him. This thing between us feels so good.

He follows me after another slow, languorous thrust. The air is filled with our ragged breathing. Ash presses a kiss against my shoulder before he pulls out.

"Well, that was unexpected," he says after disposing of the condom.

I pull up my panties and re-tie my scrubs, then giggle when I look around. "No kidding. I think my brain short-circuited when I saw you. I can't believe you're here. Aren't you exhausted?"

"Not anymore." He tugs me to him and brushes his lips over mine. "How long do you have for break?"

"Thirty minutes minus however long that took."

"So twenty-eight or twenty-nine more minutes." He grins impishly. "Not my best work."

"No complaints here."

He takes my lower lip between his teeth and then kisses me again. "Can I see you tomorrow?"

"I have classes and then I need to sleep for a few hours and study. I don't work tomorrow night though."

"I have a team community service thing in the evening."

"Oh." My disappointment is palpable.

"Come over after class. You can sleep and study at my place. I can't go another day without seeing you."

"Okay," I say, lacing my hands around the back of his neck. I really love Ash's bed. Mostly because it's his.

He must have expected me to say no because his eyes widen with delight. "Really?"

"Yeah. I can't go another day without seeing you either."

The next afternoon after a glorious nap in Ash's giant king-sized bed followed by an hour of naked time with him giving me multiple orgasms, we set up in his living room. I'm studying on the couch and he's in a big arm chair watching game film.

I look up and find him watching me. A playful smile teases his lips, and he drops his gaze back to the iPad.

When it happens a second time, I laugh. "What?"

"Nothing. You just look damn good wearing my clothes and sitting on my couch."

I stole a thin, faded college T-shirt from him and sweats that I had to roll at the waist to keep from falling to my ankles. They even smell faintly like him. "I may never give this shirt back."

"Looks better on you anyway." He sits forward and drops the tablet on the coffee table. "I have an interview in a few minutes. I'm gonna go in the office so I don't bother you with the noise."

"Okay." I nod as he stands. He drops a kiss on my lips before going upstairs. I still haven't been up there, but he told me there's three guest rooms and an office.

I try to study, I really do, but after thirty minutes without remembering a single thing I've read, I give up and quietly head upstairs.

Ash is easy to find. I follow his voice to a room at the end of the hall. The door is open an inch and Ash is sitting in a tall, office chair in front of a desk. He has in headphones so I can't hear the person on the other line.

He smiles as he speaks, talking about the team with enthusiasm that's contagious. I don't move, but he must sense me because he glances back and spots me.

I lift a hand in a wave and start to retreat, but he waves me in. Quietly, I enter. His phone is on the desk, face up. No video, check.

Ash pulls me down onto his lap, never faltering while he talks.

I straddle him, appreciating his broad, naked chest. He places a kiss on my lips and whispers, "Hi."

I get lost listening to his voice and soaking up his presence. When the interview is done, he ends the call and tosses his headphones on the desk.

"I got lonely downstairs by myself."

"Sorry it took so long. Done studying?"

"No, but I need a break."

"And how would you like to spend this break?" He waggles his brows. "I have a few ideas."

"I bet you do." My stomach flips. I can't seem to get enough of him. I trace the outline of one of his tattoos with my finger. "Why a butterfly?"

The blue of its wings matches his eyes.

"My sisters wanted us all to get something. It was a butterfly or a flower."

"That's sweet," I say with a small laugh, then move my attention over to the words over his chest. "And this one?"

"It's something my grandfather always said. I guess it stuck with me."

"I like it."

"I like you." His arms circle my waist, and he pulls me farther onto his lap. "What are you going to do tonight?"

"Lane is having a party at his place. I think Everly wants to go for a while. I probably won't stay long, but the three of us haven't been out since Ev's birthday." My pulse speeds up for reasons I don't understand until Ash smiles.

"Sounds fun," he says.

Just like that. No comment on me going out without him or trying to talk me out of it. I know Ash isn't Gabe, but I guess I haven't completely stopped expecting him to react like Gabe would have. Then again, Ash and I aren't in a relationship. We're casual. Both of us are free to do what we want. Somehow, I don't think that matters. Ash doesn't strike me as the kind of guy that wavers on his affection because of a label. He's in this. And so am I.

"What about you?"

"I'm gonna crash early. Game tomorrow. But if you want to send me some sexy, drunk texts later I won't be mad about it."

"I'll see what I can do."

CHAPTER TWENTY-SIX

Ash

CASUALLY OBSESSED

I see Bridget every second my schedule will allow, and we text constantly. I am a man obsessed.

We have a home game tonight. After our morning skate, I went directly to her house and we haven't left her bed since. My phone alarm goes off for the third time and I shut it off with a groan.

"I don't wanna go," I tell her as I drape an arm around her middle.

She wiggles out of my hold and stands next to the bed. "Oh no. I'm not going to be the reason you're late. The whole city will hate me if you get benched or something."

I sit up reluctantly. She's not wrong. Coach will not be happy if I'm late.

"Plans later?" I ask as Bridget pulls a T-shirt over her head.

"No. I don't think so. Why?" She gives me a playful smile as I gawk at her half-naked body. "Want to hang out?"

"Actually, I was also hoping you'd come to watch me play."

She pauses, sliding her panties up over her toned legs. "I don't think that's a good idea."

"Why not?" I swing my legs over the side of the bed and stand. Heat flickers in her eyes as her gaze drops to my dick.

Whatever this is might be casual, but she can't get enough of me and the feeling is mutual. Casually obsessed.

"You know why. Gabe—"

"Doesn't own the arena." I really hate that prick and hate even more that Bridget still feels like she needs to walk on eggshells to keep him happy. "I get that you don't want to see him, and you don't want him to know about us, but it isn't like we're going to be fucking on center ice." Though that sounds interesting. I step to her and rub my hands up and down over her arms. "Ev and Grace are going, right?"

"Just Everly. Grace is going out with Lane tonight."

"It's highly unlikely you'd run into Gabe. He'll be in the press box, and I can get you seats all the way across the arena. If by some chance he randomly spots you—because let's be honest, you do stand out, babe. You'll easily be the hottest woman there. Then stick with Everly. She'd love to give him a piece of her mind."

"I want to come, I do. You in your little hockey getup is seriously hot." She does another slow appraisal of me. "But I just can't. I'm sorry."

It shouldn't disappoint me. I've never cared that much about my family or girlfriends being there. Sure, it's fun to have them in the stands, but we play more than eighty games a year. Even some of the wives don't make it to every single home game.

Still, that feeling stirring in my chest is achingly close to disappointment. I try not to think too hard on why I want Bridget there so badly. Especially knowing that it puts her in such close proximity to the douchebag ex. My selfishness shouldn't trump her comfort.

"Nah, I get it," I say. "We're just coming up on another long road trip and I was hoping to spend some more time with you first."

"Sitting in the same arena is hardly spending time together." She drops her arms over my shoulders and laces her fingers together behind my head.

"I'll take you as close as I can get you." I brush my lips over hers.

We get lost in kisses and soon we're back in bed and naked. I'm disturbingly good at pushing away all thoughts and worries when her legs are wrapped around me and I'm buried inside her.

Eventually we do have to get dressed and leave the house though—real bummer. I head home for my usual meal and power nap before the game.

Hours later when I get to the arena, I go straight to the locker room. Slipping into my routine has helped me forget about my disappointment but when I see Gabe, those feelings are back and tinged with anger.

He's standing in front of one of the stalls talking to Lewis as the latter removes a name plate and tosses it to the ground, then places a new one in its spot.

I drop my bag on the bench in front of my locker. Leo looks up, then turns his gaze to where they're readying the new spot.

"Traded," he says quietly. "We got Nick Galaxy from Chicago, which should help with scoring."

I nod and swallow the lump in my throat. More guys have come and gone in the three years I've been with the Wildcats than I can count. We're all professionals and most of us know what it's like to be the new guy so we don't spend a lot of time mourning the guy that left because we're too busy figuring out how to adjust to the change.

Our job is to win despite everything else. I never resented it so much until now.

Lewis finishes changing out the stall and picks up the discarded pieces on his way out. Just like that it's done. Gabe is all smiles as he talks with Nick.

"Galaxy played on the junior team Gabe worked for before he was drafted to Chicago."

It's a reminder of Gabe's influence over who comes and goes on this team. A pit forms in my stomach as I watch the new guy and Gabe's easy camaraderie. Eventually Gabe shakes his hand and leaves Nick to settle in.

Leo doesn't waste any time. He stands and walks over to Nick. If I know my buddy, he's welcoming him to the team and shooting the shit, trying to ease the nerves and bring him into the fold quickly.

I'll do the same. He's a good player and a huge get for us if he can come in and help put pucks in the net.

Gabe's steps slow as he approaches me.

"Kelly," he says, shoving one hand into his tailored pants pocket. "How's it going?"

"Fantastic." My voice drips with sarcasm. I don't bother asking how he is. Don't give a flying fuck. "What can I help you with?"

"Just checking in and making sure everything is all right with you." His attempt at genuine concern is almost believable if it weren't for the words that follow. "Your stats are down from this time last season."

Of-fucking-course they are. I missed four weeks because of my shoulder.

"Only one goal in the last four games." He cocks his head to the side. "Jim thinks you can turn it around, but I'm not so sure. Maybe what you need is a change of scenery. Dallas is nice this time of year."

I keep my mouth clamped shut, knowing there's nothing I can say. Guys like him feed on control and feeling like they have the upper hand. I refuse to give it to him. Maybe I should talk to Jim though. If he has concerns, I want to address them. But even doing that feels like giving in to whatever twisted power trip Gabe is on. My jaw tightens. I'm going to crack a molar if I don't get away from this guy.

"How's Bridget doing?" he asks.

"Probably great now that she's away from you," I say with a smile. If anyone saw me talking to him or overheard, they'd think I was joking.

The flicker of anger that crosses his face is smoothed out quickly.

"Hey." Jack walks up, glancing between us and reading the tense situation. Neither Gabe nor I look at him. "Need something, Gabe?"

"Just making sure everyone's all set for tonight."

"Appreciate it," Jack says. "But we've got it from here."

It's a dismissal that's polite enough that Gabe obeys but icy enough that I know my captain has my back.

As soon as he's gone, Jack looks to me. "What was that about?"

"My shitty season stats and a thinly-veiled threat of being traded."

He curses under his breath. "You can't let him get under your skin. Especially right before a game."

"I know," I say, feeling the annoyance thrum through my blood. Fuck. He's right. "I know."

Nick jumps right in like he's been with the team all season. Coach mixes up the lines to put him with Leo and Jack and our first line gets most of our shots on goal. They don't score, but they're getting looks. The other change is that I'm moved to center on the second line with Maverick and Tyler. I've played center before, but it isn't where I'm most comfortable. I try to push Gabe's words out of my head but at the end of the second period, I've not contributed a damn thing.

In the locker room, I take off my jersey and fling it down hard at the ground in front of my stall. I keep my pads on but take off my skates. We have just a few minutes to rest and cool down before we head back out.

Usually, the coaches don't come in during intermission until they've met to discuss the period, but I'm not that surprised when Coach Miller follows the last guy in.

He stands in the middle of our quiet locker room, hands on his hips.

"That sucked," he says quietly.

"No shit," someone murmurs.

Coach Miller lets his arms drop to his sides and he scans the room. I glance down when he holds my gaze too long.

"You're too talented of a team to be struggling this much. Get out of your heads. Tonight is one of those nights that shots don't want to go in. That doesn't mean to back off. The first line looked good. Keep putting it on net and something will get by. Nick, nice job coming in. Leo and Jack, good job communicating. Second line…"

When I look back up, Coach turns his gaze at me again. "Keep at it. We may switch some things up again to see if we can find a better fit than having Ash at center, but I like the three of you together. You're fast and finding each other out there. Let's see if we can make something happen. Everyone, give Mikey some help. It's not over yet."

Coach claps his hands once in front of him, then turns on his heel to leave. When he's gone, the chatter of my teammates begins. Leo leans over. "You good?"

I cock my head to the side to look at him. "Is your eyesight failing? Fuck no, I'm not good. That was fucking terrible. I've only taken one shot all night, and it missed the net by a mile. Goalie didn't even flinch."

I chug down some Gatorade and lean back. I close my eyes and take a few breaths, trying to find some calm. Visions of Bridget flash through my mind. Her smile, her laugh, the way she looks at me when I bring her to orgasm, that goddamn hair. As quickly as they float through, I push them away, but they do the trick, and I feel a little more ready to get back out there and figure out how the fuck to help my team and keep myself from being traded.

CHAPTER TWENTY-SEVEN

Bridget

WE'VE GOT COMPANY

Everly: Wish you were here!
Me: Me too. Cheer extra loud for me.
Everly: Already on it.

The game is on while I paint my toenails in the living room. I don't know a lot about Colorado, or really any of the teams, but they seem good. At the start of the third period, the Wildcats are down by three goals and the announcers keep talking about how they need to shake off the first two periods and come out strong.

A fierce protectiveness rages inside me when they mention that Ash has been struggling since his return. But when they zoom in on him after an icing call, I can see the tension in the set of his jaw.

Guilt gnaws at me. He wanted me to be there, and I said no. It isn't like I didn't want to go. I don't think Ash realizes just what lengths Gabe will stoop to get what he wants.

He said he understood, but I still feel crappy. And it makes me hate Gabe that much more. And, okay, myself a little. I was so glad to be free of him, but he's still this annoying, silent presence keeping me from living my life.

The Wildcats do pick up a little momentum (according to the sportscasters) as the third period winds down. Jack scores, then less than a minute later Maverick does as well, but Colorado follows it up with one of their own, and with one minute to go, they're still down two goals.

Me: Do you think the guys will go to Wild's after the game?
Everly: I doubt it. They don't usually go out after a loss.
Me: Oh. Okay.
Everly: You want to go out? I think I heard that Kappa is having a party tonight.
Me: No, I don't really feel like partying. I was just curious.
Everly: OMG were you going to surprise Ash?
Me: I feel bad for not going to the game. It's probably a terrible idea anyway.
Everly: NO WAY. He'll be so excited. He can probably use some cheering up. You HAVE to go.
Me: You just said they weren't going out.
Everly: Not to the bar. Surprise him at his house.
Me: That sounds a little presumptuous. Maybe I'll just

text him and see if he wants to hang out.

Everly: Are you kidding? He'll love it. Ash loves a surprise. He'll be so stoked to see you.

Me: What if he made other plans or just wants to be alone? Or what if he brings another girl home?

Everly: I would kill him for cheating on you, but he would never.

Me: We're not together so it's not cheating. Appreciate the loyalty though.

Everly: Always.

Nerves have me fidgeting while I wait parked in front of Ash's house. The entire street is dark and quiet. I feel like a total lurker. Dropping my head to the steering wheel, I contemplate leaving for all of two seconds before I talk myself out of it. No. I should have showed up for him at the game and I didn't. Even if he doesn't want to hang out, I want to see him long enough to tell him how much I regret not being there.

Lights flash through the windshield and I glance up, squinting to identify the vehicle. Ash's truck slows and turns into the driveway in front of me. I can't see through the tinted windows, but my heart races, knowing that he's in there and there's no turning back.

I swallow down my nerves and get out of the car. Ash is already walking around behind his truck when I shut my door.

"Hey." I give him a wobbly smile. "Surprise!"

He's in joggers and a sweatshirt, with a black Wildcat hat pulled low over his eyes, making it hard to read his expression. His long legs eat up the space between us before I can decipher if he's happy to see me or freaked out.

When I finally do get a glimpse of his face, my chest tightens at the serious and focused glint.

Shit. Not cool, Bridget. So not cool. What guy wants you to show up unannounced after he just had a crappy day at work?

"I'm so sorry—"

His mouth crashes down on mine before I can get the full apology out. His giant hands frame my face and he tilts my head to deepen the kiss. His tongue strokes mine, needy and frantic.

I'm breathless when he pulls back, and his chest rises and falls in the same rhythm.

"I guess it's okay I showed up without warning then?"

"I think my heart catapulted out of my body when I realized it was your car. It's really you?"

"In the flesh."

His gaze dips to my bare legs. I hadn't planned on standing outside in a skirt, but the look he gives me makes it well worth braving the freezing temperature out here. Ash reaches down and scoops me up into his arms.

I let out a little squeal as he swats my ass. He starts for the house, bypassing his truck.

Laughing, I try to wiggle out of his hold. "Ash. Wait. You left the door open."

"Left all my stuff in there too. Don't care."

"What if someone steals it?"

"Ah, shit. I need my keys." He backtracks and carries me to the truck instead. He sets me on the driver's seat. The cab of the truck is still warm. "I missed you."

"It's only been a few hours," I say, but his words make me giddy inside.

"I stand by my words." His palms glide down my thighs to my knees and then back. "Did you have a good day?"

"No, not really."

His brows furrow.

"I felt like shit for not coming to the game. I shouldn't have let Gabe scare me away so easily."

"You were right to say no. It wasn't fair of me to ask that of you. I underestimated what a prick he is."

My body tenses. "Did something happen?"

"Nothing important."

I cock my head to the side.

"Everything is fine," he says. I'm not convinced, but he leans in and kisses me again and all my thoughts of Gabe, or anyone else, are gone.

Ash steps between my legs, pushing them farther apart as his fingers drift up under my skirt.

"I'm sorry about the game."

He hums, then the tips of his fingers graze the lacy material between my thighs. His lips go to my neck and work their way down to my collarbone.

"You'll get them next time, or whatever they say in this scenario." I jolt when his thumb strokes my clit over my panties.

"In *this* scenario, the only thing I want you to say is my name, babe."

"Ash," I say, far breathier than intended.

"That's it." His fingers slip underneath the material. "Lie back, baby. I need to taste you."

"Here?"

"Right fucking here. I can't wait." He hooks one leg over his shoulder as I lean back over the center console. He tosses his hat onto the dashboard.

Any uncertainties are quickly erased when his lips brush over my aching core.

"Ash."

He moves my panties over to the side and then places another kiss in the same spot. I'm vibrating with a need so big it feels impossible to quell.

"Fuck, Bridge. You're so wet. So ready for me." His eyes lock onto mine as he covers me with his mouth.

"Yes." I reach out for him and pull at the front of his joggers. I need more. I need him. Sex with Ash is unlike anything I've experienced before. He's playful and fun but surprisingly tender and attentive too.

"I don't have any more condoms in my wallet."

"I'm on birth control and I haven't been with anyone else since…" I don't say his name, but Ash nods in understanding.

"I get checked regularly."

"Okay," I say breathlessly.

He dips back down between my legs and nips at my inner thigh. "But first I want to feel you come apart on my tongue."

This time when his mouth covers me, his touch is hard and demanding. His hands hold me in place as he alternates sucking and licking my swollen clit.

I'm gasping and writhing beneath him. It's too much and not enough.

"I need…I need you," I rasp.

"You want this." He stands tall and lets his hard cock nudge against my throbbing pussy. He's still wearing his joggers, but I'm so close it sends a wave of pleasure through me.

"Yes." I arch into him, but he pulls away.

I whine, out of my mind with how turned on I am. How much I want him. How much I need him.

He drops a quick kiss against my lips and murmurs, "Come for me, Bridget. Then I'll take you inside and fuck you so hard you won't remember anyone but me."

Oh, I remember the others, all right. Remember how none of them ever made me feel like this. Even without his talented tongue, huge dick, and dirty words, Ash puts every other experience in a column labeled *Nowhere Near as Good as This*.

When I shatter for him, it's with the knowledge that he'll always stand apart for reasons I don't fully understand and couldn't explain.

My legs are still trembling around him when Ash adjusts my panties and pulls my skirt down. "Uhh, Bridge?"

His tone, full of hesitation and apprehension—two things Ash is not—makes me sit up quickly. "Yeah?"

"We've got company."

"Company?" I squeak as I finally notice the headlights pulling to a stop on the curb in front of my car.

"Hey," Leo's deep voice calls from the open window. "Everything okay?"

"Yep. Everything is great." He motions with his head for me to step out.

I shake my head. I cannot imagine what I look like right now.

"It's just Leo," he says when I don't move.

Another head shake.

"He knows I'm not over here talking to myself, babe."

Reluctantly, I shimmy forward. Ash is impatient, though, and decides to lift me out and set me on the ground in front of him. He wraps his arms around my waist. "Bridget came by to surprise me."

Leo's smile widens. "Hey, Bridget."

"Hey, Leo." Heat hits my cheeks. I wave, then smooth a hand over my messy hair.

Without another word, he rolls up the window and pulls into the driveway across the street.

"Oh my gosh. I'm going to kill you. I'm so embarrassed."

"He knows I make out with girls. I think you'll survive."

"Yeah, but not in your truck with the door open in the middle of the driveway." I wave my hand around dramatically, then groan again.

"You're cute."

"I am mortified."

He chuckles, then wipes a thumb under my left eye where I'm sure my makeup is smudged. "Well, put that mortification on hold because I sort of promised him and Scarlett I'd come over for a bit tonight."

"I thought you might have made plans. It's no big deal. You should go. I just wanted to drop by and tell you I'm sorry for not going and that it was a tough game."

His face twists in confusion. "You're not going anywhere, babe. You're coming with me."

"Are you sure?"

"Positive. Scarlett will be thrilled." He circles my waist and pulls me flush against him. "Besides, we have plans later."

CHAPTER TWENTY-EIGHT

Ash

RAZZLE DAZZLE UNICORNS

At five o'clock on the dot, I walk outside of my house to meet Leo. He's waiting at the end of my driveway with Callum sleeping in a stroller next to him. I pull my sweatshirt over my head and then a cap down over my ears. We haven't had any snow the past week, but it's still freezing outside.

"Are we not running this morning?" For the past two years, we've done this damn near every day. It stopped being about conditioning a long time ago, though that is a nice benefit. Staying in shape year-round has made me faster.

"No, we are. Check it out. It's a jogging stroller." My buddy beams harder than he did when he bought his first nice vehicle as he pushes the fancy contraption around in a circle.

Chuckling lightly, I smile as I take in the change in him. Pushing a stroller on our morning runs? That's not something I ever saw in our futures.

We take off on our usual route. The quiet morning stretches in front of us. Callum is fast asleep, and Leo and I are both lost in our own thoughts.

He's the first to speak. "It was fun hanging out last night. I like Bridget. Scarlett does too."

"Yeah. She's cool." The thought of the woman still lying in my bed makes me instantly wish I were back there. The hours we get together are few and sometimes far between. She's got school and work, and we've had two weeks of some brutal travel for games.

"It was good to see you two out together. It was starting to feel like Talia all over again."

My hackles rise instantly. "Bridget isn't like Talia."

Talia wanted to date a hockey player because of how she thought it made her look. She liked going to fancy events and big parties, but otherwise, we didn't really date publicly. It was casual sex when our schedules allowed. That's not what is happening with me and Bridget. She's guarded and hesitant, but it's not because she doesn't feel strongly about me. Even if she won't say it, I know it. I *feel* it.

"Don't glower at me." Leo laughs softly. "I just mean that you mostly go to her place or yours and it's nice to see you two out. You dig her and we all just want to get to know her better."

With Talia it was basically just about fun and sex. Sure, we went on dates occasionally and she came to some games, but I never felt like we were a couple. Not like I do when I'm with Bridget. Though Leo is right, we haven't really left the house together.

"She's still pretty hesitant about us being seen together because of Gabe," I admit. "I should probably be worried too based on how poorly I've been playing. I've got a giant target on my back, and he'd love to take me out."

One brow rises. "Do you really think Gabe would do something shady just because you're dating his ex?"

"I don't know, but I don't trust him." Even if he's not prepared to trade me, the threats are enough to tell me he isn't focused on the well-being of the team when it comes to me.

We fall back into silence. Leo's pace is slower this morning and I glance back as we make the turn at the halfway point to head back home. "Everything okay? You're dragging."

"You try pushing a stroller up that last hill."

"Are you seriously trying to blame your baby right now? What does he weigh, ten pounds?"

"More like seventeen."

"Yeah, but he's on wheels."

Leo angles the stroller toward me. "Let's see you do better."

With some trepidation, I take Callum from him. The stroller is light and glides over the pavement nicely. It takes a little getting used to, but soon I've got the hang of it.

Leo picks up his pace with a wicked grin. "Race you back."

He takes off, leaving me and Callum to chase after him.

By the time we make it back, I'm questioning my earlier statements.

"What are you two feeding this kid?" I ask, panting as I come to a stop in front of my house.

"I told you."

I blow out a breath and peek over the top of the stroller at Callum. His eyes are open, but he's just laid back, chubby fingers in his mouth and completely unfazed. "It's a good thing you're so cute or I might have left you a couple miles back."

Leo chuckles and takes the stroller back from me. "Same time tomorrow?"

I don't bother responding as I lift a hand in a tired wave and head inside.

I find Bridget in the shower. She smiles shyly as I step in to join her.

"Hi." She rubs sudsy hands over her stomach and breasts. "Tough run?"

"I learned a hard lesson about physics and weight distribution."

"O-kay." Her brows scrunch together.

"Leo brought Callum in a jogging stroller. It's harder than it looks," I explain.

A smile spreads across her face. "I cannot picture you running with a stroller."

"I looked cool as hell. I've got future DILF written all over me."

Sliding a hand over her wet skin, I rest my hand on her hip and pull her closer. My lips brush over hers quickly. I know she doesn't have time for what's on my mind so I let her go.

"I was thinking, we should go on a date."

"A date?"

"Yeah, a date. We put on clothes, leave the house, go eat some food, maybe see a movie or…whatever."

The spark in her eye is at odds with her initial hesitation. "When?"

"Tomorrow night? We don't have a game and you're off work, right?"

"Okay." She moves to stand under the spray of water, rinsing off the soap. "You're not worried about being seen out with me? You're kind of a celebrity around this city. Even if we don't run into Gabe, it's possible it'll get back to him."

"It won't. Trust me. I know just the place to go."

When I pull up behind the building twenty minutes outside of the city, Bridget looks unsure.

"Where are we?"

"You'll see." I hurry out of the truck and around to her.

Together we walk, hand in hand, into the old ice rink. It's a far cry from the big and fancy arena where the Wildcats practice and play, but the sounds and smells are the same.

The game has already started, but we find seats behind the bench of the Mini Mite team.

Bridget's mouth hangs open as she looks from the little kids skating around the ice to me. "What is this?"

"The Razzle Dazzle Unicorns."

She laughs. "I'm sorry, what?"

"That's the name of the team." I unzip my jacket and show her I'm wearing a purple T-shirt that has the team name in bold across the front.

"How? And why?"

"I help coach when I have time." Which lately hasn't been much. "They're actually pretty good. Watch number eleven."

Beatrice Fisher, Tris for short, is five years old and can skate as well as half the guys on my high school hockey team. She's incredible. I have no doubt someday I'll be watching her dominate leagues. The skill level at this age varies greatly. A lot of them are still learning how to stay upright while navigating around teammates and defenders, or they shoot with so much strength it throws them off-balance. But they never fail to bring a smile to my face.

"Ash, this is so cool." Bridget drops one hand to my knee but keeps watching the action on the ice.

I stare at her hand for a few seconds before threading my fingers through hers. We sit that way, holding hands and watching the game. A simple thing maybe, but after hiding away for weeks, it feels big.

A few of the players spot me between shifts, but their excitement at seeing me has nothing to do with me being a professional hockey player and everything to do with the promise I made them at the beginning of the season: Win more games than they lose, and I'll get them onto the ice at the Wildcat arena. A promise it's looking like I'm happily going to get to make good on.

Bridget squeezes my fingers when Tris skates down the ice on a breakaway, and stands and cheers when the puck slides in between the goalie's legs. It feels so damn good being with her, watching her enjoy something that I love.

I turn to smile at Tris' parents sitting a few rows behind us. They're cheering so big. That's the thing I love about hockey at this age. It's all for fun and the love of the game. Don't get me wrong, I'm happy to do it as a career, but it's a good reminder of why I started playing. I love it down to the very core.

And sharing that with Bridget feels so perfect.

CHAPTER TWENTY-NINE

Bridget

ONE MORE STOP

"That was unbelievable. I can't believe how well some of them play already." The wind whips around my head, blowing my hair around my face, but I'm too excited to care.

Ash nods proudly as I go on and on about the Mini Mite hockey game. Never in a million years did I expect him to take me to watch four and five-year-old kids play hockey, but it is somehow still so him.

"How did you get started coaching and how long have you been doing it?"

He runs a hand over his jaw. "Not long. Last summer Maverick asked if any of us wanted to help with a hockey camp that his buddy was running. It was a few weeks, no big deal. The camp was all ages, so we got split up and I ended up with the youngest group." One shoulder lifts in a small shrug. "I enjoyed it and asked around about places I might be able to help. Rhett, that's Maverick's friend, put me in touch with the league president and that's pretty much it. I don't get to too many practices, but I try to make any games that I can. They're a trip."

"I loved it. Thank you for bringing me here." Every little thing I learn about him has me falling harder for him despite all my misgivings.

We come to a stop next to the passenger side door of his truck and I wrap my arms around his neck and kiss him like I've wanted to do for the past hour.

He makes this little humming noise deep in his throat when we break apart. "You're welcome, but it's not over yet."

"It's not?"

He shakes his head. "Nope. We have one more stop."

"Is it your bed?" I ask hopefully.

Silent laughter makes his chest rise and fall and a wolfish smile takes over his face. "Make that two more stops."

We drive back to Ash's house, but instead of parking his truck at his place, he pulls up to the curb in front of Jack's.

"I'm intrigued," I say hesitantly as Ash grabs a bag from the back seat and gets out.

We head around the back of the house instead of going in the front.

"Uhh...do I need to worry that this night is going to end in the back of a police car?"

"Jack's not home and he knows we're stopping by."

I still feel like I'm doing something I shouldn't be as Ash leads me into the backyard and then to a gate at the other side of the property. He tries the handle and then clicks his tongue when it doesn't budge.

"I forgot the key."

"The key to what?"

"I'll give you a boost over." Ash laces his fingers together and looks at me expectantly.

"You want to toss me over the fence first? Do I look gullible to you?"

"I promise I'll be right behind you." He gives me a quick kiss before resuming his position.

With a whole lot of nerves, I put my foot in Ash's hands and let him help me over the fence. I land with a thud, ungracefully but unhurt thankfully. I stand and brush off the back of my jeans as I take in the sight in front of me.

"Heads up," Ash says before launching the bag and then himself over to join me.

My gaze is glued to the darkened courts. The lines and net are barely visible in the moonlight, but my heart races.

"Ash," I whisper, turning my head slowly to look at him. His cocky smile mixed with the sweetness of him bringing me here has warmth spreading through me.

"Pretty cool, right?" He moves over to a metal box and flips a door open, clicks a few buttons, and lights flood the tennis courts. There are two, side by side. The green and blue surface has white lines. It's even covered.

All of it looks new, or barely used, which Ash confirms when he says, "He just built it last year. He's always adding on something in the off-season. A pool house, a jogging path around the lake, and basketball and tennis courts. "I thought he was crazy, but turns out he just had really good foresight."

With a wink he goes to the bags and pulls out rackets and balls. I'm still overwhelmed by all of it. Him, the hockey game, the fact he remembered something I said months ago—all of it.

I swallow around a lump in my throat as he extends one racket to me.

"Try to take it easy on me."

My fingers wrap around the handle and my chest tightens. The weight of the racket in my hand is familiar and comforting. "I haven't played in so long. I don't think you have anything to worry about."

He spins his racket and bounces a ball, looking like a pro. I have no doubt he's good. Ash doesn't strike me as someone who does anything badly.

We hit the ball back and forth without keeping score. I'm rusty, as I expected. And as expected, Ash is pretty good. Neither of us are going that hard though and it feels nice just to be playing.

"You're incredible," Ash says when we stop to catch our breath. My stomach flips at his compliment and the genuine delight in his eyes. "How long has it been since you played?"

"I can't even remember. A year, give or take."

His brows lift. "That long? I'd never know it. You're really fucking good."

I tap the racket against my thigh and look at the ground. "Thanks."

"Do you miss it?"

"Yeah. I don't think I even realized how much," I say honestly. "I shouldn't have quit."

"Why did you?"

"I don't know. I was decent, but I was never going to play beyond college or anything." I keep staring at my feet. "It was a big time commitment and with school and work, it seemed like the logical thing to cut."

I can still see Gabe's unimpressed, condescending smile when I told him I was going to cut back my hours at the hospital so I could make it work. 'It's a waste of time. You're not talented enough to make it professionally, so what's the point?' He'd always try to soften the blow by adding, 'I'm not trying to hurt your feelings.'

In hindsight, that's exactly what he was doing.

Ash steps forward. He ducks down to catch my eye. The lights hit his face and he shoots a concerned and questioning smile at me. "What's going on in that head of yours?"

"Sorry. Being here just brings up a lot of memories. I thought I had come to terms with not playing anymore."

"Do you still enjoy it?"

"Yeah." I nod. "I do."

"Then you should do it more. Who cares if you're not going to make a career out of it?"

"Says the guy who gets paid to play hockey," I say.

"I'd do it for free." His face tells me how sincere he is about that statement. Then he grins. A grin that pushes the past out of my mind. "But it is a lot cooler that they pay me for it."

"Thank you." I tap my racket against his. "This was the best date I've ever been on."

"Same."

We hit the ball around a little while longer and then head back to his truck. He turns the heat on full blast, and we warm our fingers in front of the vents.

"Can I ask you something?"

"Yeah, of course. What's up?" He takes my hands in his and rubs them.

"Did something happen with Gabe last night?" After the game he seemed to have a different attitude about my ex than before.

"Not exactly." His jaw works back and forth before he speaks again like he's carefully considering his next words. "He made a few comments about my stats being down this season and how maybe I need a change of scenery."

My stomach drops and I pull my hands away. "Oh my god. Why didn't you say something?"

"You don't need to worry."

"Not worry? He's threatening your career because of me."

"I can handle him. I've struggled to get back in a rhythm since my injury, but I'll get there."

I feel like crying or screaming.

"Hey." He takes my hands again and brings them to his chest. "Everything is going to be fine. All right? There's nothing for you to worry about."

He doesn't move until I nod. Then a boyish grin takes over his face. "Come on. I hear the best way to warm up is to get naked and share body heat."

CHAPTER THIRTY

Bridget

NOT FOOLING ANYONE

"I'm so glad you came!" Everly throws her arms around me in the little booth we're sitting at in the back of Wild's. The bar is packed tonight after the Wildcats' win. I skipped the game but met up with Ev and some of the wives and girlfriends after it was over.

I lean my head against her shoulder. "Me too."

"Thank god they won," Scarlett says across from us with Jade, Declan's wife. "Between my dad and Leo worried about the season to Callum teething, my life has been filled with grumpy men."

Cheering in front of the bar alerts us to the entrance of the guys. Jack, Tyler, Maverick, Leo, Declan, and Ash walk in one after the other. Most people just lift their drink in greeting, but a few pat them on the back or crowd around, making it hard for them to pass by.

"I'm gonna go save my man," Jade says. "He looks like he needs to feel me up in a dark corner somewhere."

"Get a room!" Scarlett calls behind her, but she's smiling.

Everly nudges me. "Are you going to say hello to Ash?"

I shake my head. "We've decided to play it cool in public. Especially this close to the arena and after a game."

I look up at where he's standing at the bar waiting on a drink. It's only been a few weeks since we started hanging out, but I've come to know so many things about him. The easy way he makes conversation with anyone and everyone. His genuine love of people and wanting to know their story. The way one side of his mouth pulls a little higher than the other when he smiles. How he can make my entire body light up with a simple touch. All the sweet and thoughtful things he does to show me how much he cares. The way he can flip from playful to demanding when we're kissing. And the way that he's staring at me now tells me he's picturing me naked.

He winks from across the room and my stomach does a series of Olympic-size somersaults.

"You two aren't fooling anyone," Everly says, arching one brow.

Heat creeps up my neck and I force myself to look away.

"You came to the bar just to be in the same place as him, but have no intention of talking to him or kissing him or interrupting that girl that's trying to get his attention?" Scarlett asks.

When I glance back at where Ash stands, he is indeed talking to a girl.

"Want me to go tell her to get lost?" Ev asks me.

"We're not exclusive," I say as jealousy sweeps through me. "And yes, I know it isn't ideal, but I want to support him even if it means we can't make out in the corner like Jade and Declan."

"Oh, honey, that is just about the sweetest thing I've ever heard." Scarlett reaches over and squeezes my hand.

She and Everly are both giving me weird looks.

"And to hang out with you guys," I say quickly before taking a drink. "Do you want to play pool or darts or something?"

"I'm gonna go to the bar." Scarlett tips her head toward where the guys are. "Leo and I only have about an hour before we need to go pick up Callum."

"I'm in." Ev finishes off the last of her soda and then stands. She grabs my hand and pulls me to my feet. "But first we need to get another drink."

I have no idea why I'm nervous as Everly tugs me behind her toward the end of the bar where Ash is standing with Jack and some girls I don't recognize. My friend obviously is not because she marches right up between Jack and Ash.

"Hey. Nice game," she says to them. She moves closer to Jack, forcing him to make room and then uses our joined hands to pull me beside her.

"Congrats!" My smile is timid, but my heart is beating so fast as I get a whiff of Ash's cologne.

"Thanks," he says, then turns sideways to lean one hip against the bar. He tips up his beer with long fingers and stares at me. I watch as his throat works. One day. It's only been one day since I've seen him, but it feels like an eternity. Dating a hockey player means lots of time apart when the team travels. A month ago that seemed like no big deal. Those were simpler times back when I didn't know how hard Ash Kelly could make me come. Or how many times. Or...

Ev breaks me out of my daydream by squeezing my hand. "Do you want something to drink?"

"Oh. Yeah. Chardonnay," I say to the bartender.

"Same," Ev tells him.

"One Chardonnay and one Pepsi," Jack orders the guy behind the bar while giving Everly the side-eye. "Put their drinks on my tab."

"Having a good night?" Ash asks. He leans an inch closer, and I can feel the heat of him. I'd think he were completely unaffected if not for the way his eyes hold me captive and the tension in his shoulders. He wants to throw me over that tense shoulder and get out of here. I want that too. So badly.

But Ev has been giving me shit for not going out with her and Grace more since I started seeing Ash. And I know that somewhere, deep down below the sex haze we're in, Ash wants to celebrate the win with his teammates too.

"Pretty average so far," I say with a small shrug, fighting a smirk.

He invades my space so quickly it catches me off guard and I inhale sharply.

"I have a few ideas on how to improve both our nights," he whispers, breath tickling my neck and making goosebumps dot my skin.

He pulls back as quickly as he came. Everly hands me my wine. I take a large sip, but it doesn't do anything to cool the warmth flooding my body.

After a few more torturous minutes of talking with Ash and Jack, Everly and I leave them. The dartboards are occupied, but Ev recognizes a couple of guys from school, and they let us join them. She introduces me, but I barely catch their names. Ash and Jack have attracted more people, mostly women, and I want to claw their eyes out.

He isn't even paying them that much attention. Every time I look up at him, he's staring back. And I know Ash well enough to know he isn't going to hit on anyone in front of me or do anything to purposely hurt me. That isn't him.

Blowing out a breath, I do my best to ignore my hot man at the bar (for now) and hang with Ev and get to know her friends. They turn out to be pretty nice. I think they both like Everly, but that's not all that surprising because she's beautiful and fun and has that air of confidence that guys love.

We play two games, then go to sit at a table with them across the bar.

I can't see Ash from here unless I crane my neck over the crowd of people between us.

My phone buzzes in my pocket.

Ash: Where'd you go?

Me: With Everly at a table in the front.

Ash: Meet me by the jukebox

"Is there a jukebox in here?" I ask the table.

Everly nods. "Yeah. It's in the far-left corner. You want to play a song?"

"Maybe. I'm not sure."

Her gaze narrows, then she glances at the phone in my hand and her lips curve up. "Tell him I said hello."

The jukebox isn't hard to find, but Ash isn't there. I turn in a circle looking for him, then open our text chain again in case I misread it.

I'm tapping out a reply to ask him where he is, when warm arms wrap around my waist from behind.

"Hey," he rasps. "Don't freak out."

"Why would I—" My sentence is cut off when he picks me up and carries me down a long hallway.

He kicks open the men's bathroom and then sets me down. It's empty and cleaner than I would have expected.

"Really? The bathroom?"

"I know, not romantic at all, but I couldn't wait to kiss you any longer." He backs me up against the door and both hands frame my face. "You're so fucking beautiful and I've had to watch you talk to every other guy in the bar while I kept my distance. I hate it."

Jealousy is a very good look on him. It's not mean or fueled with angry words.

His thumb strokes the corner of my mouth. "But I'm so glad you're here."

My pulse races and my breaths come in quick, shallow gulps. "Me too."

His lips drop to mine in a soft kiss, but that tenderness only lasts a moment before we're both frantically trying to press our mouths together harder. His hips pin mine and his hard length pushes against my stomach.

One hand drops to the top of my jeans and a long finger curls under the material and pulls it away from my body. "I hate that I can't claim you like this out there where everyone can see."

His words make my heart soar. I shouldn't want to be claimed. Not by him. That's not what this is. We agreed to casual. But it feels so much bigger than that.

He pops the button and undoes the zipper of my jeans slowly as he continues to kiss me, then Ash shoves his hand down the front. The tips of his fingers brush against the silky material of my panties and then lower until he's cupping me. He kicks my legs farther apart and then one finger is dipping inside me.

He pulls back to watch me as he pumps in and out of me with his long, strong fingers. First one, then two.

The door handle moves a fraction like someone's trying it from the outside, then there's a knock.

"Go the fuck away!" Ash calls without removing his eyes from me. The heel of his palm presses down against my clit and my eyes slam closed with pleasure.

The beat of the music in the bar filters through, drowning out the little moans and pants slipping from my lips.

"Come for me, Bridget. It's all I've thought about for the past twenty-four hours."

He removes his fingers from my pussy and strokes those two long fingers over my clit until my body goes rigid against him. My head falls back, and he drops his mouth to my neck. He sucks hard on the sensitive skin above my collarbone as his fingers glide over the sensitive bundle of nerves until I cry out his name.

His fingers don't move until I'm limp and quivering against him. I'm thankful for the wooden door to lean against because my legs are wobbly.

"I missed you." He places a sweet kiss on my lips.

"I kinda got that," I say, smiling, eyes still closed. When I open them, he's grinning back at me.

"What time do you want to get out of here?"

"You want me to stay with you tonight?"

"I always want that."

I'm still not quite used to that. For a guy that's only ever done casual relationships, he's pretty into hanging out whenever he's free.

"Okay. Well, whenever you're ready, I guess. Just text me and I'll leave a few minutes after you."

"Babe, I was ready as soon as I walked in."

My face must show my surprise because he adds, "Did you really think I'd rather be here than at my place fucking you?"

"Ummm….Yeah, kind of. You won. You should celebrate with your teammates."

"I love my teammates, truly, but the only thing I want to do for the rest of the night is listen to you scream my name over and over again."

Heat creeps up my neck.

Ash flips the lock on the bathroom. "I'll go get my truck and pick you up out front, so you have a few minutes to say goodbye to Ev."

"I drove. My car is in the lot across the street."

"It'll be fine until the morning."

"I have class in the morning."

"I don't mind."

I cock my head to the side. "Do you even need to come back here tomorrow? I thought you had the morning off before the flight to Toronto. If I take my car then you don't need to make an extra trip."

"What I need is for you to ride with me so I can make you come with my fingers again before we get to my place."

I squeeze my legs together to ease the ache that's started up again.

"Okay by you?" he asks.

I nod and swallow the lump in my throat. Yep, absolutely fine by me.

Ash makes good on his promise and makes me come again in the truck. I made him wait until we were parked in his driveway. Safety first. Then he carried me inside and got another orgasm out of me with his tongue before we made it out of the entryway.

I'm not sure I'm capable of more when he pulls me into his bedroom, but I owe him several. He helps me get him out of his shirt and pants. I spend a few seconds gawking at his body every time I see him naked.

"See something you like?" He strokes himself slowly.

"Maybe," I say with a coy edge to my voice and a little indifferent shrug.

He growls as he playfully narrows his eyes at me. "I'll make you pay for that, babe."

I don't know what he has in mind, but before he has a chance to move, I drop down to my knees in front of him. When I glance up, his gaze is dark. I open wide and he feeds his dick carefully between my lips.

He's too big to take completely, but I wrap my mouth around him and swirl my tongue.

"Fuck me." His hands slide into my hair and he rocks his hips slowly.

Tears prick my eyes as he hits the back of my throat. He's being gentle, but he's just so big.

He pulls out and motions for me to stand. "Come here."

"I wanted to return the favor," I tell him.

"Getting you off isn't a favor. It's a gift. Lie down, beautiful." One arm circles my waist and he places me on the edge of the bed.

Ash kisses me, pushing me onto my back as he covers my body with his. I missed him. Missed this. Missed being here.

Despite the number of orgasms he's already gotten out of me tonight, I'm panting and writhing beneath him quickly.

"One sec," he says, reaching toward the nightstand for what I assume is a condom or lube or something, but Ash reaches under the bed and pulls out something I haven't seen before. The metal bar is about a foot long with cuffs on either end.

"Trust me?" he asks.

"In theory."

He chuckles, places a kiss to my lips, and then moves down my body. Carefully, he puts a cuff around one ankle, then does the same to the other. I can't close my legs and the bar is sturdy enough that Ash uses it to pull me closer to the edge of the mattress.

He lifts the bar, and my legs, off the bed and then somehow extends the bar so my legs are pushed farther apart. I let out a little gasp that makes him chuckle again.

I'm spread out for him. Vulnerable in a way I couldn't have imagined letting anyone but him make me feel. I'm safe with Ash. I know he doesn't realize how much that means, but it's something I'll be forever grateful to him for giving back to me.

"You take my breath away, Bridge," he says, voice husky as he stares down at me.

Ash lowers the bar and climbs onto the bed. His nose grazes the inside of my calf, and he kisses my knee as he moves higher. His touch makes goosebumps rise on my skin. On instinct, I try to clench my thighs, only to be met with the resistance of the bar. The sensation is overwhelming.

My core throbs with anticipation. His long fingers splay out over my leg and drag upward so slowly that I moan in frustration.

"Ash." His name comes out breathy. "I need you."

"You have me." He kisses my stomach and then lower, flicking his tongue over my clit.

My hips jump.

"I need your dick," I clarify in a bossy tone.

I get another laugh out of him, but his eyes darken as he leans back and scans my body. "Fuck. Okay. I can't wait either."

He lines up the head of his cock at my entrance. I'm already so wet that the thick crown slides in easily. He pushes in gently, groaning as if the restraint to not go faster is physically painful.

I'm helpless to do anything and safe to feel everything.

My mind is on a loop, playing out the last few weeks—all the fun and sexy times we've had—as Ash pounds into me at a steady and torturous pace.

The orgasm I was sure wasn't possible forces my back off the bed. Ash follows me over the edge seconds later.

We lie together in a sweaty heap, catching our breath for a moment before he undoes the cuffs on the spreader bar. He gives each ankle a kiss as he goes, then tosses the bar on the ground beside the bed.

He falls onto the bed next to me and I curl up to face him. Boneless and tired but satiated in a way I've never been before.

"I want you to be mine, Bridge," he says quietly as the pad of his thumb drags over my bottom lip. "I know we said this was casual and there are reasons that we can't be together right now, but I don't want anyone else but you and I'm hoping you feel the same way. We can deal with whatever happens together."

My heart beats so loudly I'm certain he can hear it. The people next door can probably hear it.

By 'whatever happens' he means Gabe. I don't know for sure what my ex would do if he knew we were together, but I don't want to find out and risk Ash getting dragged into it.

I like him too much to pretend I don't feel the same. I like him so much. He's reminded me that there are great guys out there and that relationships don't have to be a roller coaster. Every day just gets better than the last.

"I don't want to be with anyone else either. You make me very happy."

He smiles and brushes his lips over mine again.

My chest tightens. "But for now, I think we should keep things casual and discreet. At least until the season is over."

That's a few months away and if we both still feel the same, then we can figure it out. When it will make the least waves possible. I would never forgive myself if being with me caused problems for his career. I know what hockey means to him.

"Exclusively casual?" I ask, hopeful it's enough for him for now.

A flicker of what could be disappointment flashes across his face and then he nods. "Yeah. All right. Whatever you want, babe, but I'm yours."

The next morning I wake up to the smell of coffee and bacon. I pull on one of Ash's T-shirts, brush my teeth, and then head out to find him in the living room. He's on the couch with an iPad on his lap. He's shirtless with sweats and no socks. He looks so adorable and at home that it makes the furrow between his brows more pronounced.

"Morning," I say as I walk in.

His expression shifts and he smiles as he sets the device beside him. "Morning, beautiful. There's coffee and food in the kitchen."

"Exactly how long have you been awake?" I climb onto his lap, straddling him as I lean in to kiss him.

"Awhile," he admits. "I couldn't sleep, and I didn't want to wake you with all my tossing and turning."

"Is everything okay?"

"Yeah," he says, in a tone that's not at all convincing. "I was just watching some clips from last night's game."

I glance down at the iPad beside us. A frozen image of little green men on the ice. Sliding off him, I pick it up and press play. There he is, speeding down the ice with the puck.

"It's pretty impressive," I say.

"What's that?" He smooths my hair away from my face with a hand he rests along my neck.

"You. Your job. Being a professional hockey player. It's a cool job and you're amazing."

He smiles and a soft chuckle rumbles in his chest. "It is a cool job, but I'm not really that *amazing*. Not like Jack or Leo or some of the other guys."

Confusion knits my brow. "Is that like saying you're the worst of exceptionally talented players? Because that still makes you amazing."

He laughs again and takes the iPad from me. "I just mean I'm not a guy that makes a difference out there in the same way. Without Jack or Leo, the team would fall apart. Jack is our captain—he keeps everyone motivated and happy, whatever the cost, and he's one of our top scorers every season. Leo is a quiet, natural leader. Guys look up to him. And we can always count on him in the playoffs. The man has another gear in the spring."

I wonder if it's something Gabe said that has got in his head. I know how easy it is to let other people's opinions create self-doubt, but I never would have thought my cocky Ash would doubt how absolutely incredible he is. "You're wrong. What you bring to the team is just as valuable."

He smirks, obviously amused by my comment, but there's a glint of hope and vulnerability that pushes me to keep going.

"I don't know hockey that well, but I see how you are with your teammates. They love and respect you. Not because they have to, but because you're good and loyal. You make people feel seen and capable, and it pushes them to be better. That's such a rare quality. Don't undervalue yourself."

"You're something, you know that?"

"I do," I say proudly. Thanks to him.

He tosses the iPad to the far end of the couch and then brings a hand up to caress my neck.

"You gave me a hickey," I say as he lets his thumb glide along the mark on my skin.

"I know." A real smile finally pulls his lips apart. He shifts so he's on top of me. "And I plan to give you another on the other side before you leave here."

CHAPTER THIRTY-ONE

Bridget

NICE RIDE

I have an eight o'clock class, but I'm dragging my feet to leave Ash's house. I'm sitting on the bed while he's packing his bag. The team flies to Toronto tonight for a game tomorrow afternoon. Two days apart shouldn't seem so long, but I'm already dreading it.

"Are you working tonight?" he asks.

"Yep."

He goes over to his dresser and pulls out a book and tosses it to me. "Can you give that to Liza for me?"

I stare down at the Sudoku puzzle book. "How did you know she's back at the hospital?"

"She started following me on Instagram."

Laughing, I nod. "I'll give it to her. It's sweet of you."

He lifts his brows and gives me a sexy smirk. "You're off Thursday night when I get back though, right?"

He zips up the bag and tosses it by the door.

"Mhmmm." I move to my knees and grab the front of his shirt.

"Good. That means you can be waiting right here when I get back."

"I'll see what I can do."

He lunges for me, kissing me hard and taking us back down on the bed. His phone vibrates in his front pocket.

"Do you need to get that?"

He shakes his head and keeps kissing me, but when his phone doesn't stop, he finally pulls back.

"What's up?" he answers, not moving off me.

He kisses me while he listens to whoever is on the other line, pulling back to say, "Shit, man. I'm sorry. I need to drop Bridget off at her car. I don't think I have time. Did you try Jack?"

"I can call Everly or grab an Uber," I whisper.

He shakes his head at me. "All right. Yeah. Sounds good."

When he hangs up, I ask, "Who was that?"

"Maverick. He was hoping to catch a ride. His father-in-law is in town and borrowed his SUV. I didn't catch all the details. He's calling Jack."

I glance at the time. "If you go now, you can pick him up."

"I'm not leaving and making you catch an Uber."

"I will be fine. Go. Seriously." I wiggle out from underneath him and stand.

He gets to his feet slowly. "Okay, but under one condition."

"No. Absolutely not." I start to walk away but Ash grabs my hand and keeps me from fleeing.

He's holding back laughter in front of his shiny silver Mercedes G-Wagon.

"I'm not driving that."

"Why not? It's a nice vehicle."

"Exactly."

"You'll be fine." He forces the key fob into my hand. "It's just a car."

A very expensive car. It doesn't feel as "him" as his truck, but it's gorgeous and has AK53 on the plates. And did I mention it's expensive?

"Come on. It'll be totally painless."

"I'm gonna throw up," I say as he opens the driver's door for me. It still smells like new.

"Don't do that." He kisses me. "I gotta go. I'll see you tomorrow night."

He jogs back to his truck, calling over his shoulder, "Try not to crash it."

"Ha ha," I mutter to myself.

For the first few miles, I go so slow that if the police were following me, they'd probably pull me over for driving too far under the speed limit. Eventually, though, I start to relax. The roads are quiet and the sun is shining.

My phone rings, Ash's face filling the screen. I accept the call and put it on speaker.

"Better be important, Kelly. I'm focusing here."

His deep chuckle relaxes me a fraction more. "How's the car?"

"Good, I guess. It's your car."

"I don't drive it that often. I like my truck better."

"Yeah, don't think I didn't notice the odometer has less than ten thousand miles."

"Well then, do me a favor and enjoy it instead of driving it like a grandma."

"How do you—" I glance up into the rearview mirror. Ash waves from behind the wheel of his truck. Maverick is in the passenger seat.

"I drove ten minutes in the opposite direction and still caught up to you. You won't hurt it. And if you do, just don't hurt yourself, okay? Mav says hey. Gotta go. See you tomorrow night." He signals and exits toward the arena.

I don't speed up that much, but I do decide to stop for coffee near my old apartment. I park the SUV and head inside.

I haven't been back since I moved in with Everly and Grace, but I recognize the same baristas behind the counter. I order my coffee and a scone, then head back outside. I stop beside his SUV and snap a selfie. I send it to Ash, who hearts it immediately, then sends a pic of him with the team jet in the background. Show-off.

God, I like him. I run my finger along the screen. Like maybe love him like him.

"Bridget?"

I slide my phone into my back pocket before looking up. My stomach drops as Gabe comes stalking down the sidewalk. He tears his gaze away from me to stare at the car I'm standing next to. Oh shit. What are the odds he thinks I'm just posing here in front of a nice vehicle or that I won the lottery?

"Gabe," I say curtly. The only way to flee is to get in the car, but that means stepping closer to him.

He whistles. "Nice ride. Screwing a professional hockey player has its perks."

I say nothing but my heart races and hands tremble as he takes another step toward me. We might be on a public sidewalk, but we're alone and I vowed never to be alone with this man again.

I crowd the SUV, staying as far from him as I can while I try to move around to the driver's side, but Gabe sidesteps to block my path. "What are you doing messing around with that loser, anyway? He's a talentless hack that should have been traded years ago."

"Get out of my way. I'm not doing this with you." Blood roars in my ears and a lump lodges in my throat.

He grabs my forearm. "I could ruin him. You know that, right? One call and he's gone."

"Let me go, Gabe."

His grip tightens. My bones feel like they're going to crush under his hold.

"Or we could work something out." His nose grazes my cheek. "Come back to my place and I can fuck you good while your boyfriend is away. Don't tell me you don't miss it. We were good together."

"Not a chance in hell." I shove at his chest.

He grabs my other arm with the same force, and I drop my coffee on the ground. He jumps back as it splashes at our feet, and I use the distraction to pull away from him.

"Fuck," he mutters, glancing down at the mess.

I throw open the driver's door and get inside with my heart racing and hit the locks. With one more glance at him glaring at me through the windshield, I pull away.

"Bridge, you have to tell him." Ev brings me an ice pack for my arm. I hadn't even planned on telling them about Gabe, but I was shaking so hard when I got home, it was obvious something was wrong.

Grace nods her agreement.

"No. It will just make things worse." I know Ash. He'll want to do something and that something could blow up his career.

"What if Gabe really does try to have him traded?"

"He won't." At least I hope not. "He just wants to intimidate me."

"Have you considered going to the police?" Grace asks.

"So they can ask me a million invasive questions and then give him a slap on the wrist?" I shake my head. "No. I just need to stay away. I was stupid to go back to that coffee shop."

"You're allowed to go wherever you want, babe. Gabe doesn't own this town."

"It's scary how far he's willing to go to get you back," Grace says, brows furrowed slightly.

"That's the dumbest part. He doesn't even want me. Not really." Maybe he thinks he does, but you don't treat someone like he did me and truly love them.

Grace stands and comes over to hug me. "I'm glad you're safe. I have to go to class, but text me if you need anything."

"Thanks. I'll be okay."

When she leaves, Everly comes over and sits next to me on the couch. She leans her head on my shoulder. "I'm so sorry."

"I'm okay."

"Can I ask you something?"

"Of course."

"This isn't the first time Gabe hurt you, is it?"

My eyes sting and I squeeze them shut so I don't cry. Nope. He gets no more tears from me. I shake my head. "No."

"I want to murder him." She wraps an arm around my middle. "I'm so sorry, babe."

"He doesn't get to win." I swipe at a tear that falls. "I'm not going to let him get to Ash through me."

"Good." She sits up and looks out the front window. "Also, can we talk about the fact he let you borrow his G-Wagon?"

I parked the SUV in our driveway. There was no way I was leaving it on the curb.

"I should have taken an Uber."

"He really likes you."

"I really like him too." I sigh. "But I don't know. Maybe it'd be easier if we—"

"Don't even say it." She shakes her head. "Do not let that asshole Gabe win."

She's right. Ash hasn't done anything but make me feel wanted and happy, carefree and hopeful. He wants to be exclusive, wants me to come to games, and to claim me in front of the world. I want all of that and so much more. I see a real future with him. It's scary and exhilarating. I'm tired of Gabe being the thing getting in the way of my happiness. Not anymore.

I just don't know how to get what I want and keep Ash safe too.

CHAPTER THIRTY-TWO

Ash

GODDAMNMOTHERFUCKERSHITFUCKDAMMIT

I pull the front door open, and I swear my heart lurches in my chest at the sight of Bridget. "Finally, woman."

She squeals when I scoop her up and kiss her hard.

I fumble with the door, closing it with a foot, and then carry her into the living room where I dump her onto her back on the couch and then hover over her.

"I've been home for five minutes. Five looong minutes all alone."

Her smile is soft. "I'm so sorry."

"I know how you can make it up to me." I waggle my brows.

Her arms drape around my neck and she pulls me down to her. Thirty-six hours and I was ready to fly the plane home myself to get to her.

"I told you I have to study tonight."

"I know. I know." I nuzzle into her neck and hug her, breathing her in. I am totally gone for this girl. "I can be really quick though."

She giggles. "That isn't usually something guys brag about."

I kiss her until we're both panting and I'm real close to getting off without even being inside her. I pull back with a groan. "How long do you need to study?"

"An hour or two."

I want to be good for her. I really don't want to be the reason she fails a class. My schedule is nuts and I know she can't drop everything when I'm available.

I sit back and pull her upright. "All right, but I'm setting a timer. In two hours and one minute, you're mine."

While she gets settled in my favorite spot on the couch with her textbooks and laptop, I find a new favorite spot—sitting on the opposite end staring at her.

I watch a little TV then decide to play video games, but I'm struggling to focus. I'm antsy.

She looks up and meets my gaze. A shy smile pulls at the corners of her mouth. "What?"

"Nothing." I pick up the video game controller again. "Do you have plans on the third next month?"

"I have no idea."

"There's this event at the arena. The Wildcat Foundation is hosting it and I need to stop by for a bit. I'll be in a tux. You could pull out that old prom dress and come with me."

"You know I can't do that."

I groan. "Fucking Gabe."

"I could come over after."

"Yeah, of course. I'd love that."

She smiles and then goes back to studying. I try to focus on video games but fail.

"You graduate in May, yeah?"

"Yep." She focuses on the computer screen. "Three more months and then I'm done."

"Do you already have a job lined up at the hospital?"

"Not yet. I'll try to get moved to pediatrics when a spot opens up, but it could be a while."

"But you're definitely staying here after college?"

"That's the plan."

Relief floods me. Thank fuck for that.

She finally meets my gaze again. "What about you? Is this where you'll stay after hockey is over?"

"Absolutely. I've lived a few places, but this one is by far my favorite. The city, the lakes, my teammates and friends…you sitting on my couch. I can't imagine it getting any better than this."

Her smile is accented with a blush. Our gazes lock and she bites the corner of her lip. I break eye contact just long enough to check the time on my phone. "One hour and three minutes."

"Maybe a quick study break?"

I'm on her so fast, she doesn't have time to react.

One of her books falls to the floor and I shove her laptop out of the way. Giggling underneath me, she slides her hands up the front of my T-shirt.

"You don't have to ask me twice."

"I see that."

I sit back and grab her forearm so I can pull her up and onto my lap. I freaking love when she straddles me. Bridget yelps and pulls away from my touch.

"Oh shit, babe. I'm sorry. Did that hurt?"

Her face pales. "No. I'm fine."

She sits on my dick, but there's still a weird look on her face.

"Let me see." I reach for her arm.

"I'm fine. Really." She tugs at the sleeve of her sweater and smiles at me.

Something doesn't seem right.

"Bridge?"

Her lips fall into a straight line, and she cradles her arm protectively. "It's nothing. I hurt it yesterday."

Carefully, I pull up the sleeve, revealing bruising a few inches from her wrist. It's red and purple, splotchy like someone wrapped their fingers around her delicate skin and squeezed. My stomach bottoms out.

"Fuck, Bridge. Did I do that when we were having sex?" I try to think back to the other night. I'm sure I pinned her hands above her head at some point.

"No," she says quickly, then her voice lowers. "No. You didn't do it."

The wheels turn slowly. I didn't do it. But someone did.

"Bridge…" My pulse quickens and heat climbs up my face.

Tears fill her eyes.

"Who did this?"

It takes everything inside me not to rush her to talk, but I can see her working up to saying more.

"Yesterday when I left here, I stopped by the coffee shop in my old neighborhood."

"Right." She sent a cute pic of her with coffee standing beside my SUV. It's the new wallpaper on my phone.

"After I sent that picture, I ran into Gabe."

Goddamnmotherfuckershitfuckdammit.

My body is eerily calm as I rage internally. "Gabe did this? He put his hands on you?"

"I was just trying to get away from him."

"This is not your fault," I say too quickly, showing some of my anger.

She tenses.

"Baby." I place both my hands softly on her face and look her in the eye. "Whatever happened, there's no excuse for it ending with you having fucking bruises on your arm."

Her lip trembles. "I'm sorry. I shouldn't have gone there. He saw the SUV. He knows that we're seeing each other."

"Listen to me, Bridget. You have nothing to apologize for. Can you tell me what happened?"

"Not much. I saw him, he said some terrible things about me and you, and then said that he'd ruin you unless I had sex with him," she whispers. "And then I dropped my coffee on him and got away."

Ruin me? That'll be hard to do with two broken legs and a smashed jaw.

I kiss her forehead and then move her to the couch beside me. "I need to call my agent."

"No, no, no." She holds on to me to keep me from moving. "Please don't tell anyone. I didn't even want to tell you."

"I always want you to tell me."

"You know it's complicated. He isn't just some jerk ex-boyfriend. He can damage your career."

Like I give a fuck right now. "This has gone too far. He doesn't get to talk to you like that and he definitely doesn't get to put his fucking hands on you. Are those the only ones?"

She hesitates, then shows me the other arm. It has similar bruising.

Motherfuckingcockfuckasshole.

"I'm fine, okay? I made a mistake going somewhere that I might run into him. I knew he went to that coffee shop sometimes. You going to talk to him or making a big scene will just make things worse. I thought about it all night. If he was going to trade you, he would have by now. He's just trying to scare me."

A slow unsettling rage fills me as I realize two things at once. One: Bridget's been trying to avoid Gabe since we started dating. I already knew this, but suddenly the not going to games or out in public together looks different. I thought I understood it before, but I was only thinking about what it meant for me if he saw us together. She was telling me, and I didn't hear her. She didn't want to see him. Which leads to number two: This isn't the first time he's hurt her.

I feel like my legs have been taken out from underneath me while skating hard down the ice.

"How many times?"

"What?"

My brows lift and I hold her gaze. "How many times has he put his hands on you in anger?"

She looks away first. "Twice. The first time he swore it would never happen again. When it did, I broke up with him."

A memory of the first night I saw her outside the bar makes my stomach twist. He grabbed her arm and she winced. It was right there in front of my face.

"I wanna fucking burn him alive." I wrap my arms around her and pull her tight against my body, wishing I could turn back time and keep her safe. I can't change the past, but I can protect her now.

"If anyone gets to do the honors, it should be me."

"I'll hand you the matches."

She sighs into my chest. "We have to be more careful. We've been spending so much time together that we've gotten sloppy in trying to hide it."

"Fuck that. I'm not hiding you anymore."

"Ash," she says quietly. "This was only ever supposed to be casual for this very reason."

"Is that what you want?"

"It's what's best for both of us. I won't let him destroy your career because of me."

"I can handle myself." I lift her chin up. "Do you want this to be over?"

She shakes her head.

Relief washes over me. "Good. I was going to have a real hard time letting you go."

A hint of a smile graces her lips.

"I'm so sorry."

She nods in acknowledgment and then presses her lips to mine. "Make me forget."

I stand with her in my arms and carry her into my bedroom. I place her on top of the comforter, then remove my T-shirt. She looks up at me, eyes still a little glossy but sparking with heat.

I undo her pants and she helps me get them off, then she sits up and removes her sweater. My gaze drifts to the bruising again. I lie down beside her and kiss the spots he touched.

I'm slow and unhurried despite the way everything inside me feels amplified and urgent.

"Don't you dare treat me differently," she says, her voice finding some resolve again. "I won't break."

"Never, babe. You're the toughest girl I know."

CHAPTER THIRTY-THREE

Bridget

THINKING OF NABBING ONE?

It's still dark outside when I wake up. Ash sits on the edge of the bed, leaning over to tie his shoes.

I roll over on my side. "What time is it?"

"Early. Go back to sleep."

"Where are you going?"

"For a run."

"Can't sleep?"

He shakes his head. The ramifications of my past with Gabe feel like a wrecking ball for the people around me. I don't regret telling Ash, but I hate the position I've put him in.

"Can I come?"

"You want to go running?"

"I run sometimes." I fight a yawn. "Okay, I walk quickly sometimes, but I do know a cool place if you're up for a change of scenery."

It's still early so only a few other people are out, but we see a cute Cavalier and two Yorkies walking along the path around the park.

"I love coming here," I tell him. "It's great for dog shopping."

"Thinking of nabbing one?"

"No." I laugh lightly. God, it feels good to laugh today. "Just window shopping. My dad is allergic, so we never had one growing up. I used to spend hours looking at puppy ads online, but then I discovered that if you go to a park early enough in the morning you can see them in person."

He chuckles. "Wonders of the world."

"And this way I get to see what their personalities are like. Did you have any pets growing up?"

"We had cats, mostly, but when I was about nine, my parents rescued a little lab and pointer mix. She was already six so we didn't have her that long, but she was cool. I took her skating with me all the time." He smiles wider. "I forgot about that."

We're both quiet for a few minutes as we walk along the path, watching the sun rise.

"How are you feeling this morning?" Ash asks, taking my hand as we move over to the side to let a bicycle pass.

"Okay. Relieved in some ways and not so relieved in others."

"Does anyone else know?"

"Grace knows about yesterday and Everly knows everything."

"No one else?"

"I lost touch with my friends when Gabe and I started dating."

"What about your parents?"

"They loved him. He's really good at charming people when he wants." I bite the inside of my cheek. "And I guess I was ashamed that I let things get so bad. I know it wasn't my fault, but there were so many red flags that I ignored."

His thumb strokes the outside of my hand. "I'm not sure the best way to navigate this, so bear with me, but have you considered talking to someone? A therapist or something? Or trying again with your parents? If it were my sister or mom, I'd want to know."

"Maybe." My throat tightens.

"Whatever you need, I'm here. I could ask the team doctors for recommendations."

"That's okay, but thank you."

"And I'll go with you, if that's something you want. I don't want to screw this up."

"You won't. You've done more than enough already." I try to laugh it off, but the sound is weak and brittle.

He stops and steps closer. "Last night you said this was supposed to be casual but, Bridge, the way I feel about you isn't casual. It never was. I want to be with you. I want to take you on dates and vacations and out with my friends. Hell, I woke up yesterday morning thinking about asking you to move in with me. I'm sure that freaks you out right now, but I want you to know where I stand. I'm crazy about you and I'm not giving up. We're going to figure this out."

Panic fills my veins not because I don't want those things too but because I don't know how to get there without blowing up his career. He thinks it'll all be okay, but he can't know that for sure.

"Come on. I promised you a run." I start jogging down the path before the tears can fall, and a few seconds later, Ash falls into step beside me.

CHAPTER THIRTY-FOUR

Ash

BITCH SESSION

"That is seriously fucked up," Leo says, leaning on his hockey stick. He and Jack met me at the rink to burn off some rage. It's mostly turned into a bitch session while I fire pucks at the net, pretending it's Gabe's face.

"What are we going to do?" Jack asks. He looks like the wheels are already turning.

It doesn't escape me that he's ready to go to war with me. I love him for that. "Nothing."

"Nothing?" Jack lifts a dark brow.

"Bridget doesn't want me to say or do anything. She was cool with me telling you guys because I swore you also wouldn't say or do anything," I say pointedly.

"Fuck you," Jack says. "You can't tell me something like that and expect me to sit on it."

"I think he's right, man," Leo says, skating around me. "At least consider telling Coach."

"We'll back you up on this. Everyone will."

"I appreciate it. Truly. But this isn't something I can dictate. I need to let her decide when and how to tell people."

"And you just have to keep your mouth shut and pretend like you don't know the guy abuses women?" Jack breaks his stick over his knee.

My chest tightens. Doing and saying nothing is the last thing I want to do, but I don't want to fail her. She trusted me with something she's only trusted one other person with.

"He'll get what he has coming to him eventually." We leave today for a three-day road trip and Jack assured me that none of the GMs are coming with us this time. Me and Gabe trapped together at ten thousand feet is a very bad idea.

"What if Jack and I go talk to Jim without you? We won't name names, just give him a vague idea of what's going on." Leo's offer is tempting.

I consider it briefly. Could it be that easy?

"Nah. You know they'll want more information before they do anything. They'll ask questions and that'll probably just piss off Gabe more. And then, what if he tries to go after her again? No. No way."

"Fine. I'm just gonna punch him and say it's because I don't like him, then." Leo's jaw is set hard.

I can't help but laugh at him. "You've got a wife and kid to think about. Don't do anything stupid. I can handle it. As soon as we get back from our road trip, I'll go to Jim and tell him I'm struggling to work with the guy." I have no idea what I'll say if he presses me for more details, but I've got a few days to figure it out.

We leave the ice with enough time to shower and head to the team jet. It leaves in thirty minutes. First stop is Dallas.

Bridget has classes today, including a test in one, so I can't call to check in and let her know I'm thinking about her. How I feel about her is so simple and yet I can't find the path forward for us that doesn't compromise her safety and sanity or my career.

Nick is in the locker room.

"Hey," he says when he sees the three of us walk in.

"What are you doing here?" Jack asks him, walking over to give him a fist bump.

"Working with Shane before we head out."

Jack nods.

I give the new guy a head nod. He's been good for the team, but I've kept my distance. Anyone that's tight with Gabe isn't someone I want to spend any more time with than I have to.

He shoulders his bag. "See you guys in a bit."

"Later," Leo says.

As soon as he's gone, I breathe a little easier.

I shower and change, then sit down with my phone and fire off a text to my girl. Hopefully she'll see it between classes. I can't go all day without knowing how she's doing.

Me: Hey, gorgeous. Hope you're having a good day.
Nurse Bridget: Hey! Just finished with my first class. Are you in Dallas already?
Me: Heading to the jet now. Seventy-six hours and counting.
Nurse Bridget: Can't wait!

Jack and Leo get called into Coach's office and I kick back, texting Bridge while she walks to her next class. The tension I've been carrying since last night loosens.

Which is why when someone comes through the door, and I glance up to find Gabe, the anger I'd felt earlier pushes to the surface with renewed fury.

"Ash Kelly," he says coolly.

I don't trust myself to say anything. I slide my phone into my pocket and grab my bag. I need to get the fuck out of here before I do something I regret.

He heads to the equipment manager's office across the locker room. They already left to load up everything on the plane so we're alone.

Before I can escape, he calls out to me, "Did Bridget tell you I ran into her the other day?"

I stop and ball my hands into fists. Turning to look at him is a mistake. He stands there all smug.

"No?" he asks like he's surprised. "Well, I shouldn't be surprised that she wanted to keep it a secret." He stalks toward me slowly. "I forgot how gorgeous she looks when she comes."

"Fuck you. I know she didn't sleep with you. She can't stand you."

Surprise flashes in his eyes momentarily before he smooths it back into that smug smile. He leans in and lowers his voice. "Are you sure about that? You might be fucking her, but how well do you really know her?"

"I know her better than you ever will."

He snorts a laugh. "Don't flatter yourself, Kelly. Bridget and I have real history. You're just some guy she's screwing to pass the time. I wonder what she's doing this weekend?"

The thought of him touching her makes my blood boil.

"Stay the fuck away from her."

"Or what?" He laughs. "You're not going to do anything to risk being traded and we both know it. I've got you by the balls."

"If you ever put your hands on her again, I will end you. You don't know shit about what I'm willing to risk." I try to walk away, but he takes another step closer to me, blocking my path.

"Don't worry, I'm not interested in keeping her now that she's fucked her way around the city, but one last time oughta scratch the itch. She might be a slut, but she sucks cock like a champ." He laughs as he says the final words and drops a hand to my shoulder.

I snap and shove him off me. He stumbles back and trips over a chair onto the floor. The anger on his face is quickly replaced by obvious glee at pushing me over the edge.

"What the hell is going on in here?" Coach asks. I look up to see him, Jack and Leo standing in the doorway. Coach's face reddens when he looks from me to Gabe sprawled out on the floor. No one says anything for several long seconds.

Coach's voice breaks the icy barrier first. "Kelly. Get to the plane."

Gabe sneers up at me, a pleased smile on his face. *Fuck. What have I done?* My feet don't move.

"NOW!" Coach bellows.

CHAPTER THIRTY-FIVE

Bridget

DON'T FREAK OUT

After classes for the day are over, Everly, Grace and I go to Scarlett's house to watch the game.

"Hi." Scarlett hugs me, catching me a little off guard. She's been so lovely and welcoming each time we've hung out, but I'm still not used to it. "I'm so glad you came."

"I brought wine." I hold up the bottle.

"You didn't need to do that." She takes it with a smile and heads into the kitchen. I follow her, and my roommates go to the living room with Piper and Jade.

"Can I help with anything?" I ask, spotting Callum in his highchair. He has dark hair that sticks up all over the place and these big blue eyes framed with long lashes.

She's right. I didn't need to bring wine. The counter is lined with bottles far nicer than the one I brought. And food. So much food. It's all catered and smells delicious.

"No. I think I got it. Help yourself to food and drinks. I need to feed this little guy first before I join everyone."

A timer goes off at the same time Callum drops his pacifier and starts to cry. Scarlett glances from the oven to Callum.

"I got it."

She hesitates but then nods. "Thank you. I already burned one batch of cookies."

While Scarlett stops the timer and takes out the cookies, I rinse off Callum's pacifier.

"Hi," I say softly to him as I squat down and hand it back. He stops crying immediately, and I'm rewarded with a slobbery smile and a peek at two little teeth on the bottom gum.

He swats at my hand still resting on the top of his high chair tray and curls his little finger around my thumb.

"You're good with him," Scarlett says as she comes over to check on him. She helps him put the pacifier in his mouth. The cute little thing looks up at his mom adoringly.

"Thanks. I've always liked kids."

"Do you want your own?"

My stomach flutters as I get a picture of Ash chasing around a blonde-headed little girl or boy. He's so good with the kids he coaches that it's an easy image to lock on to.

"Yeah. Eventually." I smile at Callum and then stand tall. "Are you and Leo planning to have more?"

"We've talked about it, but probably not for another year or so. Callum keeps us on our toes and Leo's gone so much. Well, you know what it's like."

"I don't think Ash and me are the same as you and Leo."

"Not yet." She smiles at me. "Speaking of, have you talked to him today?"

"Ash? Yeah, earlier." My stomach swoops as I think about the last twenty-four hours. It all made me realize just how much I like him. Scarlett is staring at me like she's waiting for me to say more. "Is it hard doing it all on your own while Leo's gone?"

"It's obviously easier when he's here, but no. I have Jade next door and Dakota and Piper a couple of blocks away. Everly and Grace… you. We all look out for each other. The guys are more family than teammates and that extends to us. There's nothing we wouldn't do for each other. If you need us, we're there."

I feel the impact of her words. She means it. I've felt it from all of them.

"Game's about to start," Everly calls from the living room.

We all pile into Scarlett and Leo's living room. Callum plays on the floor in front of the TV and the rest of us sit on couches and chairs.

"Is Meredith coming?" Jade asks.

Scarlett shakes her head. "No, she's working tonight. Twins have a pre-season practice or something."

"Spring training," Grace says, mumbling as she chews a pretzel.

"Thank goodness." Jade pulls a pillow onto her lap.

"I thought you liked Meredith," Scarlett says.

"I do, but I have to censor every word I say when she's around."

Our host laughs quietly. "She's not a spy."

"No, worse. She's a reporter. A *sports* reporter."

"For the Twins. She doesn't care about hockey."

Jade doesn't look convinced. "Uh-huh. I know media. I'm a writer. She would care if the story was juicy enough."

"I like her," Everly says.

Everyone goes quiet and turns to her.

"You do?" Jade squeaks out.

"Yeah. Why do you seem so surprised?"

"Because she's dating Jack."

"Aaaaand?" Ev's brows rise.

Jade laughs. "You know what? Never mind. Someone pass me the bottle of red."

The camera is aimed at center ice. The Wildcats are in their green jerseys and Dallas in white. Someone is singing the national anthem and occasionally it cuts to them or the team benches. I don't see Ash immediately, but the cameras move too quickly to capture every single guy.

"I'm here. I'm here." The front door shuts and then Dakota comes rushing into the living room. She's the cutest pregnant woman I've ever seen. She's all bump. "Sorry. I sat down and fell asleep."

"Feeling okay?" Scarlett asks.

"Yeah, just exhausted all the time. This little monster inside me better love me more than Johnny. Did I miss anything?"

"No. You're just in time," Everly says.

The teams get set for face-off and then they're off. Ash said Dallas would be a tough matchup. I hope he has a good game. I know how stressed he's been about how he's playing. I wish he could see what I do. He's this amazing force. Maybe he's not the top scorer but he has this energy about him. I've seen it when he's talking to people and when he's on the ice with his team. He matters. They need him.

"Where's Ash?" Everly glances at me, brows furrowed. "I don't see him out there."

"Uhh…I'm not sure." The camera pans the bench again. "Are you sure he's not on the ice?"

"Yeah. Positive. He's been playing on the second line with Nick and Johnny but they've got Travis out there instead."

"Maybe he ran back to the locker room with the trainer for something," Grace says. "Is his shoulder giving him trouble again?"

"No. I don't think so." A sinking feeling washes over me.

Scarlett leans forward and tops off my glass of wine. I can tell by her expression she knows something.

"What?"

"Maybe drink that first?" She tries to smile, but it's more like a grimace.

I take a sip and then set it on the coffee table. "What do you know?"

"Ash didn't say anything?"

"About what?"

She blows out a breath that puffs out her cheeks. "Okay, don't freak out but Ash and Gabe got into some sort of fight in the locker room before the team left."

"What?" The girls ask all at once. My voice doesn't work.

"I don't know all the details, but there was some sort of altercation. Leo said my dad was talking about benching him for the night. I didn't want to say anything until I knew for sure, and I didn't know if you knew. I'm so sorry."

"Oh god, this is all my fault." My stomach cramps so hard I lean forward.

"No, it isn't," Everly says and glares at me. She's the only one that knows the full story with Gabe.

"The Wildcats will be without forward Ash Kelly, who is sick, in tonight's game against Dallas," Jade reads from her phone.

Sick. Like I feel right now.

I know he was upset and that he wanted to go after Gabe last night, but this morning he seemed okay about standing down. Dammit. Maybe that was asking too much of even a cool-headed guy like Ash.

"Excuse me." I hurry out of the living room and down the hall into the bathroom.

I close the door and then turn on the sink. Leaning forward, I stare at myself in the mirror. This is all my fault. No, fuck that. This is Gabe's fault, but it's also mine for getting Ash involved.

I knew it was a bad idea to date him. I knew it and I did it anyway.

"Bridge?" Everly knocks on the door.

I shut off the water and stand tall.

When I open the door, she and Grace both stand there.

"I'm so sorry." Ev rushes forward and hugs me.

The three of us huddle together in the bathroom.

Grace rubs my arm and Everly takes my hand.

"This is not on you," Ev says, like she can read my thoughts.

"I shouldn't have gotten involved with him. I knew what Gabe was capable of. I knew and I did it anyway."

Everly scoffs. "The only person responsible for this is Gabe. I mean honestly, if I'd run into the guy, I would have had an altercation with him too."

"But it's his career. This team and this place mean everything to Ash."

"So do you." Grace squeezes my arm.

"If he were to lose his spot on the team because of me...I couldn't live with that."

Scarlett peers in from the hallway. "Are you okay?"

I nod even though I'm not sure.

Jade, Piper, and Dakota are right behind her.

"I don't know the whole story, but your ex sounds like a real piece of shit," Jade says.

That makes an unexpected chuckle slip from my mouth.

"Whatever happened, we'll figure it out, okay?" Scarlett smiles. "If my dad didn't suspend him immediately then it couldn't have been too bad."

I blow out a breath. "I should go. I don't really feel like watching the game anymore. Thank you for inviting me over."

"You are always welcome," Scarlett says. "I meant what I said earlier. We've got your back. Ash adores you and so do we."

"You're stuck with us, don't try to fight it." Dakota winks at me, which does ease a little of my anxiety. A little but not enough.

"Thank you. I just want to go home and take a long bath."

"I'm coming with you," Everly says.

"Me too. I'll grab our stuff." Grace brushes past us out of the bathroom.

"No, you guys should stay." The last thing I want on top of everything else is to ruin their night.

"We love you," Everly says. "You're upset and we want to be there. You don't have to talk to us or even be in the same room as us, but we're going with you because that's what friends do."

A tear betrays me and falls down my face. "Damn you for being such good friends."

She grins. "Just giving it back the same way you give."

I spend the rest of the night an anxious mess. What am I going to say to him? I'm sorry doesn't feel like enough. I compose a dozen text messages that I don't send. Should I walk away? Everly says that's letting Gabe win, and that isn't what I want either. Ash always plays it off like everything will be fine. I love that he has this unwavering loyalty and determination to stand up for what's right, but I know how much his team and hockey mean to him.

At midnight, exhausted from crying and worrying, I finally send one of the many texts I've composed.

Me: Maybe we should cool things off for a while?

Or maybe for good? I can't help but think that none of this is fair to him. My throat is thick with emotion while I wait for his response. He's said so many times that he wants me and that this isn't casual, but that was before it was impacting his job. I wouldn't blame him for protecting that.

CHAPTER THIRTY-SIX

Bridget

PAIN AND PUNISHMENT

I skip classes on Tuesday. I can't remember the last time I did that. I woke up to a single text.

Ash: It's going to take a lot more than some asshole ex-boyfriend to scare me off.

I was relieved until Everly showed me some articles that popped up this morning, circulating rumors that the Wildcats are working on a trade that'd send Ash to Chicago or Dallas.

My feelings have morphed from sadness and guilt to anger. And I know just who to take it out on.

"Are you sure you don't want me to go with you?" Scarlett asks. "Or wait until Ash gets back."

She looks a little nervous on my behalf.

"No. I need to do this on my own. Thank you for getting me in."

"Of course." She walks me past security to the elevators. "Get off on the top floor. Third door on the right. He should be there now according to my sources."

I don't ask who her sources are, just nod.

"If you're not back in ten minutes, I'm sending security."

"I'll be fine," I say more for my benefit than hers.

The top floor of the building is quiet when I step off onto the marble floors. Framed photos of the team line the wall. I even see one of Ash. He has his hands raised over his head and a huge smile on his face. It's a good reminder of why I'm doing this. For him, because he loves this team more than anything. And for me, because I want to put the past behind me and plan a future with Ash.

I don't bother knocking when I find the office I'm looking for. I don't even give myself time to think, I just push open the door.

Gabe sits behind his desk with a large, curved monitor in front of him. His expression switches from surprise to barely contained glee when I close the door behind me.

"Bridget. To what do I owe this surprise visit?"

My stomach twists. It's not the same fear I had the last time I saw him, but I won't lie, he does scare me. But I know he gets off on that fear and I refuse to let him see it. Not anymore.

"Cut the crap, Gabe. You know why I'm here."

"I did hear something about a disciplinary meeting with your boy toy and Jim." He clicks his tongue. "I knew you'd run and cry to him. I've gotta say, he has more restraint than I thought. I had a hard time getting get him to crack."

"You wanted him to hit you?" I'm such an idiot. I fell right into his trap.

"With the shitty stats he's put up this season, it's probably enough to finally get him out of here. I've been pushing for a trade for months, but the organization is split. What Jim and Coach Miller see in him, I don't know."

"Of course, you don't. You are pathetic. God. I wish I'd never met you."

His face reddens. "Is that what you came to say?"

"No. I came to say this. Whatever game you're playing, it ends right now. You and I are over. Trading Ash isn't going to change that."

"Don't flatter yourself. I'm doing this organization a favor by getting him out of here. But you should thank me. That guy is trash on and off the ice."

"Ash is twice the man you'll ever be."

"I think you've been spending a little too much time with the other puck sluts, Bridge." He rolls his eyes.

"What is wrong with you? Seriously? Why are you such an asshole?"

"You can hate me all you want, but your boyfriend is washed up. He's on the downhill slide of his career and my job is to make sure we have the best players money can buy. This has nothing to do with us."

"Nothing to do with us? You used me."

"I did what I had to. You didn't really think I wanted you back now that you've whored yourself around, did you?"

I huff a bitter laugh. "You're delusional."

The proud smile on his face fills me with so much rage. Every cell in my body screams at me to leave, but if there's any chance I can change his mind about trading Ash, I need to take it.

"I don't know that much about hockey or stats, but I know that if you think trading him is best for the Wildcats, then you are even dumber than you look. He's the heart of this team. You can't replace what he brings to this organization with stats. The fans love him. His teammates love him. This whole city loves him. He is so much more than you give him credit for."

More than he even gives himself credit for.

"If you're done getting up on your ridiculous soapbox, then I think it's time for you to stop wasting my time and leave." His grip tightens on his pen. "I have a job to do here."

"And if I don't? Are you going to hurt me again?" My heart is beating so fast, feet begging me to run in the opposite direction.

It's the first time I've ever stood up to him and he's as thrown by it as I am to be finally saying it. He doesn't move, but a muscle in his jaw flexes. "I don't know what you're talking about. If I hurt you, it wasn't intentional."

Of course, he would deny it.

"You have a problem, Gabe. But you'll never lay a hand on me again. I have people in my life now that have my back and you better believe I will not hesitate to tell them and anyone else that will listen just what a sleaze you are. You think you can ruin Ash? Ha! He's irreplaceable, but you're just another mediocre guy with a fancy office on a power trip."

"Get the fuck out of my office, Bridget."

"With pleasure, but first I want to tell you how things are going to go between you and me from now on. I'm going to walk out of this office, and I never want to see you again. Do not call me. Do not try to talk to me. If you see me walking down the street, turn around and go the other way. Because if you so much as look at me ever again, it won't be just Ash coming after you, it'll be the entire goddamn team. I know where their loyalty lies and it sure as hell isn't with you."

Bluffing? Yes, but it has the desired impact. His jaw is so tight.

Good. I hope he cracks a molar.

I turn and place a hand on the doorway. My fingers are trembling. "And find a new coffee shop."

As soon as I'm out of the office, I slump against the wall and let a whoosh of air out of my lungs.

"Wow. That was amazing," Scarlett says slowly. Her brows are raised, and she has a shocked smile on her face.

"What are you…" I start to ask as I realize she was out here the whole time. I cringe a little at some of the things she overheard.

"I wasn't leaving you alone with that prick, are you kidding me?"

I crush her against me in a fierce hug. "Thank you."

She laughs as her arms tighten around me. "You're welcome. Are you okay?"

"Yeah. I'm good." A slight fib, but I will be.

We head back downstairs and out of the building. Neither of us speaks again until we're in her car.

Scarlett looks over at me as she starts the engine. "You know, you were absolutely right back there."

"About?"

"We all have your back."

"Oh. Yeah. I embellished a smidge. I just wanted to scare him a little."

"I know, but it's true. I said it before and you didn't believe me, but I'm going to keep saying it. We're here for you. If Gabe touches you again, it won't just be Ash or the guys he'll have to worry about." She pulls her sunglasses down over her eyes and a wicked smile takes over her face. "Hockey wives are much scarier and far more creative with doling out pain and punishment."

CHAPTER THIRTY-SEVEN

Ash

YOU'VE WORKED TOO HARD

"How'd it go?" Jack stands. I'm not sure I've ever seen him look as nervous as he does now.

"Everything's good, right?" Leo has a similar anxious expression.

Jack and Leo are joined by Declan, Tyler and Maverick. These are my brothers and I know what I have to tell them isn't going to be easy.

As soon as we got back today, I had a personnel meeting with Jim to discuss the other day's altercation. "I have to pay a fine, but they aren't making me sit out any more games."

They all relax a fraction, until I add, "I asked him to trade me."

"You did what now?" Mav's eyes widen. The rest of the guys are stunned silent.

"I talked to my agent this morning and I'm going to take a few teams off my no-trade list and see if we can find somewhere for me where Gabe isn't."

Jack turns and puts a fist through a picture on the wall behind him. The glass shatters and the frame falls onto the ground.

Leo, always the rational one, says, "There has to be another way."

"Did you tell them what he did?" Tyler asks.

I shake my head. "It's not my story to tell and even if I did, it might not change anything. I shouldn't have let him get at me like that at work."

"Gabe should be the one leaving, not you. This is bullshit." Jack's eyes are almost black when he's pissed…and he is pissed.

"I respect it, but fuck, man." Declan's jaw tightens after he speaks.

"I'll be okay, and so will the team. You guys have a shot of making it back to the playoffs, but not with all the distractions happening lately." We only managed to get one point on our road trip. Three games, two losses, and one tie. This team is too talented to be playing so badly.

"I'm going to talk to Jim," Jack says.

I hold up a hand to stop him. "Let it go, all right? It's for the best."

He flicks his gaze away. "I like Bridget, so I mean no disrespect, but don't throw away everything for her. You've worked too hard."

"I'm not throwing anything away." I clap my hand on his shoulder reassuringly. "I love this team. A few months ago, I would have said I loved it more than anything, but now… I love her more. I can't ask her to have a future with me when it means she has to see that prick. And with me gone, maybe you guys can get back to focusing on hockey."

I drop my hand from him and give my buddies a smile. I'm gonna miss the fuck out of them.

I know in my heart it's the right thing, even if it's going to royally suck to start over with a new team. "I need to find her. I'll catch you guys later, all right?"

Each of them hugs me on the way out.

Leo hangs back. "Scarlett brought her to see Gabe yesterday."

"She did? Why?" The idea of her being in that jerk's presence makes my pulse kick up.

He nods. "Not sure, but Scarlett said she let him have it." He smiles proudly. "Your girl is tough as nails. And so are you. You'll be okay, but fuck I'm going to miss you." He slings an arm around my neck and hugs me again.

I swallow the lump in my throat. "Right back at ya."

Instead of calling Bridget, I drive over to her house. Our texts have been few and far between. I wanted to show her instead of tell her how much she means to me. She's it for me.

Everly opens the door, hugs me, and says, "She's in her room."

Bridget's door is open. She's standing at the edge of her bed shoving a pile of clothes into an overnight bag. My heart squeezes in my chest at the sight of her. Any hesitation I had that I made the right decision is completely erased. She glances up as I fill the doorway.

"Hey." I walk in slowly.

"Hi." She drops her bag on the bed.

"Going somewhere?"

"I was going to drive up and stay the night with my parents for a few nights. I confronted Gabe. It's time I told them everything too."

"I heard. I'm proud of you. That couldn't have been easy. I hope you didn't do that for me."

"I didn't. Well, not just for you. It was time."

"I could come with you." I shrug. "If you want. I don't have anywhere I need to be for a day or two. The team has a break for the next two days and by then I might be heading somewhere else."

Her face falls as the meaning registers. Tears fill her eyes. "Ash.

No. He can't do this. The team means everything to you. You can't let him trade you."

"He didn't do this. I did. This team did mean everything to me, but this thing between us…it means more."

Her face twists in pain.

I close the distance between us and raise a hand to her cheek to catch a tear with my thumb. "This is a good thing. I can't ask you to make a life with me when it means having him in our lives, and Bridge…I want to make a life with you. I know you have a few months left of school, but once I get settled somewhere then maybe you can look for a job there. Or we'll do long distance. It's all negotiable except you. I love you so damn much and I'm really hoping you feel the same. I want to date you and tell the whole damn world that I've fallen for you. I don't want to hide."

Instead of saying the words back, she kisses me. The stress of the past few days lessens. It doesn't mean I won't miss this place, but I know I made the right decision. I can't play hockey forever. Maybe someday we can come back. My mind is already conjuring up the next twenty years with this woman. I don't know what the future has in store, but today it's me and Bridget against the world. And I wouldn't have it any other way.

CHAPTER THIRTY-EIGHT

Bridget

A PROPER SEND-OFF

Ash and I spend the rest of the day in bed. The sun is setting when my stomach rumbles loudly.

Ash's mouth curves into a smile. "Wanna grab some food and then head to your parents?"

"I should probably wait until tomorrow now. They'll be in bed by the time I drive there."

"Okay. We'll go in the morning."

"You really don't have to come with me."

"I want to be there. I'll stay in the truck while you talk with them if it's something you want to do on your own. I just can't stand the thought of you being alone afterward."

I nuzzle into his chest. Guilt still weighs heavily on me. I believe that he loves me and that he wants to be with me, but I worry that while Ash has been this amazing addition to my life, the things I've brought him are clouded with all that he's lost.

A knock at the door makes me sit up.

"Come in," I call.

Everly opens the door and pokes her head in. "Hey. You two decent?"

"Yes," I say at the same time Ash says, "Never."

Everly laughs quietly. "We have company."

Ash and I exchange a glance.

"Who?" I ask.

"Yo, losers." Mav tosses an arm around Everly's shoulders, looking as casual as if he lived here. "Time to party."

"Party? Where?"

"All shall be revealed in time." He chuckles and flashes a mischievous grin. "I'm here to make sure you both get there. My SUV is outside."

"We'll follow you," Ash says. "I'm not getting in a vehicle with you without a lot more details."

"Just trust me."

The party, as it turns out, is at Ash's place. His living room is filled with Wildcat players.

"There he is!" Tyler calls as he raises a beer.

"You fuckers are throwing me a goodbye party at *my* house?" Ash asks with an amused smile.

"It deserves a proper send-off just like you." Leo hugs him.

Jack hangs back, a glass of whiskey in hand. "I'm here under protest and it's not a fucking goodbye party."

"Thanks for coming, man," Ash says, smiling.

Jack tips his head at me. "Hey, Bridge. Good to see you."

I'm not sure if he means that or not, but he's here for Ash and that's all that matters.

"You too."

He stands tall and points to a basket filled with phones. "Drop 'em."

"Seriously?" Ash asks. "You know my agent is going to be calling."

"It can all wait until tomorrow. Tonight we're all going to be present and distraction free."

I toss my phone in there and Ash reluctantly does the same.

Jack finally smiles. "Enjoy your party."

Ash wraps an arm around my waist and places a kiss on the top of my head. "I have a feeling things are about to get weird."

My heart squeezes in my chest. "They just want to say goodbye."

I let the guys have him and find Everly in the kitchen.

"He's really going?" she asks me. Her eyes are red-rimmed and her usual winged eyeliner is missing.

"Yeah, I think so."

"And you too?"

"I don't know yet, but you're stuck with me until at least May."

She stares down at the can in her hand. "I know that we haven't known each other all that long, but I thought we'd be friends forever."

"We will." I hug her. "Forever. I promise."

She hugs me back and when I pull away, she shakes her head like she's snapping herself out of it. "Okay. Let's do this night up right for your man."

We definitely do it up right. No one leaves until well after one in the morning. Even Leo—though he and Scarlett kept switching off on carrying Callum around in a little baby carrier.

The guilt I felt earlier tonight starts to wane as I watch Ash throughout the night, but in its wake is sadness. Maybe this is the right step forward for him and for us, but it isn't the way I would have wanted it to happen.

Ash falls into bed with a happy, drunk smile. "Why aren't you naked and on top of me yet?"

"I can't find my favorite sleep shirt," I say as I rummage through my bag.

"There are no clothes required for this ride," he says with a cocky smirk.

I'm about to give up when my hand brushes against something hard. A smile spreads across my face as I close my hand around it.

"Hey, remember the first time we met?" I ask him and walk over to the bed with it behind my back.

"Mmmm." He hums. "You had on a black sweatshirt and a bunch of rings and I kept moving closer, trying to figure out what color your eyes were. You didn't want to give me the time of day. It was a real ego hit, babe."

I sit on my knees beside him and Ash crooks a hand behind his neck.

"You took off your jersey to give it to a little girl in the crowd and I thought it was the cheesiest gimmick I'd ever seen. I really wanted to find you both annoying and unattractive."

He laughs.

"Now I know that's just who you are."

"Annoying and unattractive?"

"No." I shake my head. "You work so hard at making the people around you happy. By your words and your actions."

His smile is shy and crooked.

"You make me so incredibly happy."

"Same, babe."

I move my hand around and open my palm. He stares at it a beat, then takes it and runs a thumb over the Wildcat hockey logo.

"You kept the puck I gave you? You said you gave it away."

"I didn't even know you, but I wanted to keep some piece of you with me. Now that I do know you and your big heart, I want to keep all of you."

He stiffens. "Does that mean you'll come with me?"

"Yeah."

He circles my waist and pulls me down onto the bed with him.

"Oh, and one more thing," I say. "I lied to you once. Actually twice."

His brow quirks up.

"My best kiss…you. And my favorite celebrity crush is…also you."

Instead of the cocky retort I was sure was coming, his face softens. "I love you."

"I love you too."

We wake up the next morning to the doorbell incessantly ringing combined with pounding on the front door. Ash groans.

I didn't drink as much as him, but it's way too early for this.

"Want me to get it?" I ask him.

"No." He groans again.

He gets up and pulls on a pair of sweats before trudging out of the room. I quickly dress and follow him. He's opening the door to Leo and Callum when I catch up.

"Finally," Leo says as he barges past Ash with his little boy in his arms. "Do you not answer your phone anymore?"

Ash runs a hand through his hair. "I don't even know where my phone is right now."

"Have you seen this?" Leo shoves his phone toward Ash.

Ash stares at it for a few seconds. His expression morphs from sleepy to wide awake in seconds. "Is this real?"

Leo shrugs. "I came straight here as soon as I saw it."

"Is everything okay?" I ask tentatively.

They both look at me.

"What?" I ask, nerves making me want to run away instead of move closer when Ash holds out the phone to me, then hurries over to the basket for his abandoned device from last night.

My jaw drops at the headline. I glance quickly up at Leo, who is staring at me like he's waiting for a reaction.

I can't even guess what my expression looks like. I avert my gaze just as fast and skim through the article. After I've read it once, I start back at the beginning. I go through a series of emotions. Confusion, relief, unease, and the scariest emotion of all—hope.

"But how…" I trail off. I know Ash didn't say anything and neither did I, but here it is the top story on the site: *Wildcat Assistant GM Rumors of Harassment and Assault.*

"Jack," Ash says. "It had to have been."

I stare at the little picture of Meredith under the headline. I only met her a couple of times, and I never mentioned Gabe or my previous relationship with him.

"Makes sense." Leo bounces in place with Callum. "If he didn't leak it to her, he's going to be pissed. Have you heard from him?"

"No. I've got a bunch of texts and missed calls from my agent though." Ash focuses on me. "Are you okay?"

The article doesn't name me at all. Meredith only says that a top player's girlfriend was assaulted and continues to be harassed by Gabe. She also mentions that many of the players on the team are aware of the situation and it's made the mood in the locker room tumultuous. The most surprising part is that Meredith claims there are others. Specifically, someone from when Gabe was working as a scout for the Penguins' junior hockey team. I never thought about the idea that he'd treated other women the same way. I guess that makes me selfish, but I was too caught up in it.

"Yeah." My throat is dry as I swallow. I briefly wonder what my friends and family will think, but I'm tired of feeling shame for his actions. I blow out a breath. "Yeah. I'm okay. Are you?"

I have to think that this kind of attention on the team is going to make a lot of his bosses really unhappy.

His phone rings before he can answer me. "It's Jim."

"Answer it," Leo and I say at the same time.

Ash's face pales as he accepts the call and puts the phone to his ear.

The conversation doesn't last long, but those minutes drag on with excruciating thoughts of worst-case scenarios. I've already cost him so much.

When he finishes, he drops his arm, still clutching his phone and runs a hand through his hair with the other.

"Well?" Leo asks, with as much impatience as I feel.

"He's gone." Ash's face brightens. I don't think I realized how much of the spark in him was missing until now. His gaze locks on me. "He's fucking gone."

I let out a whoosh of air. They believed me. I hadn't even put a voice to that fear, but I acknowledge it now. Ash, Leo, Jack, Meredith, and now Jim...they all believed me, even if they didn't know it was me, and because of that, he's really gone.

"Does this mean you're staying?" Leo asks, hope making his voice climb higher.

Ash looks to me, and I let the relief and hope breakthrough in my smile of agreement.

CHAPTER THIRTY-NINE

Ash

THE UNNAMED SOURCE

The next few days go by in a blur of meetings and phone calls. Gabe is gone, I signed a new contract with the Wildcats, and Bridget and I are no longer discreet, aka we're kissing anywhere and everywhere.

Her parents were shocked by the article. I went with her to talk to them, and I could see the genuine regret on their faces. They were confused why she never said anything and a little blindsided that they were so wrong about his character. There's still some hurt there, but my girl is tough. She'll get through this and I think her relationship with her family will continue to improve over time.

Today I brought my Mini Mites to the Wildcat arena to skate and play around. The guys stopped by too. They might not be impressed by me, but when Jack stepped out onto the ice with me, the kids stared at him in awe.

A bunch of them are teamed up, trying to steal the puck from

Leo, and the others are shooting at our goalie, Mikey, trying to get one past him.

I skate over to the bench where Jack is signing a bunch of merch I bought to give the kids.

"Thank you," I say.

"Of course. This was fun."

"Not for this. Well, not just for this. I meant for the article." I haven't had a chance to talk to him one-on-one since it came out.

"I don't know what you're talking about." He refuses to make eye contact with me.

There isn't a player I know that'd willingly give a reporter locker room gossip. Not only could it hurt their career, but it can also turn teammates on you in a hurry. No one wants to look over their shoulder all day. What he did was risky.

"I don't know how you got her to do it, but it means a lot."

He snorts. "If you want to thank someone, thank Nick." His gaze drifts to where the new guy is on the ice. He brought his son, who is just a year or so younger than the other kids.

"Galaxy? Why?"

"Penguins."

"*He* was the unnamed source?"

Jack shrugs. "He'd heard rumors when he was there but brushed them off. He mentioned it to me after your fight in the locker room, and I might have let it slip over dinner with Meredith."

"How'd you know she'd run it?"

"I didn't." His jaw hardens. "Not for sure anyway."

I curse under my breath. He did exactly what he swore he wouldn't do—he gave his reporter girlfriend a hot scoop. And she did what he feared, but in this case also wanted—she ran with it.

"We broke up," he adds.

Yeah, I'll bet. "I'm sorry."

"Don't be. Writing it was the right thing. It saved you, and Gabe got what he had coming. It all worked out for the best. I owe Meredith a lot for that."

"Then why'd you break up with her?"

He tips his head to the seats where Bridget is sitting with Everly. "You were ready to give it all up for her. I can't fathom that." He laughs softly. "I put myself in your situation and I couldn't say the same. Maybe that kind of relationship is out there for me too."

I arch a brow. "Wow."

"You've got a good one. Don't fuck it up and make me regret all this. And don't tell anyone about that last part. I'm sure the feeling will pass."

I laugh. "I won't."

Nick skates by.

"You misjudged him. He's a good guy," Jack says as if reading my thoughts.

"I'll talk to him."

"Good. And invite him to your party."

"My party?"

"Yeah, we should throw another one after the game tomorrow night. The last one was all doom and gloom. I'm in the mood to celebrate." He skates off without another word.

My pulse races as we walk down the tunnel. With every step, the noise of the crowd gets louder. I hold my stick horizontally across my body, twirling it to release some of my nerves.

I let out a breath, roll my shoulders, and force my mind to focus. My eyes are locked on Declan in front of me. His broad back is all I can see, but when the first guy's skates touch the ice, I know it. The roar inside the arena vibrates inside of me.

One by one, my teammates take the ice in front of our home crowd. The buzz of excitement in the arena is electric. The night is ours and this moment is magic.

The music is loud, the announcer louder, and my heart thumps wildly in my chest, nearly drowning out everything else.

When it's finally my turn to take the ice, everything gets quiet. I go through my usual routine: skating around, finding a puck, and then firing it at the net before I skate back to center ice. Slowly, things come back into focus. That's when I look for Bridget.

She's standing with thousands of others, but I could pick her out even if I didn't know exactly where to find her. She's my heart existing outside of my body.

When I meet her gaze, she holds up the sign in her hands. "I Wanna Puck #53!"

Chuckling, I skate over to her. She comes down to the front of the plexiglass.

"Is that a request for a souvenir or did you just proposition me at work?" I point to the sign.

"Everly dared me."

Her friend waves from their seats a section up.

I flip the puck up with my stick and catch it. "I'll puck you any time, babe."

"What about your jersey?"

I blanch.

"I tried to get one in the gift shop but they were all sold out." She bats her lashes.

Fuck me.

Bridget holds back a laugh as I strip off my jersey. I toss both it and the puck over to her. She clutches them to her chest with a satisfied smile.

"I'm gonna get you back for this," I promise her.

Screams around the arena pull us out of our bubble.

"I didn't think this through," she says, glancing around at the fans cheering at my half-naked performance.

"Don't worry, babe. I'm all yours." I tap my hand onto the glass and then skate over to the bench.

CHAPTER FORTY

Bridget

MY GIRLFRIEND DOESN'T LIKE TO SHARE

"Can we talk about Ash's Instagram page?" Everly turns her phone around to show me the screen. "It's basically a shrine of you."

She's sitting on my bed while I get ready. "I'm serious. Here's one of you two at Wild's last week, another at the arena. You in his T-shirt, you in your scrubs, you, you, *you*." She scrolls, calling out recent photos Ash posted. In the weeks since Gabe was fired from the Wildcats, we've been enjoying dating in public. And kissing in public. We're the obnoxious couple holding hands and kissing everywhere we go, and I love it. I can finally shout how great he is to anyone that will listen, but as usual, Ash is one-upping me.

"This one is just a picture of you sleeping." She huffs a laugh. "You two are disgustingly cute."

"Thank you." I spin in front of the full-length mirror in my bedroom to face my roommate. "Do I look okay?"

"No, babe, not *okay*. You look stunning." She sits up and crosses her legs. "Where is he taking you?"

"He wouldn't say." I turn and smooth a hand over the silky red material. I bought the dress especially for tonight. It's simple, but formfitting. The straight top cuts low over my cleavage and the hem falls well above my knees. A slit over my left thigh shows a flash of upper thigh. Ash said he wanted to take me on a fancy date, and I was so excited about the idea, I got a little carried away with my outfit. Somehow, I don't think he'll mind.

My phone buzzes somewhere. Everly moves around a few articles of clothing to uncover it and hands my phone over.

As I read the text, my stomach flips with excitement. "He's here."

I slip on my shoes and grab my purse. Everly follows me out to the living room and opens the door. My boyfriend steps inside in black slacks and a white sweater. His hair is tucked behind his ears and his face is scruffy with the start of a beard.

We stand there gawking at each other for long enough that Everly erupts into giggles.

"Have fun you two." She whispers as she walks past me, "I predict that dress is off in under five minutes."

I grab my coat off the hook and shrug it on.

"I am going to have a very hard time being a gentleman," he says, running a hand over his jaw. "My girlfriend is the hottest woman alive. Or dead. You're the hottest woman to ever exist."

Ash drops a soft kiss to my lips, groaning as he pulls away. "All right. You ready for this?"

Hand in hand, he leads me outside. It's early evening and the sun is just setting. The sidewalk is empty except for two guys standing next to a flashy, turquoise sports car.

They turn as Ash and I walk toward them.

"Dude, sweet car," one of them says. "I've never seen a McLaren in person before. I'll give you my life savings if you'll let me sit behind the wheel."

The other nods. "I'll give you my girlfriend for a week if you let me drive it. She's flexible as fuck." The other smiles, then glances at me. "She's brunette. You'll have one of each."

I think the kid is joking, but it's hard to tell. My grip tightens on Ash's hand, and I hear him chuckle quietly.

"My girlfriend doesn't like to share," he says, brushing past them. Ash opens the passenger door for me. It lifts instead of swinging out, revealing a snazzy leather interior.

I take a seat and he closes me in, then goes around the front and takes the driver's seat.

"Did you buy a new car?" I ask, taking in all the shiny knobs and buttons.

"Just borrowing it for the night."

When he starts the engine, my heart races. Ash waggles his brows with a grin.

He takes me to a new restaurant that opened last week. We're led to a table near the back and instead of ordering, the chef comes out and says he's prepared a tasting of all his favorite dishes. My boyfriend does fancy well.

"I have a surprise for you," he says after we're alone.

"Another one?"

"Check it." He removes his left arm from the sweater and lifts it up.

I'm temporarily distracted by his half-naked body, but then he turns and lowers his shoulder. A red heart about three inches tall and wide covers the top of his arm. "It's you. I mean, it's in the spot that brought me to you."

"Ash." His name is the only word I manage to get out. It's so sweet and perfect.

Giggling nearby catches my attention and I look over to see two women staring at my boyfriend. Ash notices at the same time and quickly puts his sweater back on with a knowing smirk.

"Always showing off for the ladies."

"Nah, just for you now, babe."

After dinner, Ash brings me to an outdoor skating rink. We trade our shoes for skates and I let him lead me around the circle with other couples and families.

"I haven't skated in a long time," I admit.

"You're a natural." He skates ahead of me and turns backward to stare at me.

"Show-off."

He stops and when I reach him, he slides his arms around me. "I used to dream about the person I'd end up with, and about bringing them here, skating around the rink together while holding hands. Being that cheesy couple that stops every few minutes to kiss."

He kisses me before continuing. "And then someday bringing kids here, teaching them how to skate, and boring them with memories of dating their mom in this very spot."

"It sounds perfect."

His grin widens. "I think I'm living it right now and it's even better than I imagined."

I have butterflies in my stomach. He's right. It's all been so much better than I ever dreamed it could be with someone.

"By any chance did your dream include a gaggle of teenage boys tripping over themselves to say hello." I tip my head in the direction of the group heading for us.

"Someday all that will fade. But me and you…I can see us in the distance."

My heart flutters and I skate backward to make space for the kids to approach him. "Then you better enjoy it now."

For several minutes, Ash chats with the boys, smiles for photos, and signs autographs.

He glances over his shoulder at me, and I give him a reassuring smile. I could watch him like this forever. He's so good and wonderful, and I'm thrilled that other people get to experience it.

"I gotta get back to my girlfriend," he says finally. "Nice to meet you guys."

He skates back to me, smiling in a content way that he does when he's playing hockey or interacting with fans. It truly lifts him up.

"Sorry."

"Don't be. You made their day."

He joins our hands and then lifts them to place a kiss on my fingers.

"I used to dream about the kind of guy I'd end up with, too. What he'd look like, where he'd take me, and all the sweet and romantic things he'd do."

"Yeah?" One side of his mouth quirks up.

"Yeah." I nod. "And you're so much better."

EPILOGUE

Bridget

TO ASH AND BRIDGET

The bar erupts in cheers as the guys walk into Wild's. Tonight they secured a spot in the playoffs. And my man made the winning goal.

Ash smiles as people call out to him and pat him on the back. He takes it all in and even stops a few times, but I can feel his urgency to get to me. A thread pulling us together whenever we're near each other.

When he finally gets through the crowd of fans, he scans the bar. His lips pull into a wide smile when he spots me.

"Congratulations!" I wrap my arms around his neck as he picks me up and spins me around.

When he sets my feet back on the ground, I peer up at him. "You were incredible. I'm so happy for you."

His teammates gather around. Someone gets a pitcher and a round of shots. Ash keeps one arm around me as everyone talks at once, toasting and talking about the game.

I soak it all in. Him. His teammates. Our friends. This little family unit he has that has started to feel like mine too.

"I gotta get going." Ash's newest teammate, Nick, stands.

"Boooo," Maverick bellows with one hand cupped around his mouth.

"The babysitter is expecting me," he says.

Ash tips his head to him. "You wanna bring your boy to practice with Razzle Dazzle tomorrow?"

"Yeah. He'd love that." With a salute, Nick leaves.

Jack buys a round of tequila for everyone. Everly tries to grab one and he smacks at her hand with a playful glare.

"Ugh. You're a pain in my ass, Wyld." She pushes her chair back. "I'm going to play darts."

"I'll come with you," I offer.

Ash leans over and nuzzles into my neck. "Meet me by the jukebox in fifteen?"

I look at the many empty shot glasses on the table. Leo's already bringing another round. Champagne. Fitting, but odd considering the beers and tequila to start. "I don't think you're getting up from this table for a while."

"Okay, but before you run off, can you reach into my pocket and get something for me?" He shifts onto his right hip.

Confused, but not thinking too much about it, I slide my hand into his left front pocket. "What exactly am I looking for here?" I ask as my fingers touch a cool metal circle.

He grins as surprise makes me freeze. I pull out the ring with shaky hands. Ash takes it from me and gets down on one knee. The guys are already cheering around us.

"Not even in my wildest dreams did I imagine loving someone as much as I love you, Bridget. I didn't know it was possible, and yet somehow, I know I'll love you even more tomorrow. I thought I had everything I wanted before I met you. A great job, an awesome family, the best teammates." His buddies all cheer again and Ash chuckles softly before he continues, "but these past few months have been the best of my life. You're it for me. I knew it from the first time I saw you. Marry me?"

We've attracted the attention of the entire bar at this point. Someone yells out, "Say yes!"

I'm almost certain it's Everly. But I can't tear my eyes off this amazing man kneeling before me.

"Yes." I nod and a tear slides down my face. "I'll marry you, Ash Kelly."

Everything he said—I feel that too. So much better than my wildest dreams. He pushed past every wall I tried to build around myself and in return, he's given me everything.

He gets to his feet and kisses me. The bar erupts in shouts and cheers. Ash slides the ring onto my finger, and someone thrusts a glass of champagne into both of our hands.

"A toast." Jack lifts his glass. "To Ash and Bridget."

PLAYLIST

Paint The Town Red by Doja Cat

Single Soon by Selena Gomez

Alone by Kim Petras feat. Nicki Minaj

Bad Idea Right? By Olivia Rodrigo

Mona Lisa by Dominic Fike

2 die 4 by Addison Rae feat. Charli XCX

Cooped Up / Return of the Mack by Post Malone, Mark
Morrison, Sickick

Dance the Night by Dua Lipa

All My Life by Lil Durk feat. J. Cole

Feels This Good by Sigala, Mae Muller, Caity Baser,
Stefflon Don

Do It Better by Beachcrimes, Tia Tia

AM:PM by NOTD, Maia Wright

They Don't Love It by Jack Harlow

Alright by Sam Fischer, Meghan Trainor

My Bad by The Chainsmokers, Shenseea

The Girls by Blackpink

Lavender Haze – Snakehips Remix by Taylor Swift,
Snakehips

Ferrari by James Hype, Miggy Dela Rosa

Carried Away (Love To Love) by Surf Mesa, Madison Beer

Wildest Dreams Taylor's Version by Taylor Swift

ALSO BY REBECCA JENSHAK

ABOUT THE AUTHOR

Rebecca Jenshak is a USA Today bestselling author of new adult and sports romance. She lives in Arizona with her family. When she isn't writing, you can find her attending local sporting events, hanging out with family and friends, or with her nose buried in a book.

Sign up for her newsletter for book sales and release news.